A

Road to Blissville
STORY

Inside Out

AIMEE NICOLE WALKER

Dedication

To Brittany Cournoyer for her encouragement, love, and friendship. This book might never have happened if not for your support, cheerleading, and tough love when I needed it. Love you, Brit! Romeo and Julius forever!

Other Books by

AIMEE NICOLE WALKER

Only You

The Fated Hearts Series

Chasing Mr. Wright, Book 1
Rhythm of Us, Book 2
Surrender Your Heart, Book 3
Perfect Fit, Book 4
Return to Me, Book 5
Always You, Book 6
Any Means Necessary, Book 7

Curl Up and Dye Mysteries

Dyeing to be Loved
Something to Dye For
Dyed and Gone to Heaven
I Do, or Dye Trying
A Dye Hard Holiday
Ride or Dye

Road to Blissville Series

Unscripted Love
Someone to Call My Own
Nobody's Prince Charming
This Time Around
Smoke in the Mirror

The Lady is Mine Series

The Lady is a Thief
The Lady Stole My Heart

Queen City Rogue Series
Broken Halos

Standalone Novels
Second Wind

Coauthored with Nicholas Bella

Undisputed
Circle of Darkness (Genesis Circle, Book 1)
Circle of Trust (Genesis Circle, Book 2)

Inside Out

Chapter One

"Wisely and slow. They stumble that run fast."
~William Shakespeare

*"Think things through before you commit to something
you'll regret, dumb ass."*
~Romeo Bradley

"THE SCHOOL YEAR KEEPS STARTING EARLIER AND EARLIER. IT'S still summer for crying out loud and my grandkids are starting back to school in a few days," said an older gentleman sitting at the table beside mine at Books and Brew. Hidden behind the pages of the Blissville Daily News as I was, the guy had no idea the superintendent of schools was in earshot of his rant.

"The buildings are air-conditioned these days, Howie," his table mate countered wryly. "It's not like back when we were in school."

"You make it sound like we went to a one-room school like *Little House on the Prairie*, Irv," Howie countered. "I just don't understand why they're starting earlier if they're going to school for the same number of days. I think the teachers are lazy and want to start their summers early."

"Teachers aren't lazy, and they aren't the ones setting the calendars or curriculum. Take your concerns to the school board, but don't blame the teachers."

"Sorry," Howie grumbled. "I didn't mean *your* daughter."

"It's not an easy job, you know? Some of those kids don't have a great home life, and their parents don't really care if they eat properly or get a good education. My Cindy practically lives at that school when classes start up. There's always some event taking place where the teachers try to foster good relationships with the parents and community. Back in our day, they didn't even do parent-teacher conferences, and now, they have three of those a year, plus the fundraising events, music, band and theater productions, and—"

"I get it, Irv. I'm sorry."

"Their pay is total shit too," Irv said vehemently. He wasn't wrong. "I just hate it when people blame the teachers for everything they see going wrong. It's like blaming the foot soldier for losing a battle that was poorly planned by a general. They do as they're told and so do teachers, Howie." Irv was my kind of people.

"They don't mind paying big money for a big city superintendent," Howie said. "Mr. Fancy Pants Doctor of Education."

Fancy pants? I slowly lowered the newspaper and cleared my throat, giving the gents a fair warning that the Fancy Pants in question had overheard them. One man colored immediately while the other grinned. Howie at least had the good fortune to look embarrassed, while Irv found the situation amusing.

"Your analogy comparing teachers to soldiers and the school board to generals was impressive, Mr...." My voice trailed off, inviting him to share his last name.

"Rosenblum," he said, getting to his feet to firmly shake my hand. "Irvin Rosenblum, but please call me Irv. My daughter teaches at Blissville Elementary, sir. She loves her job, so please don't confuse my concern as her father with dissatisfaction on her part, Dr. Bradley."

"Call me Rome," I told him. "Cynthia Wilson is your daughter, right? She has identical dimples to yours."

"That's my baby girl," he said proudly.

"My Doctorate in Education means it's my job to solve problems in the education system. Teachers like your daughter are what's right about our system, and it's my job to give them the best tools and resources available. I encourage anyone who has concerns or issues about our school district to attend the board meetings and voice their opinions."

Howie mumbled something beneath his breath.

"Excuse me, sir?" I asked patiently. "I didn't quite make out what you said."

"I said it would be a complete waste of anyone's time," Howie said stubbornly. "Our cares and concerns fall on deaf ears."

"Howie," Irv chastised.

"Sir, I can assure you the school board, district staff, and I do care what parents and grandparents think about our schools. We do listen when concerns are brought up at the meetings."

"Since when?" Howie challenged.

"Since the residents voted in a new school board and hired a new superintendent of schools," Irv said, shaking his head. "Maybe pay attention to what's going on around you before you grumble about things."

"I'm late for golf," Howie said, rising from his chair and walking out of the café without so much as saying goodbye to his friend.

"I'm sorry if I ruined your chat with your friend over coffee."

Irv shrugged. "He's not really my friend. Our kids are married to one another, but we don't see eye-to-eye on much."

"I could tell."

"It's gotten progressively worse since his wife died. She used to temper his grouchiness by injecting positivity into his life. I'm trying to be a friend to him, but it feels like I'm losing the battle."

"I'm truly sorry for his loss," I said, feeling my irritation fading on the spot.

"He's not coping well," Irv admitted, glancing at his watch. "I must be going too. I'm taking Cindy's kids to Kings Island for the day so she can have a day of pampering at the Curl Up and Dye salon before the big day. It was very nice meeting you, Rome."

"It was nice meeting you too, Irv. I hope Cindy has a wonderful day."

Once he was gone, I entered a note into my phone to seek Cindy out after the first week of school. I'd made it clear to the board and the district staff that I would have an open-door policy and they were welcome to bring issues to my attention. I wanted to foster a healthy relationship to encourage the best possible atmosphere for our district. Everyone had nodded and said the right things, but I could see in their eyes they had no intention of knocking on my door. Fine. I'd go to them, starting with Cindy.

I settled back in my chair and resumed reading the paper. I sat there grinning while I caught up on small-town gossip, learned how to get mustard stains out of my clothes, and perused the fall sports preview insert for the junior high and high school teams. Of course, the order of teams wasn't lost on me. Football was the most popular high school sport and therefore took up the biggest portion of the preview with soccer and volleyball tied for second place in popularity, leaving only a few pages to cover the rest of the activities. It was like the kids who participated in golf, cross-country running, or tennis didn't matter as much since they were crammed onto the same page, and the marching band and flag corps weren't listed at all.

I'd heard the arguments time and time again in every district I'd ever worked. Football made more money for the school than almost all other sports combined, including the winter and spring sports. That's why so much of the budget was allotted toward football equipment and advertising in the papers. I understood all about budgets and the necessity of bringing in as much revenue as we could to keep the stadium lights on and the grass trimmed. I also remembered what it was like to play sports that weren't as respected and pouring my heart and soul into a role for the school play that hardly anyone attended. I knew there had to be a compromise that made everyone happy.

My eyes were drawn to the photo of the handsome advanced

chemistry teacher who also coached the tennis team. Julius Shepherd was the most beautiful man I'd ever seen. His medium-brown skin with bronze undertones and jet black hair made a delicious contrast to his tawny hazel-brown eyes that sparkled with intelligence and good humor. The school board had hired us both on the same day in the spring. I'd introduced myself to him as the new superintendent then shook the hand he'd offered me. The engaging smile on his face made it impossible for me to look away from his lips. Butterflies took flight in my stomach the second his warm skin touched mine. It wasn't a foreign feeling, but it had been a very long time since I'd experienced anything like it. It felt so damn good that my hand automatically tightened around his. Julius's eyes had widened, and the smile faded from his lips, but he didn't make a move to pull back from me. Instead, he narrowed his eyes and studied me intently, making me feel like a specimen beneath a microscope. He must not have liked what he saw because he stiffened and removed his hand from my grip.

"Um, sorry about that," I stammered. My reaction to the younger man left me feeling unsettled. It was just as obvious how uncomfortable I'd made him.

"I need to get going," he told me, taking steps backward to put distance between us. "I need to check out some places to rent before I return to Philly."

"You're not sticking around?"

"I need to finish out the school year, and then I'll move," he replied. "I guess I'll see you around."

"You will," I assured him, hoping I didn't sound predatory.

I expected it would be months before I saw him again, but I ran into him the next day when I got my hair cut at the same salon Irv mentioned. The adorable receptionist, Dare, turned out to be Julius's new landlord, and he'd stopped by to finalize the paperwork so he could get on the road. Wren, the barber who cut my hair, looked like a younger, sexier version of Fabio, and he made it clear Dare was off-limits by explaining he previously rented the same apartment from

Dare. It was only available for Julius to lease because the beauty and the barber had recently moved in together.

My exchange with Julius in the salon was brief and mostly one-sided, but I didn't miss the way he nervously licked his lower lip when I approached or how his pen trembled when a deep chuckle rumbled out of me over something Dare said when I paid him for my haircut. Maybe he wasn't as immune to me as I had first thought. I had worried about accepting a job in a small school district because returning to the closet wasn't something I was willing to do at forty-five years old.

It turned out the newly elected school board didn't care a bit about my personal life; they only cared about my professional credentials and whether I was the best candidate for the job. Once I accepted the position, I looked around the quaint town and realized just how happy Dolly, my five-year-old Dachshund, and I would be strolling down the picturesque streets. Then I learned there were several gay couples already living in Blissville, including the salon owner and his detective-turned-police-captain husband. While I couldn't say that Blissville was Palm Springs, it was close enough for this guy and his four-legged best friend.

I'd only seen Julius a few times once he moved to Blissville until all the required pre-planning meetings for the school year started. Each time I was near him, I managed to stumble, spill something, or do something equally as embarrassing. I hadn't realized he was also hired as the tennis coach because he'd only been introduced as the newest chemistry teacher. I nearly drove into a parked car when I saw him on the tennis courts. The man had sexy, toned legs that stretched for miles. Luckily, the chirping of a car alarm caught my attention before I made a fool of myself or hurt someone. Julius mostly dodged me whenever he could and spoke the least amount required when avoiding me wasn't possible. It was frustrating as hell, but it didn't stop me from fantasizing about the two of us tangled together, kissing, touching, and making love. I knew he was much too young for me, but I didn't see how dreaming about something that would never happen could hurt anyone but myself.

I don't know how long I sat there staring at his smiling photo before new voices from the table beside me caught my attention.

"Clara, calm down. It's not Mrs. Frazier's fault that she went into labor early. We'll find someone else to direct the school play. We should be more worried about little Max right now. He only weighs two pounds."

"I am worried about Max, Ellie. I can worry about more than one thing at a time. It's called multitasking."

"How can you guys even be excited about going back to school?" a teenaged boy asked. "You two look to join everything you can, while I look for excuses to cut class and sm—"

I lowered my paper and cleared my throat before he could finish, saving him from confessing to smoking cigarettes or weed. "Hello," I said. The three of them reminded me of Veronica, Betty, and Jughead from the Archie comic series.

"Oh, Dr. Bradley," the Veronica lookalike said. "I'm Clara Simpson, and these are my friends Ellie Pedersen and Curtis Langston."

"Hiya," Ellie said, wiggling her fingers in a wave.

"Hey," Curtis said like he'd rather be anywhere else than talking to a boring adult.

"Guys, this is the superintendent of Blissville Schools," Clara said, beaming. That got Curtis sitting up straighter.

"Your mom is Caitlyn Simpson, right?" I asked her. Caitlyn was the president of the school board, and Clara looked just like her.

"Yep, that's my mom. Have you heard the news about Mrs. Frazier and little Max?"

"I have. It sounds like Max is little but mighty. So, you're worried about the school play?" I asked her.

"Yes," she admitted hesitantly.

"No, we're not," Ellie replied, giving Clara a reproachful look. "I'm sure Mrs. Frazier will be back in plenty of time."

I knew that wasn't true but didn't think it was my place to make that announcement yet. Tammy Frazier had just talked to the board earlier that morning and requested a leave of absence for the school year.

"Ellie, she's not coming back until next year. We'll have graduated by then."

"I'm sure there's someone qualified to direct the school play," Curtis said drolly. "How hard can it be?"

"Harder than you think," I told him. "There's a lot more to it than holding auditions and telling people where to stand."

"Yes, there is," Ellie agreed, studying me closely. "You sound like you have theater experience."

"Some," I acknowledged with a slight tilt of my head. I had decades of experience, but I played it cool. "Had Mrs. Frazier picked out a play for this year already?"

Ellie and Clara smiled at one another while Curtis groaned miserably. I suspected he was sick of hearing the theater talk.

"We wrote our own play, Dr. Bradley," Clara said. "It's kind of like a modern version of *The Outsiders*, but it delves deeper than just the differences between income brackets."

"Right," Ellie added. "We looked at things like gender, race, and sexual orientation too." She leaned over and patted Curtis on the shoulder. "Curtis wrote the music." Ellie smiled at her friend and added, "They're the most beautiful lyrics I've ever heard."

"That's amazing," I said. "I've worked in several school districts, and never once have I seen a group of kids write their own production."

"We've been working on this since eighth grade when Curtis came out," Clara told me. "We've tweaked and fine-tuned it until we felt it was perfect."

"We even got the school board to approve the production," Curtis told me. "And now…"

The three kids wore matching looks of disappointment on their

8

faces. They were so close to seeing their dreams realized and felt that Mrs. Frazier's leave of absence would prevent it from happening.

"Surely there is someone else qualified to direct the play," I said. "What about the music teacher, Mrs. Hoffenburger?"

"She's like seventy or something," Curtis said with a slight sneer.

"She doesn't need to be able to do backflips to direct a play," I replied mildly.

"Her taste in plays concerns me more than her age," Ellie injected. "If she takes over the theater department this year, we'll be stuck doing an old play that no one our age can relate to or will want to see." I hated that her positivity from earlier had disappeared.

"The woman hates me," Curtis whispered.

"Who will be Mrs. Frazier's substitute?" Ellie asked hopefully. "English teachers make excellent directors. They understand the nuances hidden in words."

"Mr. Weatherby." Clara answered her friend. "That's not going to work either."

"Oh, hell no," Curtis said. "Anyone who sounds like Ben Stein doesn't inspire young actors to get into character."

"It's a lost cause," Clara said.

"I'll direct the play." I should've thought more before I spoke, but the temptation of directing a play written by them was more than I could resist. I had both the skills and time to devote to the project. It felt like it was meant to be.

The three of them looked at me silently for a few heartbeats while they tried to determine if I was teasing them. Once they decided I was serious, the girls jumped up and hugged each other while squealing happily. Curtis leaned forward, offering his fist for a bump.

"You won't regret this, Dr. Bradley," Clara said once she settled down. "I promise you."

"We need to go create casting sheets for auditions. Let's set up a Facebook group once we pick a cast so we can share all the information in one place," Ellie said.

"Great idea!" Clara exclaimed.

"I need to find a few more musicians who can help me create melodies to go with some of the songs."

"What about Mr. Shepherd?" Clara asked. My ears perked right up.

"Your tennis coach?" Curtis asked.

"He's also our chemistry teacher," Ellie told him.

"And a classically trained musician who was accepted at Juilliard but chose chemistry and science over music," Clara told them.

No one asked how she knew. Her mother had read Julius's resume then apparently shared the details with people in her life, including her teenage daughter. It wasn't like she could use something so innocent against Julius in class, but what other kinds of school business did her mom discuss in front of her?

"Dr. Bradley," Ellie said, interrupting my thoughts. She smiled when she gained my attention. "How soon can we come to your office to begin working out a schedule?"

"How about five o'clock this evening before we have the mandatory fall sports meeting with coaches, parents, and players?"

"That sounds perfect. Come on, guys," she said to her friends. "Let's see if we can catch Mr. Shepherd at the school. He said he would be setting up his classroom this afternoon."

The three of them darted out the door without saying goodbye. Two thoughts slammed into me as I watched them walk toward the high school: *What the hell were you thinking?* and *Please let Julius Shepherd agree to help them—us.*

I picked up my phone and dialed my secretary, Priscilla. If there was one thing I knew for certain, she didn't like it when I forgot to update her with any changes to the calendar she kept for my daily commitments. And by calendar, I meant one of those big desk calendars where she could pencil in my appointments. Priscilla was old school. She didn't do electronic calendars, email, or even voicemail. My calls went through her rather than to me on a direct line. Her message system consisted of those pink "While You Were Out" message pads. I thought it was odd at first and worried I'd have a hard time adjusting, but she filtered out the bullshit calls and redirected them when needed. Priscilla might not have been tech-savvy, but her fifty years of experience working for the school district was invaluable.

"Hello, you've reached The Dragon's desk," she answered, making me snort. She must've seen my number on her caller ID because that wasn't her usual greeting. Priscilla Marshal was the epitome of little but mighty. She was only five feet tall and probably weighed ninety pounds, but the woman was fierce. She guarded my door like a dragon, and no one got in to see me without an appointment. "How may I help you?"

"Dr. Fancy Pants calling. I need to add an appointment to my calendar for this evening."

"You already have the sports meeting," she reminded me. "What's this Dr. Fancy Pants bullshit?"

"It's just a name I overheard someone call me. I've been called much worse. Anyway, I know I have the fall sports meeting, but this will be a brief gathering at five to go over some production plans for the school play I've agreed to direct."

"You? When did this happen?"

"Thirty seconds before I called you," I answered patiently. "I know this is your night to play bridge with the ladies, so don't worry about staying late."

"You're damn right I'm not staying. Beatrice Abernathy is going down tonight. I have your appointment marked on your calendar. I'll see you tomorrow, Dr. Fancy Pants."

"You bet, Dragon."

I loved my new town with its quiet, tree-lined streets more than I could ever have imagined, but the best part by far was the quirky residents. One particular resident was my favorite, and my heart raced at the prospect of working closely with him on the school play.

Please say yes, Julius.

Chapter Two

"Any fool can know. The point is to understand."
~Albert Einstein

"Knowing and understanding are not the same thing."
~Julius Shepherd

"ARE YOU EXCITED FOR WEDNESDAY?" MOM ASKED WHEN I ANswered my phone.

I looked around my barren classroom and puffed out a breath. "Excited? Yes. Ready? No."

"Have you been putting off until tomorrow what you should've been doing all week?" she replied in the tone I knew so well. Sherise Shepherd was a no-nonsense, own-your-shit kind of woman, and I adored every molecule in her body.

"It's only Monday," I said with a warm chuckle. "Today was the first day we were permitted to set up our classrooms. I guess it took longer than they anticipated to give the walls a fresh coat of paint and polish the floors."

"Well, it's already one o'clock in the afternoon. What have you been doing all day?" Before I could answer, her warm laughter floated through the phone like a beautiful melody. "For once, I'm just messing with you, Jules."

"I know, Mom. I do need to kick it into high gear before open house tomorrow night."

"You seem to have adjusted to your new town remarkably well for a guy who was so used to big city life. Still no Door Dash?"

"Still no Door Dash," I confirmed, though I was probably better off without it. It was much too easy to order unhealthy food when I was pressed for time and have it delivered to my front door. "I rented some cookbooks from the library and—"

"Oh my God!" she exclaimed. "I never thought I would see the day."

"'If you can read, you can cook.' Sound familiar to you?"

"It's true," Mom said, owning her words. "Are there no decent places to eat anywhere?"

Okay, she had me there. I was disciplined, inquisitive, and adventurous in many aspects of my life, but not when it came to cooking or love. Why spend all that extra time cooking from scratch when you could buy a frozen version for half the cost and cook it in a quarter of the time it took to shred this or dice that. And love? Don't get me started on that train wreck.

"Edson and Emma's diner serves up the most delicious food."

"Better than mine?"

"Of course not," I replied too swiftly.

"Liar," she said with a laugh.

"Okay, they make some things better than you do," I amended. "I can't wait to take you there and show you around the tiny town when you come for a visit. You'll love the little shops and quaint feel of the town."

"I can't wait to see your apartment, your classroom, and meet the landlords you can't stop talking about."

"Are you excited to see me too or just my surroundings?" asked the proud mama's boy who would always want his mom's approval.

Mom tsked. "Son, what would be the fun in seeing those places and meeting those people without you being there too?"

"Just making sure I'm still your favorite."

"You're my favorite oldest child, and your brother is my favorite youngest child. I'd love to know when my adult children will stop fighting over who I love the best." The answer was never. It was a game we'd played since we were old enough to know it got under her skin. "In all seriousness, Jules, I'm over the moon whenever I hear you sounding so happy. I admit I had my concerns."

"I did too, but so far, everyone has welcomed me and treated me well." Our biracial family had seen plenty of ignorance lobbed our way, and there were times Marcus and I didn't feel like we fit in anywhere. People made snide remarks about our parents for marrying outside their race. I didn't want my good mood to turn sour, so I steered the conversation back to a safer subject. "So, when can I expect this visit?"

"I am going to let both my boys get settled with their classes first." Marcus, a standout football player, was in his senior year at the University of Cincinnati. My brother had been encouraged to enter the NFL draft as soon as he became eligible, but he wanted to complete his degree more than he wanted to enter the early draft.

"You're welcome here anytime, and I know Marcus feels the same way. No two bigger mama's boys walk this earth, and you know it."

"I do know it," she agreed, humming her approval. "I also know you've avoided mentioning that sexy, silver fox again since the first time you brought up his name in a conversation. I know that's not an accident."

"I didn't want you getting the wrong impression."

"Oh, Jules," she said wistfully. "You meant to say you didn't want me to get my hopes up that a grand love awaits you. Baby, I'm never going to stop wishing that for you. I'm also going to keep asking why you're not pursuing him. I heard something extra in your voice when you said his name, and a mama just doesn't let that go for long." I wasn't surprised to hear my voice sounded different when I said his name, because I'd felt a jolt of electricity when he touched me. I'd never felt anything like it with another man. I'd felt lust and raw desire before, but this was…different. I felt it down on a molecular level.

"He's the superintendent of schools, and I'm a teacher, Mom," I said as if that explained everything.

"Is there anything in your contract that states you're not allowed to date anyone in the administration? I looked him up on the school's website, by the way." I groaned, but she didn't acknowledge me. "His silver hair looks as soft as silk, and that square jaw just begs to be nibbled on. And those eyes. Mmm-mmm-mmmm. He has those penetrating eyes that make you think he can read your thoughts. Better shield yours just in case, baby boy."

"Mom," I cautioned. "I know how to act like a professional, and I haven't exactly searched my contract to see if it prohibits me from getting involved with him."

"Because you don't want to know. You'd rather play it safe."

"And if I do?"

There came a deep sigh from her end of the call. I wouldn't say it was disappointment, per se, but she wasn't happy with me. "No mother wants her children to have loveless lives, Julius. Love is worth the risk."

"How can you say that?" I asked, remembering the devastation etched on her face when my father died suddenly and unexpectedly from a ruptured aneurysm.

"How could I not say that?" she countered. "You saw how much your father and I loved each other. There was no level of hatred we would allow to come between us. Every day with that man was a gift, and even though I miss him with every breath I take, I wouldn't trade the love and life we shared to avoid feeling the hurt. I know that's hard for your scientific brain to compute, but I know your musician's heart knows precisely what I mean."

"Mom," I began to say but didn't get any further.

"I hope you take a chance someday, Son. And I think that's where we'll let this conversation end because we both have work to do."

"Yes, ma'am," I replied. "I love you, Mom."

"I love you too, Julius."

My mom's words played over in my brain while I unpacked boxes and tried to make my classroom both a place to educate and also a place that incited the desire to learn and explore. I needed more than a periodic table to grab their attention and hold it. I knew the success of my classes depended on my teaching style rather than the appearance of my room, but I felt it was a great idea to set the right tone. I'd slipped my AirPods in my ears and turned on some Bach to chase away the wispy tendrils of discontent that lingered after talking to my mom. I pulled out my framed photos of my favorite scientists which included one of their famous quotes. I thought the young ladies might be inspired by Marie Curie and all of us need the reminder from time to time to never give up, which Thomas Edison is renowned for. Of course, my favorite is Albert Einstein, who looks every bit the mad scientist with his wild hair.

I looked up from the box to search the room for the best placement when I caught movement from the corner of my eye. I turned and saw three students standing in the doorway of my classroom wearing mixed emotions ranging from hopeful to wary. I pulled the AirPods from my ears and slid them inside my pocket.

"Hello, Ellie," I cheerfully said to the one student I recognized because she was on my tennis team. "I wasn't aware there were students in the building today. I'd hoped to have my room setup before—"

"We're not worried about how your room looks," said the young lady with the long black hair. Seeing them standing together in my classroom reminded me of Veronica, Betty, and Jughead. I had to bite the inside of my cheek to keep from pointing it out.

"Oh? What can I do for you?"

"First, allow me to make introductions," the Veronica looka-like said. "You already know Ellie since she's one of your captains on the tennis team. I'm Clara Simpson." Then she gestured to the male student who stood between the two ladies. "And this is Curtis Langston." I recognized their names and knew they were enrolled in my advanced chemistry class, so I anticipated they wanted to speak to me about the curriculum.

"I'll be handing out your syllabus in class on Wednesday," I said. "It wouldn't be fair if I gave you guys information before anyone else."

"We're not here about that either," Ellie said.

"What can I do for you then?"

"We need someone to help us compose the melodies to go with the original lyrics we wrote for our school play," Curtis said. "I heard you have a background in music, and we wondered if you'd be remotely interested in helping us."

"We know that tennis practice and matches would need to come first, but do you have any extra time you could spare?" Ellie asked, sounding hopeful. "We thought the opportunity to produce the play we wrote was lost when Mrs. Frazier had her baby early, but we've received a second chance."

"You wrote the play your school will perform?" I asked, sounding as impressed as I felt. That was no small feat. My respect grew when I learned how long they'd worked together on it. I noticed the way Curtis's face flushed when they talked about his coming out in eighth grade being the catalyst for their creation. I thought the play sounded unique and timeless. "And you've written the songs to go with the play?"

"I have," Curtis said humbly. "I'm not sure the songs are as great as Ellie and Clara say, but—"

"They're amazing, Mr. Shepherd," Clara rushed to say. "I mean, we could always record Curtis playing the acoustic guitar and singing the songs he wrote, but certain songs would sound amazing with strings in the background."

"Maybe we should show him the lyrics so he can see for himself."

"I'd love to read the lyrics," I told Curtis, who stood stiffly and stared at his feet like he was expecting me to reject their ideas.

Something about these kids really got to me. When Curtis raised his head, he looked hopeful and the tension had eased from his body.

"I have them saved on my phone," he offered.

"Sure," I said, meeting them halfway when they started crossing the room toward me.

Curtis clicked on his phone and opened the Microsoft Word app. "Here you go," he said nervously, and I noticed his hand trembled when he handed it to me. It had to be unnerving to let a stranger read the words he'd ripped from his soul and put on the page.

I wasn't prepared for the depth of emotion or the way his words would reach inside my chest and squeeze my heart. "Oh wow," I said once I'd finished reading the first song. "This is...this is..." I had a hard time conveying just how impactful his lyrics felt to me.

"Awful?" Curtis asked.

"Mind-blowing," Ellie supplied.

"Yes, Ellie. These words are stunning, beautiful, and mind-blowing. How many songs are there?" I asked while scrolling down to the next song.

"Five," Curtis said. "Each of the main characters has a solo performance and there are two songs for the entire cast to sing together."

I knew I was crazy even to consider composing music when I'd already committed to coaching tennis on top of my teaching duties. I knew there would be a lot of late nights ahead of me, but I already had a melody playing in my head. "Can you send me a copy of the script and the lyrics right away?"

My cell phone pinged in my pocket letting me know an email had arrived. Clara giggled, pulling my attention to her. She wiggled the phone in her hand. "Done," she said. "Your school email address is provided on the school's website. I didn't hack into your personnel files," she added when my brow lifted in question. Even though what she said was true, I was certain my musical background wasn't something the school bragged about on their website. Someone who'd read the resume I'd submitted to the board had shared the information with her. I wasn't sure how I felt about that. "My apologies if you feel I was too forward, Mr. Shepherd."

I wasn't exactly sure how to respond, so I changed the conversation back to our original topic. "I'm definitely willing to assist you with the melodies for your lyrics. Have you marked in the script where the songs will go? I really want to get a feel for the scenes."

"Yes, sir," Curtis replied quickly. "Everything you need to know should be found in either of the documents."

"We have our first planning meeting tonight at five o'clock," Clara said.

"We have the mandatory fall athletics meeting tonight," I reminded Ellie. I wasn't sure if Clara or Curtis played sports, but I knew her attendance was required as was mine.

"Yes, and we took that into consideration when we scheduled the meeting with the new director," she said cheerfully. "We only want to come up with a production timeline tonight, so we'll have plenty of time to get over to the auditorium for the big meeting."

"There is a proper chain of command we must adhere to," Clara said, deepening her voice to mimic the stick-in-the-mud athletic director.

"Oh my gosh," Ellie said, giggling. "You sound just like him."

"You need to sound drier," Curtis said. "The man always sounds like he has something stuck in his throat."

"The entire auditorium will start clearing their throats and sipping water because he sounds so uncomfortable," Ellie told me. I'd met the athletic director, of course, and noticed his dry voice. I'd have to remind myself not to smile when the guy started in on his speech.

"Okay, so where is this meeting taking place?" I asked, prodding them along. I had a lot of stuff to do between now and then.

"Dr. Bradley's office," Clara calmly said, completely unaware of the grenade she'd lobbed at my feet.

"Dr. Bradley?" I asked. "The superintendent?"

"Yes, that's him," Clara replied, searching my face. Had my voice sounded odd to her? "Is there a problem?"

"No," I said hurriedly. "I guess I just wasn't expecting the superintendent to direct a school play."

"He probably wasn't expecting the chemistry teacher to write the music for it either," she countered. "We shouldn't jump to conclusions about people." *Touché.* "Anyway, meet us in his office at five, and we should have it wrapped up in less than thirty minutes."

I should've told them I changed my mind, but my pride wouldn't permit it. I would attend the meetings, write the music, hand it over to the music department, and walk away. My interaction with the man would be minimal. "See you guys at five."

I returned the AirPods to my ears and cranked up the music to drown out my thoughts so I could continue setting up my classroom. When I stepped back at quarter to five, I was excited about the progress I'd made. It would only take me another two hours tops to get my room exactly as I'd imagined it. I hustled out of the high school and across the parking lot to reach the Board of Education building. There was no one behind the desk out front, but I didn't need anyone to tell me where I needed to go. I followed the excited voices of the three kids who'd turned my orderly world upside down in a matter of minutes.

It was hard to be irritated when the object of my fantasies glanced up at me from his desk as I lightly rapped on the open door before entering the room. The kids were so busy chatting they hadn't heard me arrive. Dr. Bradley's surprise morphed into joy as a smile spread across his handsome face. The kids stopped chatting immediately, and I felt their attention shift to see who'd stolen Dr. Bradley's attention. Hadn't they told him I was coming or had he not believed them when they did?

"Oh great! The gang's all here so we can get started," Ellie said.

"Here's what I'm thinking," Clara said, but I didn't hear a word she said after that because the bluest eyes I'd ever seen ensnared me. I remembered my mom's advice hours earlier and how I scoffed at her words.

Don't think dirty thoughts. Don't think dirty thoughts. Don't think... Too late. Romeo Bradley grinned like he knew exactly what I was thinking.

Chapter Three

"Fear me not."
~William Shakespeare

"I don't bite...unless you want me to."
~Romeo Bradley

WOULD THERE COME A DAY WHEN I WASN'T STRUCK NEARLY mute by him? It wasn't just his outer beauty either. There was a light in his eyes that spoke of intelligence and depth, and he carried himself with pride and confidence. It was the sexiest thing I'd ever seen. Right then, standing in the doorway of my office, his lips tilted up in the slightest hint of a smirk as if we'd unknowingly, and unwillingly on his part, shared a moment. I saw a flash of something else in his hazel depths, but it was gone before I could name it. The only thing I could do was smile at him because I was so damn glad to see him, even if the feeling wasn't mutual.

I was certain he would decline the kids' offer once he found out I would be directing the play. Clara nearly vibrated with joy when she told me how shocked Julius had been at the news. I'd asked if they told him before or after he committed to helping compose the music, and I was nervous when I found out it was the latter. He looked anxious and maybe a bit hesitant, but I didn't get the vibe he'd planned to pull out of the production. I knew it was up to me to break the ice and make him feel welcome.

"Thanks for joining the team, Mr. Shepherd."

He offered me a hesitant smile, but I would take it and hope to build upon it. "I'm excited to be included in the production of *Inside Out*." He then turned to look at the kids who sat around the small, round table in the corner of my office I used for informal interviews and meetings. I'd learned I would have more success in interacting with people if I was on their level, rather than sitting on opposite sides of an imposing desk. I saved the behind-the-desk approach for when I meant serious business and I needed my visitor to respect my authority.

I rose from behind my desk and walked toward the table where Clara, Ellie, and Curtis waited for us. "Join us?" I asked, gesturing to the two available chairs, which just happened to be next to one another.

"Sure," Julius said after a brief hesitation. "I'm excited to read the script and see what the three of you have created. I love the title you came up with," he told them when he sat down.

"It was Curtis's idea," Ellie said, nudging him with her shoulder.

"If you turn us inside out, you'll see that we're all the same. It's only our outer shells that are different." How very perceptive for a young mind, but some kids are forced to grow up quicker than the others. I wondered about Curtis's home life after he came out. Did he find the acceptance and support he needed? I suspected I'd find my answers when I read the play.

"Minus the differences in reproductive organs, of course," Clara added, earning a frown from both Ellie and Curtis.

"I need to read the play first which I will start tonight. I will make notes as I go about any melodies that pop into my head or questions I might have for the young playwrights. Then I will study the lyrics and compare them to the notes I made about the tone and tempo of the scenes. I should have a good feel for the music by the weekend then I can begin composing melodies over the next few weeks. Sometimes I can compose a song in a day, and other times, it takes weeks for me to piece the fragments together to form a cohesive melody. Is a month too much time to ask? I don't think it will take that long, but I'd like to do this right and not rush it."

"A month should be perfect," Clara said, speaking up for me. I could tell there would be times I'd need to remind her I was directing the play. "The play won't debut until January."

"Let's shoot for auditions at the end of September then," I said. "Have you already worked up character sheets?"

"We have," Ellie replied. "We created them as we wrote the play. As *Inside Out* evolved, so did our characters."

"I'd like to read them once more to make sure we're on point," Clara said.

"How about I go over them after I've read the play?" I asked. "It's always a good idea to have someone review them with fresh eyes."

"Because we're too close to the characters we've written?" Ellie asked.

"Yes, and it's often hard to be objective about your own work."

"I think that sounds fair," Curtis said.

"I agree," Clara said, nodding. "I can see already that you know what you're doing. I think you have more experience with theater than you first let on."

"Perhaps," I agreed.

"This play is in good hands," Clara said after studying me closely for a few seconds. I could feel her mentally placing the play in my care. I wouldn't let her down. "As is the music," she said to Julius.

"So, late September we will hold auditions then begin reading the parts as a team the first week of October. I want to be completely off script in two weeks. Mr. Shepherd will work with the band and music departments to coordinate their roles, and I will talk to Mrs. Jameson about her art classes creating the backdrops for our scenes. Who's usually in charge of costumes?"

Ellie raised her hand. "My mom has made the costumes for as long as I can remember. She's so gifted."

"That's great," I said. "I'd like to have another meeting in a month with everyone involved in the production. Would your mom be open to joining all of us."

"She'd love it, Dr. Bradley," Ellie said excitedly.

"My parents volunteered to cover the cost for printing the ads and programs," Curtis said. I partially had the answer to my unspoken question about his parents' support.

"My folks have arranged for us to perform the play at the Getty Theater in Goodville instead of our cafetorium," Clara informed me. "It's a historic theater built in 1916."

"I'm familiar with the Getty Theater," I said fondly. "She's a beauty, and I can't think of a better place to perform the play. I'll have to express my gratitude to all of your parents for their commitment and generosity."

I had noticed parent engagement with the school and staff was higher here than I'd seen in the other districts I'd worked as an educator or an administrator. I was eager to see what the new school year would bring us. Speaking of which, we needed to wrap up our production meeting and get to the auditorium for the athletic director's meeting.

"Does anyone have any questions or concerns at this time?" I asked. The kids looked at one another before returning their attention to me. The three of them shook their heads, and we all turned to look at Julius. "Mr. Shepherd?" Was it me, or was he watching my mouth form his name on my lips?

He blinked then moved his eyes up to meet mine. "I don't have any questions right now."

"Then we'll adjourn and head back to the high school for the athletic meeting." All three kids groaned as we rose from the table. I recalled from the photos in the fall sports insert that Ellie played tennis for Julius, Clara played volleyball, and Curtis ran cross country.

The kids left the room talking animatedly once more about the play while Julius and I followed at a slower pace. I wasn't sure what to say to him, although I needed to say something. The urge to reach for his hand rose sharp and swift inside me, stealing my breath.

"Are you okay?" Julius asked, sounding concerned. His brow was furrowed when I turned my head to look at him. "You sucked in a sharp breath like maybe you were in pain."

"No, I'm fine," I rushed to assure him. "I'm not hurt. A thought just came to me that caught me off guard, but I wasn't aware my re-action was audible."

"It was pretty subtle," he said then cleared his throat. If it was a subtle reaction, then it meant he was tuned in to me, picking up things others wouldn't. The uncertain smile he gave me was incredi-bly sweet, and I longed to trace the curve of his lips with my fingers. *Maybe someday I'll have the right to act on my desire.* Until then, I'd settle for friendship.

The fall athletics meeting was as boring as the kids had warned. I spoke first, and it was my first time publicly addressing the parents, coaches, and students. I wasn't typically nervous about speaking in front of crowds, because I'd been performing in one way or another since I was a kid, but I couldn't deny the jangle of nerves I felt know-ing *he* was watching and judging me just as the crowd was. There was also no denying that his opinion mattered a lot to me.

Afterward, I stayed at the school and talked to those who wanted to introduce themselves to me. I was glad to see so many people were excited about the upcoming year but ready to get home to take Dolly for a walk and start reading *Inside Out*. Dolly was my best girl and confidante. She came into my life when I needed a warm body to cuddle, and her fur had absorbed many shed tears during our time together. Her friendly little licks on the chin could pull me back from despair like no one else could. She didn't deserve to be locked in a house for endless hours, so I employed my next-door neighbor, Lily Brewer, as my dog sitter. I took Dolly over to Lily's house before heading to work and picked her up as soon as I got home. Dolly got to play all day with Lily's dogs, and I never worried about her being lonely.

Dolly happily barked as she watched my approach through Lily's glass storm door. Her tail whipped from side to side, and her silky ears bounced every time she barked. My heart swelled with love as I jogged up the steps and rang the doorbell. Lily answered the door wearing an apron covered in red splotches.

"Cooking something with tomatoes or have you killed someone?" I teased when she opened the door so I could come in. Dolly began to turn in circles while she waited for me to crouch down and give her ears a good scratch.

"Canning tomatoes, making homemade salsa, and spaghetti sauce. I make enough for two armies. Are you interested in receiving jars of any of those things?"

"I love salsa and chips," I told her.

"What's your preference? Mild, medium, hot, or great balls of fire? Perhaps you'd like my sampler. Instead of a pint of salsa, I give you one of each in small jelly jars."

I chuckled over my options. "I'll take the sampler," I said.

"Great. I'll have it ready for you tomorrow when you pick up Dolly. I'll send home a few extra goodies too. I assure you that my spaghetti sauce is the best you'll ever have. It's great to pop open a jar after a long day at work and pour over spaghetti noodles and a perfectly breaded, pan-seared chicken breast."

"My mouth is already watering just thinking about it," I told her. "How was Dolly today?" She hadn't seemed herself this morning when I dropped her off.

"She wasn't as playful as normal, but her appetite was good, and she drank plenty of water. Dogs are like people; they have moody days. They're also highly sensitive to their human's moods too. Maybe she's feeding off the signals you're putting out, even if you're not aware. Excited or nervous about the upcoming school year perhaps?"

"No more excited than usual," I replied but knew it wasn't true. I only had to think about seeing Julius and my heart raced. "We'll take an extra-long walk tonight and maybe stop for a frozen treat." The ice cream parlor in town sold treats made especially for dogs. Dolly barked sharply twice. That was her way of telling me she was down for the walk and ice cream. "We'll head out of here so you can get on with your night. Thanks for watching her later than usual."

"She's a joy to have around," Lily assured me. "See you in the morning."

"Good night, Lily."

At home, I opened my email on my phone to print out the script for *Inside Out* Clara had sent me and noticed she'd sent a new email that included the character sheets they made up for all the roles in the play. I preferred to hold a physical script in my hand so I could make notes, even though those tools were available digitally. I hit the print command for both documents then went into the kitchen to fix a light supper before we set off on our walk. I had leftover grilled chicken and decided to boil some penne pasta and make a simple and quick herb and garlic pesto to toss them with.

I slipped Dolly a few bites of the grilled chicken before I coated it with the pesto. I loved my girl, but her breath was foul enough without adding garlic to her diet. I kept my eyes on the printed script as I made notes rather than look into her big, brown eyes as she begged at my feet. After dinner, I changed into a pair of basketball shorts, a tank top, and my running shoes. Dolly dragged her leash to me when I sat in the kitchen chair to tie the laces on my shoes.

"Of course, you're going," I told her. "Didn't I say so at Lily's house?"

The leash in her mouth muffled her bark. Once I finished tying my shoes, I hooked the leash to her harness, and we headed out at a nice pace both of us could enjoy. Her little legs were too short to keep up with my morning runs so she sat those out. Nighttime strolls were all about her and the pace she wanted to go. Sometimes, she was feeling her moxie and trotted along quickly, and other times, she poked around smelling every other blade of grass. Her pace was in between those two, but I was happy to tag along while she did her thing. I knew I had a glass of chilled Chianti and a funny play script waiting for me when I got home.

The ice cream parlor, Tooty Fruity, was fairly busy when we arrived, but I figured it was everyone clinging to the last days of summer before school started. I ordered a double dip of butter pecan for me and a frozen doggy treat for Dolly. We sat beneath one of the tables shaded by a big, colorful umbrella.

I leaned over and petted Dolly's silky ears while enjoying my cone and thinking about the little bit of the play I'd already read. These kids were really onto something special, and no matter where life took them, I hoped they always held on to this creative outlet.

"Excuse me," said a gruff voice. "Dr. Bradley, is it?"

I lifted my head and looked into the solemn eyes of the man named Howie I'd seen at Books and Brew with Irv.

"Yes," I replied. "Good evening. I'm sorry, I didn't catch your last name this morning."

He cringed a bit, and his face flushed like he was embarrassed. "I'm Howie Wilson."

I extended a hand to him which he accepted. "It's nice to meet you, Mr. Wilson." His generation preferred a formal address until permission was granted to use their first name.

"Call me Howie," he said with a crooked smile. "May I join you?"

"Absolutely," I replied. "Dolly and I always enjoy good company." Howie snorted like he knew people wouldn't classify him as such. I wanted to change that because the sadness in his eyes reminded me of a time in my life that still hurt to remember. "Call me Rome."

"Is your first name really Romeo?" he asked, a crooked smile lifting the corner of his lips.

"Yes," I sighed. "My mother is a big fan of classic literature. Luckily for my sister, my dad put his foot down after I was born, and they stuck with a more traditional name for her. Of course, I told her she was named after Ashley Wilkes from *Gone with the Wind*, whom she couldn't stand." That earned a chuckle from Howie.

"I wanted to apologize for my surly attitude when we met earlier. My Miriam would be so upset with me right now. She wouldn't want me to walk through life like a zombie snapping and snarling at everyone. She would want me to look for the beautiful things around me and remember all the good times we had. Some days it just seems like a bigger task than I can pull off."

"I'm so sorry for your loss, Howie. Was today a particularly bad day?" I asked softly.

"It would've been her seventieth birthday. Instead of remembering all the birthdays we spent together, I'm thinking of all the places I never took her. God, what I wouldn't give to be able to take my wife to Paris and kiss her at the top of the Eiffel Tower. Why am I stuck in this quagmire of what should've been instead of what was? I tell you, Rome, my Miriam was the most beautiful soul you'd ever meet."

Bark! Bark!

Howie snickered then looked under the table at Dolly. "Besides you, little lady." I was pleased to see a real smile on Howie's face and shocked at how it transformed his looks. "I can't believe I've sat down at your table and just started spilling my guts. You're a virtual stranger, not a psychiatrist."

"I'm not that kind of doctor," I assured him. "However, I am a person who knows exactly what you're going through. Maybe something inside you recognized that about me."

"Maybe," he said gruffly. "You've lost someone special too? A spouse?" It was nice he didn't automatically assume it was a woman, but I was sure he'd heard about my sexuality through the grapevine. I didn't exactly blurt my orientation through a bullhorn, but I was very open with the board when they interviewed me. If they didn't think

I would be a good fit, then I didn't want the job. I felt it was better to get it out there in the open than wait for it to become part of the conversation.

"A partner," I corrected. "Peter passed away before it was legal for us to marry, but he was my husband in every way that counted."

"I'm sorry for your loss too, Rome. How long ago did Peter pass?"

"Seven years," I said. "How long has it been for you?"

"Almost two years, but it feels like it happened yesterday."

"It does for a long time, but one day, you wake up and you realize a lot of time has passed, and the memories don't hurt quite as bad as they did the day before."

"I can't imagine ever feeling that way," Howie said, eyes watering as if that would be worse than the misery of missing her. "I don't want to forget the sound of her voice."

"I wouldn't want you to either, Howie."

"She had the best laugh," he said, a single tear rolling down his face. "And her smile was so bright it could warm you on the coldest days."

"If you can, wrap the memory of her smile and laughter around you like a warm blanket. It's possible to move forward while remembering; they're not mutually exclusive."

"Is that what you did when it got hard?"

"Yes, and I adopted Dolly. I focused on caring for her instead of fostering my grief. Day by day and little by little, I started to heal. Birthdays and holidays are still hard, but I do things to honor Peter's memory. I planted his favorite flowers at my new home so I have a part of him with me. I'll fix his favorite meal on his birthday. I donate to his favorite charities at Christmastime. I do all the things he'd do if he were still around. Some people see that as clinging to the past, but I don't see it that way."

"You're still young. Do you hope to fall in love again someday?" he asked.

I pictured Julius Shepherd and recalled the way he made the blood rush through my veins from just a shy smile. "I do. I have a lot of life yet to live and many laughs to share. I'd rather not experience them alone."

"Does that mean you've already—"

"Dad?" A new voice joined us, cutting him off before he could finish his question. I was grateful for the interruption because I knew what he was going to ask but not sure how I'd answer.

"Oh, hello, Seth," Howie said, rising to his feet.

"Dad, I've been worried sick about you. I've been calling your phone for hours." Seth hugged his father tight. Howie chuckled and returned his son's embrace, clinging to him longer, like he needed the affection more than he was willing to let on.

"I took a drive to the lake and walked around then stopped to talk to Dr. Bradley when I saw him sitting here. He's the new super—"

"Superintendent," Seth supplied. "I've heard great things about you from my wife, but I've not had the pleasure of meeting you yet. Seth Wilson," he said, offering his hand to me."

"Rome Bradley. It's good to meet you."

"This is Dolly," Howie said, squatting down next to my dog. He began petting her silky ears. "I think I'd like to adopt a dog, Seth. My house is just too quiet without your mama."

"Really?" Seth looked from where his dad knelt by my dog then back at me. "I think several of us suggested that to you already."

"You did, but it had to be my idea. I think I saw a poster at the library that said this upcoming Saturday is adoption day at the shelter."

"You could always get a puppy from a breeder."

"Nah, I want to rescue a dog from heartache." I thought his new dog might rescue him in return.

Seth's eyes widened and glistened with unshed tears. "That sounds perfect. Maybe we can make a family day out of it."

"That would be great," Howie said, rising to his feet. "I need to be getting home. Thank you so much for chatting with me, Rome."

"It was my pleasure. If you and your new companion want walking buddies, just let me know. Dolly and I take a stroll every night."

"I might take you up on that. Good night, Rome."

"Good night," I said to them both.

I rose from my chair, threw away my trash, and began my trek back home where a nice glass of wine and a captivating script awaited me.

Chapter Four

*"Inherent force of matter is the power resisting by which
every body, so far as it is able, perseveres in its state either of
resting or of moving uniformly straight forward."*
~Isaac Newton

"The key to resisting the sexy, silver fox is to keep it moving."
~ Julius Shepherd

O VER THE NEXT TWO WEEKS, IGNORING MY GROWING ATTRACTION to Rome, as I'd come to think of him, was easy. I had tennis practice or matches at least six days a week, and I spent my evenings grading papers and composing music for *Inside Out*. I suspected Rome knew I returned his attraction just as he'd picked up on my reluctance to act upon it. For the most part, he respected the boundaries I'd set in place and only reached out to me through emails to talk about the play we were both reading and helping to develop. I very well couldn't ignore his communications, but I could choose not to acknowledge the personal notes he added to the bottom that complimented me on the tie I'd chosen to wear that day or mentioned he regretted missing me in the teachers' lounge during lunchtime on the days he joined us.

I had to give the man credit; he was serious about fostering a great relationship with the teaching staff in the three buildings, which included bringing catered lunches once a week. It's true that

I happened not to attend, but if he'd asked around, he would know I usually spent my lunch break in my classroom. I knew it made me look standoffish to the rest of the teachers, but my workload was going to be heavy enough without adding the play to my teaching and coaching responsibilities. I wouldn't say I felt overwhelmed, but I had enough on my mind that I didn't need to add fending off unwanted advances to the list.

Unwanted advances. That made me snicker. In the stillest hours of the early morning, I would dream of Rome and wake up hard, hot, and yearning for him. I started running more in the morning, and if that didn't drive him out of my system, I took care of business in the hot shower that followed. I used the excess energy in my classroom and on the court which meant my students were engaged and my tennis players were motivated. I was winning at this avoidance thing until Rome decided to step up his game on the third week of school.

"Knock knock," he said, standing in my open door with a carry-out container in his hand. "I thought I'd take a chance and catch you before you ate your…" His words trailed off as he tried to see what I had laid out on my desk from across the room.

"It's leftover chicken Caesar salad from dinner last night." The smells wafting across the room intrigued me, making it easy to put the lid on my Tupperware container and shove it aside. "What did you bring me?"

Rome accepted my question as the invitation I intended and entered my room. His stride was casual but powerful at the same time. The man moved with a natural grace and confidence that hinted at tightly controlled power. Was he that controlled in bed too or was it the one place he felt safe enough to free the beast he tried to hide from the world? The closer he came, the faster my pulse raced, answering the power that hummed beneath the surface of my tormentor. Rome's blue eyes locked on mine, and that crooked smirk returned to his face because there was no way he missed the desire he stirred within me. I should hate that my body betrayed my true desires and the smug expression on his face, but I had to focus all my energy on not letting my imagination run wild. Getting a boner in my classroom was a big no-no, even if the only other person in the room was a consenting adult who would love seeing the way my body reacted to his nearness.

"I brought you a little of everything since you've been so elusive in both your attendance at the weekly lunches and your email responses when I bring it up."

"Is that like Mohammed going to the mountains when they wouldn't come to him?"

"I don't think anyone's ever compared me to a prophet before, but there is a mountain of mashed potatoes in here."

I couldn't help the little hum of pleasure that escaped me. Carbs were my only vice. "Gravy too?"

"What's Salisbury steak without mashed potatoes and gravy?"

"A life not worth living," I said vehemently, rubbing my hands together as Rome set the Styrofoam container on my desk. I eagerly opened it and saw he'd brought me honey-glazed carrots and a yeast roll also. "Who is going to teach my class and coach the tennis match after school once I fall into a carb coma?"

"I could take it back and you could eat your—"

My playful growl cut him off, stunning us both. Rome's eyes widened in surprise then closed as a delicious shiver worked its way through his body. Yes, I knew the sexy man was envisioning all the ways he could make me growl. When Rome reopened his eyes, his icy blue gaze burned with intensity.

"I don't want to keep you from working," Rome said, taking two steps back from my desk. I couldn't stop myself from raking my eyes up and down his lean, muscular frame. When my eyes returned to his face, I saw that all traces of the smugness from a few minutes before were gone. Rome's jaw was clenched as tightly as his fists, and I saw his internal struggle reflected in his expressive eyes. He wanted to stay in the room with me but didn't trust himself to do it. I liked that I affected his control; I liked it more than I was willing to admit to myself. What would he do? Lean across my desk and kiss me? I wasn't ready to accept the ramifications of meeting him halfway if he did. "I just wanted to be sure you didn't miss out. Again."

His subtle rebuke made me smile. "It's not personal, you know," I said. "I rarely eat lunch in the lounge." I gestured to the stack of papers on my desk. I had started entering the grades into the website the school used to share real-time updates with parents and students before he stopped by. "These honor students fret if their grades aren't updated regularly."

"So do their parents," he said with a sly grin. "Good luck tonight."

It would be our stiffest competition of the season against our county rivals. Whoever won the most points would be in first place for the league. The highest Blissville had ever finished was second, so our team was hungry to prove we were the real deal. "Thank you, sir."

"Please call me Rome," he said. It wasn't the first time he'd asked me to be less formal with him, but it was the first time I gave it serious consideration. Of course, calling a man sir in certain circumstances could be very personal, but it wasn't something that had ever appealed to me.

"Thank you, Rome." I loved the way his name felt on my tongue, and his flared nostrils said he liked it too. "Will you be there?" I'd heard he attended as many high school events as he could but had yet to see him at the tennis events.

"I wasn't sure you would want me there," he admitted.

He was right; I hadn't wanted him to attend. Had one kind act changed my mind? It shouldn't have because I would find it even harder to ignore his presence and concentrate even after such a brief exchange. "I think the kids would appreciate your support." *The kids, huh?*

"I would hate to disappoint *them*. See you this afternoon."

"Thank you," I said, gesturing to the food I had yet to taste.

His answer was a quick wink before he turned and left my office without a backward glance. I didn't have time to contemplate what had transpired between us because I only had fifteen minutes before my next class, and I wouldn't waste it waging an internal battle when I could be eating. The steak was tender and flavorful, and the mashed potatoes were creamy and delicious with the brown gravy on top. I ate and entered grades until not even a single carrot remained. The bell for my next class rang just as I tossed the empty container in the trash.

"Mr. Shepherd, I have a question about my most recent grades," Angela Hightower said when she entered the classroom.

"Angela, you shouldn't know what your recent grades are because you're not supposed to have your phone on you during school," I said.

"It's in my locker," she replied. "I checked my grades between classes."

I was proud she took her education so seriously, but I also wanted her to laugh and live for something other than her updated grades. "We went over my policy on the first day of school, Angela. I won't use classroom time to discuss individual concerns over grades. That's not fair to the other students because it cuts into my lesson. I have a tennis match after school, but I will make myself available until three fifteen if that works for you." The young lady was upset because she earned ninety-seven points out of a hundred. As ridiculous as it may seem, I knew it was important to her, and I wouldn't belittle her concerns.

"I'll be here," she said with a firm nod before she went to her desk.

I stood in front of the class and waited for the desks to fill before I spoke. "Now that we've covered the basics of atoms, we're going to move on to atomic mass and atomic mass numbers." My announcement was met with a mixture of excitement, grumbling, and indifference. I freaking loved my job.

"Oh, yay," Ellie said excitedly. "Dr. Bradley came to cheer us on. I was starting to think he was like the rest of the pricks in our community and only cared about the football team."

"Language, Ellie," I admonished. "We all know he's been making his rounds to all the fall athletic events. It means more that he's here to cheer us on when we claim first place in the league for the first time in school history."

"You really think we're going to do it?" she asked, sounding less precocious and confident than usual. She and her teammate, Sara Devers, were our best individual players and were practically unstoppable in doubles competition.

"I know so," I assured her. "Let's make sure we have a good warmup and let's take down East Carter High."

I supervised warmups and met with the head coach from East Carter while managing not to look in Rome's direction. I needed to be at my best which meant I had to pretend he wasn't there. I couldn't ask my players to focus if I was distracted. I'd seen him when he first arrived and noticed he'd changed into a pair of gym shorts, sneakers, and a Blissville High T-shirt with our bulldog mascot on the front. I didn't need to look in his direction when I knew he had those baby blues beneath his aviator sunglasses trained on me.

Every match against East Carter was a dogfight, but I knew the night would be ours when we went into the final set. Ellie and Sara were playing their best tennis of the season, and I saw the determination on their faces when I spoke with them before they took the court.

"I see how badly you want this, but do you know what I want from you as your coach?"

"A first-place trophy at the end of the season?" Sara asked.

"I want you to enjoy every serve, volley, and point. Play as a team and have fun, ladies."

"Winning is fun, coach," Ellie said with a sly grin before she looped her arm through Sara's and pulled her toward the court.

Those ladies at East Carter didn't stand a chance against their determination. Ellie and Sara coasted to an easy victory because they played together like a well-oiled machine. We lined up and exchanged high fives with our opponents over the net before I took my team off to the side to celebrate.

"Congratulations, everyone. You played your hearts out this afternoon, and I'm so proud of you. That doesn't mean we can slack off. We might be leading the league, but East Carter is going to be hungry to reclaim the top spot. If we falter, they'll do just that. I want you to celebrate tonight but be ready to practice tomorrow after school. Bulldogs on three. One…two…three…"

"Bulldogs!" we all shouted together.

The parents who were able to attend came over and congratulated me on the victory, and I assured them the win belonged solely to the kids. I was aware of Rome's presence on the periphery and knew he was waiting for the right opportunity to approach me which didn't happen until the last parent, student, and coach left.

He slid his glasses to the top of his head and offered me a warm smile. "Congratulations, Julius."

"Thank you, Rome." I thought I was prepared for the energy that would blast through my body when I accepted his handshake, but I was wrong. It was so much more intense than the first time. "My friends call me Jules," I found myself saying.

"Are we friends?" he asked huskily.

"I…um…" I rubbed the back of my neck while trying to figure out how to answer that. We were friendly, but I couldn't say we were friends. Could we even be friends with the attraction sparking between us?

Rome began to chuckle. "I didn't mean to make things awkward between us. I guess I'm just rusty."

"Rusty at being friends with someone?"

"With someone I find attractive and would like to get to know better. Romantically," he added.

"As in date?"

"I would settle for you not avoiding me and would love to work my way up to a cup of coffee and a pastry. See where things go from there. Is that something you're willing to entertain?"

I had no damn clue how to approach the situation and decided honesty would be best. "Rome, I'm very attracted to you, but I'm not sure pursuing a relationship with you is good for me." I could tell he was trying to figure out the reasons I felt that way, but he didn't press me.

"I respect your honesty, Jules. I hope you respect that I don't give up easily."

"Fair enough."

I didn't hear from Rome for the rest of the week. He didn't email me or stop by my classroom. I thought maybe his parting words to me after the tennis match were just bluster, but it turned out he was just gathering his second wind and biding his time.

I reported for duty at the concession stand on Friday night because it was the tennis team's turn to volunteer. The kids would rather watch the game, but many of their parents volunteered their time to serve nachos, hot dogs, hamburgers, popcorn, walking tacos, and an assortment of candy and drinks during the football game against our biggest rival. The boosters were on hand to show us the ropes and determine which of us would be best with money. One of the moms was a bank teller and one of the dads was an accountant, so they were elected. I would work with the food, assembling hot dogs, hamburgers, and walking tacos. Just before the service windows opened, our final volunteer for the night showed up.

"Back again for more punishment, Dr. Bradley?" one of the moms asked.

"This is like the fourth home game in a row," another chimed in. "We've never had a superintendent work the concession stand one time let alone four times in one season."

"I enjoy it," he said. I was disappointed to find out he didn't volunteer solely to have an excuse to be with me until he turned his twinkling blue eyes on me. "I see you already have someone doing my usual job."

"I'm sure Mr. Shepherd could use your help. It's a lot for one guy to keep up with during a normal game, but things will really be hopping tonight."

"Want some help?" he asked, coming to stand beside me. God, he smelled delicious. I wasn't the only one who noticed how damn good he looked in his tight, dark wash jeans and the navy blue, long-sleeved T-shirt that clung to his biceps and pecs. That damn bulldog had never looked so fine.

"Sure," I said, playing it off like it was no big deal. "Do you prefer the hot dogs, burgers, or walking tacos?"

"Doesn't matter to me. Put me wherever you want me," Rome said softly enough that only I heard him. I had my back turned to the rest of volunteers, so they didn't see the heated flush creeping up my neck. Rome's eyes widened like he couldn't believe what he'd just said.

I handed him the tongs for the hot dogs as a chuckle rumbled out of my chest. His laughter joined mine, and I knew the rest of the volunteers wondered what was so funny. Our laughter died soon enough when the service windows opened because the boosters hadn't been wrong about the projected crowds. We didn't have a slow moment from the first customer until the final seconds of the fourth quarter when we all gathered in the window to watch our kicker send the game-winning field goal through the uprights as time ran out on the clock.

We erupted into cheers and high-fived each other as the marching band blared the fight song and the home crowd went wild. We had about an hour of cleanup once we shut the doors, but it passed by fast when we were in such high spirits. Afterward, we all walked to our cars in the parking lot which was pretty deserted by then.

"Hey, Jules," Rome said when I stopped at my car. "I'll be at Books and Brew for coffee tomorrow morning if you're free." He knew damn well I didn't have a tennis commitment in the morning. "I'll even let you buy."

I wanted to say yes, but I kept thinking that getting involved with him would be a big mistake. It was more than the fact he was the superintendent of schools where I taught; there was the age gap and race thing to consider. I would be a liar if I pretended like it didn't matter to me, but a man didn't forget the prejudices he faced growing up because his black mother happened to love a white man. On the other hand, I was never one to back away from something just because it was hard. All I owed the man was honesty, and right then, I only had one answer. "Maybe," I said, opening my door.

Rome chuckled warmly. "Fair enough. I'll be there at nine if you decide to join me. Sleep well, Jules." I knew damn well sleep would elude me.

Chapter Five

"Thoughts are but dreams till their effects be tried."
~William Shakespeare

"Wishing and hoping will only take you so far.
Sometimes you gotta take life by the balls."
~Romeo Bradley

"O NE SALTED CARAMEL COFFEE AND A CRANBERRY ORANGE muffin," said Maegan Miracle, co-owner of Books and Brew, as she removed my items from her tray and set them on the table I'd chosen in front of the bookstore and coffee shop. She and her twin brother had added the outdoor seating in the spring which made it nice on the mornings I brought Dolly with me. "And a biscuit for milady." Maegan did a cute curtsy before holding out the dog biscuit shaped like a fire hydrant for Dolly to assess.

"She prefers the biscuits shaped like stilettos or handbags," I teased. "High-dollar diva."

"A dog after my own heart," Maegan replied then scratched Dolly's ears once she gingerly accepted the biscuit. "You know, I probably should've waited for you to order rather than assume you'd want—"

"The same thing I get every time?" I waved away the thought then took a sip of my favorite coffee. "Although, I am hoping to meet someone here."

"Oh, is Howie coming too?"

It was a natural assumption since I'd formed an unlikely but meaningful relationship with the older man after our first chat at the ice cream parlor. He'd adopted a beagle named Bess and we started walking our dogs together every night. Sometimes we even met for coffee, so it made sense she drew that conclusion.

"Good morning," Howie boomed from behind me as if Maegan conjured him out of thin air. "Look, Bess, there's your best girl Dolly." It was true the dogs were best friends. I'd never seen two dogs take to each other as quickly as they did. "Maegan, can I have a black coffee and a piña colada muffin?"

"Of course," she said cheerfully then retreated inside.

"I'm glad to see you this morning since we didn't get our walk last night. How was the game?"

"I didn't see much of it because I worked in the concession stand." To be honest, the only thing I remembered about the previous evening was Julius—the sound of his voice, the crisp scent of his cologne or body wash, and the way my skin tingled anytime we bumped into each other while assembling food. He consumed my thoughts and made it nearly impossible for me to focus on anything or anyone else. That's why I made my subtle move. Julius was obviously hesitant to get involved with me even though he returned my attraction. All the wishing and hoping was making me crazy as I tried to patiently give him time to warm up to the idea of us. I needed to know if there was hope or if I should move on.

"You look wound tight this morning, Rome," Howie said, breaking into my thoughts. "I've noticed you've seemed distracted on our walks. I'm not boring you, am I?"

My heart broke right then. "Howie, I'm sorry if I've given you that impression because it's the furthest thing from the truth. Our friendship means the world to me, and our walks keep me sane."

"Man trouble then?" He'd leaned forward and lowered his voice.

He didn't do it because he found the subject awkward nor was he ashamed. We'd spent hours talking about the different experiences we'd had as gay and straight men. What he knew about gay people were stereotypes perpetuated in television and movies, and he was eager to hear what I had to say. I listened to him talk about the way he was raised and understood how prejudices and ignorance were spread from generation to generation. Howie was proud he and his wife raised their kids to be more open-minded. His lowered voice was his way of protecting my privacy.

I chuckled and tilted my head as I rolled his question around. "Something like that. I invited him to meet me here for coffee, but I doubt he shows up."

"Is it someone I know?"

"He lives locally, but we haven't talked about him," I replied.

"Is it the new pediatrician? You should hear the single ladies crying because Dr. Love is gay. You'd make a handsome couple."

"No, it's not him, but thank you."

Howie narrowed his eyes, and I could tell he was rolling it around in his mind to determine which eligible bachelor caught my eye. "That hunky fireman?"

"We have a hunky gay fireman living here?"

Howie laughed and nodded. "He's a big bruiser though." My friend's face turned bright red when he realized how I could interpret his comment. "I meant height and breadth of shoulders. I, uh, didn't mean…"

"I knew what you meant," I assured him. I saw a charcoal gray Honda Accord park by the curb down the block. Could it be? That was a common car and a popular color… My heart accelerated when the driver's door opened and Julius stepped out. I had a moment to study him before he saw me, and the turmoil etched on his handsome face tugged at my heartstrings.

Sensing my distraction, Howie turned to look down the sidewalk. "That him?"

Yes, my heart shouted. I was too dumbstruck to speak and could only nod my head.

Howie turned back to me just in time to see my confirmation. He scooted back his chair and started to rise until I stopped him by placing my hand on his arm. "Let me introduce you." I waved to get Jules's attention and was happy to see a warm smile replace his troubled expression.

"Hello," Jules warmly said when he reached our table.

Howie and I both stood up to greet him. "Julius, this is my good friend, Howie, and, Howie, this is Julius. He teaches advanced chemistry at the high school."

"It's good to meet you, Julius," Howie said, shaking his hand. "Bess and I were just keeping Rome and Dolly company while they waited for you."

"It's good to meet you too," Jules said. Then he leaned down to greet the dogs who wagged their tails excitedly. "Hello, ladies."

Maegan came outside with Howie's coffee and muffin on a tray. "Hi, Julius. What can I get for you this morning?"

"Good morning, Maegan." Julius offered her a warm smile even if a trace of uncertainty lingered in his eyes. "I'll have a gingerbread chai latte and a lemon poppy seed muffin."

"I'll follow you inside to pay for my breakfast and get a paper bag so Bess and I can get going," Howie told her. "Do you mind if Bess hangs out with you for a minute?" he asked me.

"You don't have to rush off," I said. "Stay and join us."

"Oh no," Howie persisted. "We have a big day ahead of us. We're keeping an eye on the grandkids while their parents do some shopping for the youngest one's birthday party." He shook his head. "I look forward to seeing what they come up with every year. At first, I thought making a big deal about birthdays was silly, but the kids have such a good time. Who does it hurt, anyway? It's not like they hire a circus to perform and bring in a petting zoo. They decorate the house in a theme that matches the latest craze the kids are wrapped up in and serve food, cake, and ice cream."

"No bouncy castles?" I teased.

"Well, they did that once. It was a lot of fun."

"You got in the bouncy castle?" I asked.

"I'm not always a stick in the mud, you know?"

"I do." I'd gotten to see the warm, loving man Howie truly was once he started opening up to me during our nightly walks. Grief did evil things to a person's mind, affecting every aspect of their lives.

"I'll be right back after I pay the nice lady," Howie said, following Maegan inside. She looped her arm through his and said something I couldn't hear, but it made Howie hoot with laughter.

"I didn't mean to run your friend off," Julius said, sitting in the chair Howie had vacated.

"You didn't run anyone off. I invited you, remember? Howie was walking Bess and stopped by." My eyes roamed greedily over his face, and my pulse leaped when his shy smile became a devious one.

"You didn't think I'd show up, did you?"

"It depended on the minute. Part of the time, I thought you would, and part of the time, I thought you wouldn't."

Julius chuckled. "How long have you been thinking about it?"

"I haven't been able to think about anything else since I asked you to meet me."

"Me either," he confessed, looking away briefly. "So, why did you think I might show up?"

We were two grown men and had no room for playing coy games. Julius asked me a direct question, and my response would be equally as straightforward. "I can see you return my attraction. You're starting to look less hesitant and more curious about your reaction to me. What were your reasons for wanting to come here this morning?" I wanted to reach out and cover his hand with mine but knew it was too soon.

"I don't want to live a life where I'm second-guessing decisions I made or regret letting people slip out of my life just because the situation could be difficult. What were the reasons you thought I'd choose not to come?" he asked.

"I thought my position as superintendent would be the biggest detraction, but I also worried you might think I was too old." Julius snorted. "What? How many twenty-somethings like you want to date forty-somethings like me?"

"More than you know. You're intelligent, funny, kind, mature, and you must know how good looking you are."

"I…um—"

"You have a mirror, right?"

"Yeah, but—"

"Start looking in it more often. You are one sexy man. You're the entire package." My stunned expression made him chuckle. He was so different from the man I talked to during school events. Gone was his shyness and in its place was a direct gaze I couldn't look away from. "You wanted honesty, so I'm giving it to you."

"Is it my job then?"

"Mostly," he agreed. "I'm new to this school, and I want the conversation about me to reflect on my skills as an educator, not my sexual orientation or who I'm dating."

"Fair enough."

"There's also the issue of race," Julius said. "It shouldn't matter in this day and age, but then again, it shouldn't have mattered when I was growing up and getting bullied left and right either. The crap my parents went through just for loving each other was ridiculous," he said, shaking his head. "I'm not afraid to battle hard for the things I want, but I need to make sure the person is worth the fight." I wanted to be worthy.

"I'm sorry to hear you were bullied as a kid, Julius." I decided to throw caution to the wind and cover his hand where it rested on the table. I didn't trace his soft skin with my thumb; I just let him feel the weight of my hand and learn my touch. "I'm not afraid of what people will think or say," I said earnestly. "Something inside you clicks as you get older and living for what others think no longer is important. As much as I love to please others, I care most about pleasing myself. God, that must sound selfish."

"It sounds smart and like something we should all do at an earlier age."

Howie came out of the coffee shop, approached our table, and took Bess's leash from my other hand. "I hope you guys have a great day. It was nice meeting you, Julius. Rome, give me a call or shoot me a text if you want to walk the girls tonight."

"Sounds good. I'll see you later," I told the older man.

"It was nice meeting you too, Howie," Julius said warmly.

Howie whistled as he walked away, making me smile.

"Have you been friends with Howie for long?"

"No, and we didn't get off to a very good start, either." Then I told Julius about overhearing his conversation with Irv. He threw his head back and laughed at the Dr. Fancy Pants remark. "Don't think you can start calling me that now," I warned.

"I wouldn't dream of it," Julius replied, but his wry smile said otherwise.

"His friend, Irv, explained to me that Howie hadn't been himself since his wife died, and grief is something I know well. Howie apologized to me the next time he saw me, and we struck up a conversation about life after losing someone special. From there, a beautiful friendship developed."

Julius searched my eyes, and I could tell he was curious about the special person I'd lost. He might've asked me, but Maegan approached the table with his chai latte and muffin. Julius pulled his hand free of mine to accept his breakfast.

Had he asked, I would've answered, even though it might not have been the best topic to discuss on our getting-to-know-you-over-coffee-and-pastries date. I knew in my heart Peter was looking down and smiling on me. He would've been the first person to give me a verbal kick in the ass and demand I didn't grieve my life away. He would've wanted me to live well enough for both of us.

Because I wanted to keep the tone light, I shifted gears away from heavier topics to focus on the one thing we certainly had in common. "How's the music coming along for the play?"

"I'm finished," he said after taking a sip of his latte. "These kids are crazy talented, aren't they?"

"Absolutely," I agreed. "Does the play director get to hear the music early?" I was dying to hear what he came up with.

Julius blushed and took a deep breath. "That's always the hardest part."

"Letting others hear the music you create?"

"Yes. It's so personal."

"I didn't mean to put pressure on you," I assured him.

"I have to let someone hear it sooner or later. That's the purpose of creating music, right?" Julius looked at his latte like it was the most interesting thing he'd ever seen.

"Yes, but it doesn't have to be me. I'm sure Clara, Ellie, and Curtis would love to be the ones who hear it first. It would only be fair."

He slowly lifted his head and met my gaze. The morning sun made his hazel eyes look gold. "I would like for it to be you." Excited energy pulsed through my blood because I knew what a big moment this was for us. He was trusting me with something precious. Julius pulled his phone out of his pocket and his AirPods out of another. He handed the AirPods to me, and I slid them into my ears while he worked on his phone. When he finished, he laid it in front of me. All I had to do was tap the play button on his phone and I would hear pieces of his soul.

I kept my eyes locked on his while I tapped the phone to begin. I don't know what I was expecting, but it wasn't the soulful sound of a cello and piano creating the most beautiful melody I'd ever heard. I closed my eyes and let it wash over me. I knew exactly which scenes the music went with and thought about the lyrics I had read. I heard the struggles the characters faced and the love and acceptance they found. It was pure perfection. I felt tears well in my eyes and opened them so Julius could see the way his music impacted me. He swallowed hard then smiled in relief.

Each song was more beautiful than the one before. "How?" I asked in a thick voice once the last note faded.

"I recorded the cello parts first and then the piano. Then I used software to put them together," Julius replied.

"I meant how can any one person create anything this beautiful? This is just...stunning, Julius. Can I please have a copy of the recording?"

"I will make a copy for each of us once the kids approve it. They might want to make changes." I shook my head.

"You don't think they'll want to change anything?"

Maybe they would, but that wasn't what I meant. "I want the version that came straight from your heart."

He studied me for a few more minutes. "I'll email you a link to download the music."

"Thank you." I knew it might be too much too soon, but I couldn't seem to stop myself from asking. "What are you doing this afternoon?"

"I'm going to my brother's college football game in a little bit. He plays cornerback for UC. I actually need to get going soon."

"Afterward?" I asked, unwilling to give up quite yet.

"I don't have any plans."

"What do you think about chicken Parmesan?"

Julius grinned. "I love it."

"My place at seven?"

Julius opened the notes app on his phone and asked me to enter my address for him. Once I finished, he asked, "Do you like red wine or white?"

"Surprise me."

Chapter Six

"Anyone who has never made a mistake has never tried anything new."
~Albert Einstein

"It's okay to fall on your ass. It's why we were born with a cushion."
~Julius Shepherd

"DINNER AT HIS PLACE, HUH?" MOM ASKED. I COULD HEAR the humor in her voice coming through the speakers in my car. "What's he making?"

I'd called her on the way home from Marcus's game to let her know how it went since she was unable to watch it on television. Mom was excited to hear my baby brother had a standout game against a big rival, but her attention swiftly turned to my love life. She was very excited to hear I'd accepted Rome's dinner invitation.

"Chicken parm," I replied.

"Make sure you wear good underwear."

I snorted. "Mom, it's just dinner."

"That's how it always starts. I want you to have a great night with your silver fox. Be safe, Julius."

"Always, Mom. You know, you could always find your own silver fox to lavish all your attention on."

"Julius…" she chided softly, letting her voice trail off.

"Dad wouldn't want you to spend all your time working at the hospital followed by lonely nights at home, Mom. He'd want you to have someone special in your life."

"I can finally admit he would want me to find happiness again, Jules. I promise you I will make an attempt if a silver fox comes along and catches my eye."

"You have to be looking up for that to happen, Mama. Love only miraculously finds people in those Hallmark Christmas movies. Then again, if you're watching your feet when you walk, you might run into a handsome fella who also isn't paying attention to his surroundings. Then you'll look into each other's eyes and just know."

"Listen to you now. You give in to one date after leading that man around by his nuts for months and you're a dating expert now, huh? Who the hell are you and what have you done with my son Julius? You must've been snatched out of your bed by aliens and returned to earth with one of them invading your body."

"Mom, really? An alien invaded my body and the first thing he does is start watching sappy movies on Hallmark."

"Better than Lifetime because he might want to start killing people instead of romancing them."

As was typical with my mother, our conversation had veered way into left field, or outer space if I listened to her. "I haven't been snatched by aliens, Mom. I just…" I wasn't sure how to say this without stirring up all kinds of pain. If she taught me anything at all, it was to be direct and speak with honesty. "I want what you and Dad had."

"Baby, I want that for you too. You don't know how happy I am to hear you say that. Every person needs to be loved like your father loved me, Jules. Maybe Romeo Bradley is the man to love you until you're breathless, or maybe he's not. You won't know unless you try. If there's one thing a scientist knows, it's never give up. Things don't always work out the first time in science or love, so we keep trying until we find the right formula."

I loved it when my mom put things in a scientific perspective. Of course, love is sometimes hard for scientists to grasp. Numbers, equations, and formulas we can understand. To many scientists, the heart is nothing more than the organ that pumps blood through our veins. I wasn't among them. I've felt my heart swell with pride, happiness, and love. I've also felt it break. Sure, the brain is the mainframe computer of our bodies, but I will not discredit the heart and the way it reacts to the emotions our brains detect. The two work in tandem until they're conflicted about what they want.

My heart wants Romeo Bradley; my brain thinks it's a big mistake. Will I take a chance and put myself out there for Rome or will I retreat because it's safer? Only time will tell which of those two organs would win.

"I love you, Mom."

"I love you too. Call me soon and give me the details of your night."

"Details?"

"Not *those* kinds of details, J. We have a strong relationship, but let's not get carried away. Besides, it's just dinner, right?"

"Right. I'll make sure to describe the dinner in minute detail."

"You can be such a wiseass. Your father would be so proud." The warmth and love in her voice made me smile. She would always love my dad, but that didn't mean she couldn't love someone else too.

It also reminded me of the conversation I had with Rome over coffee when he talked about Howie coping with grief. He made it sound like he too had lost someone special, and I didn't get the feeling he was talking about a parent.

"I hope so," I replied.

"I know so, J. Talk to you soon."

"Goodnight, Mom."

The thing I disliked most about fall was how early darkness fell. I found Rome's house easily based on his directions, but I shouldn't have been worried in a town the size of Blissville. Even though it was dark, I knew what his house looked like because I'd driven by it many times before without knowing it was his home I was coveting. It was a bungalow-style home painted a cool dark gray with white trim around the windows, a large covered porch, and a dark red front door. The exterior of the home was both cool and warm and combined old-world elegance with contemporary touches. I thought the dichotomy represented the man who resided beneath the slate gray metal roof.

I wasn't sure what kind of wine he liked, so I bought a bottle of white and red wine. On a whim, I also grabbed a bouquet of flowers and a toy for Dolly at the supermarket. I felt a little silly and second-guessed myself after I rang the doorbell and waited for him to answer. I looked for a place to stash the flowers until I left, but Rome answered the door before I could put my plan into action.

"Hi," he said, sounding and looking tense. Rome glanced down and smiled when he saw the flowers in my hand. "Please come in." He stepped aside so I could enter.

The living room was beautiful and immaculately decorated. The walls were painted a slate blue-gray and were decorated with black-and-white canvas prints of cities from all over the world. Rome had real hardwood floors, not the laminate that was so popular. They looked like someone had refinished them recently with a dark stain that was warm, and inviting. Throw pillows the same deep red as his front door decorated the gray and cream striped sofa and chairs. The various types of plants strategically placed around the room was a lovely touch and a telltale sign that the inhabitant was a nurturer. Dolly was nestled on a blanket in the corner of the couch wagging her tail but not giving up her cozy spot to greet me.

I handed the wine and flowers to Rome. "These are for you." He accepted them and buried his nose in the bouquet of lilies, carnations, and roses. "I couldn't decide on white or red wine, so I bought both."

"I would've been happy with either. Thank you for the flowers,

Jules. They're beautiful."

We both sounded so stiff, formal, and uncomfortable like neither of us had ever dated before meeting one another. I suspected Rome was concerned he would come across too strong. He was likely feeding off the tension I emitted. If I relaxed, then he would too.

"Your brother had a great game today. I bet he was excited for breaking the school's record for interceptions." I was surprised he watched, but then again, I wasn't. Marcus was important to me, and therefore, he'd become important to Rome if we ever got past this awkwardness.

Without thinking it through, I leaned forward and kissed Rome. The urge to cup his face and deepen the kiss was strong enough to make my knees weak, but I pulled back. I slowly opened my eyes, savoring the way my lips tingled from the brief contact. A relaxed smile and dazed eyes greeted me, telling me I'd made the right decision.

"That was lovely but very unexpected."

"You looked like you were stretched tight enough to snap, and I knew it was my fault. I wanted to put you at ease instead of us trying to make clumsy conversation."

"I truly was excited about your brother's accomplishment." I saw the sincerity in his eyes, and it only made me want to kiss him again, but Dolly barking from the couch stopped me from reaching for him again.

"I have something for you too, little lady."

I pulled the stuffed toy shaped like a latte out of the bag and walked across the room to give it to her. She sniffed it suspiciously at first then snatched it out of my hand and shook it vigorously. "I think she likes it."

"That's the cutest dog toy ever. Thank you."

"I thought it was appropriate to commemorate the first day she and I met."

Rome reached for my hand and linked our fingers, and I loved that his hesitation from before was completely gone. He acted on instinct which was exactly what I wanted. "Come keep me company while I find a vase for my flowers and put the finishing touches on dinner."

"It smells delicious," I said as he led me through a dining room and into a spacious kitchen. The cabinets had a dark cherry finish which complemented the black marble countertops. Rome's appliances were top-of-the-line stainless steel and belonged to a man who loved to cook. I loved the little pops of red color from the coffee maker, canisters, and stand mixer. The walls in the kitchen were painted ivory to balance out the darkness of the other materials. More plants sat in the window above the sink. "You have a lovely home."

"Thank you," Rome replied. "I'd love to take credit for the design, but I can't. I hired Dare to decorate it for me. He did a phenomenal job."

"Dare? My landlord?" I asked as if there were more than one living in the small town.

"Yeah, he used to work part-time as a designer at a furniture store nearby. He needed full-time work which Josh offered him as a salon manager. It has also allowed him to start his own interior design company. I was one of his first clients. The guy knows his stuff."

"He did a great job here."

When Rome turned his back on me to reach a vase on the top shelf of his cabinet, I used the time to study him. He wore a dark gray V-neck knit sweater that clung to his torso and arms and dark denim that fit him like a glove, showing off the rounded swells of his ass. Rome had long, lean legs that reminded me of a runner or soccer player. Then I noticed his bare feet sticking out from beneath the legs of his jeans. I never knew bare feet could look so sexy. Maybe it wasn't so much his feet that appealed to me, but what they signified. It meant he was relaxed and comfortable enough around me he didn't need to wear shoes, which only made his nervousness when I first arrived more endearing.

I let my eyes wander back up his legs and settle once more on his ass, which was when he turned around and caught me ogling him. I grinned unabashedly. He had a fine ass. What's not to appreciate?

"The breadsticks will be ready in about five minutes then we can eat. I'll open a bottle of wine and let it breathe. Red or white?" Rome asked me.

"You pick."

"Okay," he said then winked. "We'll save the other bottle for next time." *Next time.* Rome ended up choosing the red wine. "I'm going to put you in charge of music."

"What do you like?" I asked.

"Anything. I have very eclectic tastes. I have a vinyl record collection I've been working on all my life, more CDs than any one person needs, and I also have thousands of songs downloaded to my phone. I would love to hear more of your original music someday." And, someday, I would let him. I was more curious about his collections though. "Seriously, feel free to look around." He gestured to the huge entertainment center that took up an enormous chunk of wall space. It was too big and modern to be something he purchased from a store.

"Who made this for you?" I asked once I was standing in front of the ornate metal structure. There were typical level shelves for books, sculptures, and picture frames, but other sections had smaller shelves at angles for unique ways of stacking CDs. Sporadically placed throughout the unit were taller sections that were perfect for vinyl record jackets. The entire thing might've looked industrial if it wasn't for the intricate and delicate metalwork in between the storage units. It reminded me of the popular metal art people hung on their walls, except these were built into the unit. They weren't the typical family trees, butterflies, or flowers I was used to seeing displayed above fireplace mantels. These looked like they were tailored for the beautiful man in the kitchen. There was the half mask I associated with Phantom of the Opera, an intricate sunrise, a pair of running shoes, a convertible car that looked like an old Mustang, Brutus the Buckeye, and two entwined hearts above a picture frame that was permanently built into the structure. Inside the frame was a photo of two men dressed in suits. They stood looking at one another with huge smiles and so much love in their eyes. My heart squeezed inside my chest when I recognized a much younger Rome was the man standing on the left. He was cupping the taller man's face and looked as if he were wiping away tears of joy. I instantly knew the man on the right was the reason Rome could relate so well to Howie's heartbreak from losing his wife.

"That's Peter," Rome said softly. I was so caught up in looking at the shelf and staring at the photo of Rome and Peter I hadn't heard him walk up behind me. Rome placed his hand at the small of my back, and I relaxed into his touch. "He made this massive beast as an anniversary present. He locked me out of the garage for months while he built it."

"It's a beautiful work of art."

"Peter got so tired of me storing my records and CDs in 'the tackiest possible ways' all over our house and designed this."

"How tacky?" I asked, wanting to know that side of Rome and not just the neat and orderly vibe I picked up from him all the time.

Rome groaned, and I turned away from the picture to look into his blue eyes. "The worst! I'm talking fruit crates and any hideous thing I could find that would hold my treasures."

"You strike me more as an IKEA guy," I said, gesturing around the clean, modern room. "You're always so neat when I see you. There's never a wrinkle in your shirt or a crooked tie around your neck."

Rome snorted. "You've met my secretary. Do you think she'd let me represent such an esteemed position in a wrinkled shirt and an askew tie? I keep extra shirts in my closet because I can be a bit of a train wreck with condiments."

"Huh. I never would've guessed."

"Are we okay here? Do you have questions you want to ask?" Rome sounded worried and I wanted—needed—to put him at ease.

"About your slovenly ways?"

Rome's deep chuckle warmed me in places that had gone cold seconds before when I saw proof he was a man who'd loved hard. Was there room for anyone else in his heart? "I was talking about Pete."

"I could tell by our conversation this morning about Howie you were a man who'd experienced great love and an equally great loss."

Rome nodded. "Some days, it feels like Pete died just yesterday, and other days, I struggle to remember his voice." He shook his head. "This isn't exactly the tone I wanted to set on our first date. First, I sound and look as stiff as a robot when you arrive, and then—"

I silenced him with another soft kiss. I allowed my lips to linger a little longer than the first time, but I didn't slide my tongue between his lips when they parted to gasp in surprise. I cupped the back of his neck and rested my forehead against his. "I'm attracted to your realness."

"Maybe I should make a fool of myself more often," he said then chuckled. I hated the idea of anyone besides me in Blissville seeing this vulnerable side of him. I opened my mouth to express the sentiment, but the oven timer went off.

"How about we continue this conversation over dinner?"

"Sounds great." Like after our first kiss, Rome linked our fingers together and led me to the kitchen.

Chapter Seven

"If music be the food of love, play on."
~William Shakespeare

"Music fuels the soul and becomes the rhythm of the heart."
~Romeo Bradley

"I THOUGHT WE'D EAT AT THE KITCHEN NOOK SINCE IT'S A BIT MORE intimate than a formal dining room. Is that okay with you?" I asked Jules. God, I sounded as breathless as I felt. He'd rendered me senseless with his kisses, and I was still reeling. Then again, I liked the sensation that I was floating and the only thing keeping me tethered to the ground was his hand.

"It sounds perfect to me."

Before he arrived, I set the table with my good china and crystal wineglasses then placed the salad bowl and matching crystal carafe filled with my homemade vinaigrette dressing. I thought about lighting candles but decided it might be too much. Damn, I was so out of practice at this. I had wound myself up so tight before he arrived I practically vibrated with nervous energy while somehow managing to be rigid at the same time. It was a recipe for a disastrous evening, but Jules fixed that with a simple kiss. His lips were even softer than they looked, and I could easily spend hours kissing him, learning their shape and memorizing his taste.

"Please have a seat, and I'll bring the rest of our meal over," I said, reluctantly releasing his hand.

"Are you sure I can't help?"

Oh, there were so many ways he could help me. Take off my clothes, kiss me all over, put me out of my fucking misery by joining his body to mine. I knew that wasn't what he was offering though, so I smiled and said, "You can carry the chicken parm over to the table while I get the breadsticks if you want."

"Sure." Jules slipped his hands inside the oven mitts I'd set beside the steaming casserole and carried it to the table, placing the dish on the chrome serving rack. Jules wearing my oven mitts was such a small thing, but it felt as huge as the lump in my throat. I really liked seeing him in my space and liked him touching my things. His presence settled and grounded me in ways I never expected. Jules fit as well in my kitchen as he did the light blue sweater and dark denim jeans he wore. *Too soon, Romeo. Take it slow.*

I placed the breadsticks in the bread basket and grabbed our bottle of wine. "You have excellent taste in wine, Jules." I lifted the bottle and began pouring a fair amount in his wineglass.

"I'd love to take credit for it, but I asked the guy working the wine section what paired best with chicken Parmesan. He started talking about the different types of notes and accents found in wines then must've taken pity on me when my eyes glazed over and pulled two different types from the shelf."

"The guy knows his wine. Would you prefer to drink something else? I have a variety of beer, liquor, and soda. I never know what I'm going to be in the mood for and tend to grab a little of everything."

"This is fine, Rome," he assured me. "I enjoy a glass of good wine, but I don't know enough to choose a decent one without help." Jules took a sip of his wine then licked his lips. "This is delicious."

I wanted to lean across the table and taste it on his lips but instead picked up my glass and took a sip. "I love a good cabernet sauvignon."

Neither of us said anything while we filled our plates with perfectly seared breaded chicken smothered in Lily's scrumptious marinara sauce and melted mozzarella. I took the tongs and gave the salad another quick toss before filling my bowl and asking, "Can I interest you in a tossed salad, Jules?"

He chuckled, and a wry grin spread across his face. Jules cleared his throat then said, "I've been known to enjoy it on occasion, but I usually like to get to know someone first."

"Oh my God! Did I say something really inappropriate? Why must the younger generation take the tamest of words and phrases and turn them into something dirty? Did I proposition you without knowing it?"

Jules's chuckle turned into a deep-bellied laugh which I couldn't help answering in kind. "Kids these days," he said, imitating the shaky voice of an elderly man.

I groaned. "How bad is it?" I asked. "Did I just offer to blow you under the table?"

Jules laughed until tears ran down his face. "Not quite."

"What then?" I asked, but Jules shook his head. Groaning, I pulled my phone out of my back pocket and googled the phrase. My heart sank to my knees. According to the urban dictionary, I had just offered to give Jules a rim job. "Dear God, take me now."

"Is that my cue to pounce, or are you praying that the good Lord calls you home right this minute?"

I laughed and snorted at the same time which only added to my list of clumsy first-date transgressions. It was a miracle Julius didn't jump to his feet and run out the door. "I would totally understand if you left my house and never spoke to me again."

Julius stopped laughing and reached across the table for my hand. "I'm not laughing at you, Rome."

"You're laughing near me then?"

"You have to admit the situation is a little funny."

"I didn't want to be funny. I wanted to be suave and sexy."

"You could do that without breathing because it's part of your genetic makeup. Sometimes suave comes across as unapproachable, and I…" He let his words trail off while he carefully chose his words.

"Want to approach me?" I suggested.

"Yes, I do, and I find it easier to do that sitting in your kitchen laughing over silly phrases with double meanings than in my classroom or your office."

"I like laughing over my ridiculousness in my kitchen with you." It was the most fun I'd had in ages. "Why don't we tuck in to our dinner while it's still hot, and we can see how obvious I can make it that I haven't dated in a long time?"

Slicing into his chicken cutlet, Julius asked, "How long?"

"Seven years," I admitted.

Julius's hands stilled, but he snapped his head up to meet my gaze. "Seven years? Is that how long you've been a widower?" It was a fair question, and one he had the right to ask. I had pursued him because I wanted to get to know him better, and I'd opened the door for the line of questioning with my remark.

"I'll answer, but only if you take a bite of your dinner while it's still hot."

Julius tipped his head to the side to acknowledge my request and took a bite of the chicken parm. He closed his eyes and chewed slowly, savoring the flavors on his tongue. "This sauce did not come from a grocery store."

"You are correct. It came from my next-door neighbor, Lily. She grows the tomatoes and herbs in her garden. She gave this to me before school started, and I've saved it for a special occasion."

Julius took another bite and then another before he said, "I'm a grateful recipient of her talent and generosity." He pointed his fork at my untouched plate of food. "Your turn to eat. We don't have to talk about anything you don't want to discuss. I was just surprised to hear you haven't dated for so long."

I took my time slicing through the tender chicken then swirled it through the sauce and put it in my mouth. I'd sampled the sauce when I opened the jar and knew it was remarkable but adding in the meat and mozzarella amped the flavor to a whole other level. While chewing, I debated how much I wanted to talk about Peter on the first date with the man who finally made me feel alive. How much was too much?

"Because I'm such a catch?" I teased. I held up my hand to cut off whatever he was going to say. "Please don't answer that. It sounds like I'm digging for compliments when I was only trying to crack a lame joke." I set my fork down and looked across the table in time to see Julius do the same. This felt like a make-or-break moment to me, and I didn't want to screw it up. "Peter died seven years ago. We weren't married because same-sex marriages weren't legal in Ohio at the time. The photo you saw was taken during our commitment ceremony seventeen years ago when we were twenty-eight years old. It wasn't legally binding, but it was the best we could do at the time. The day meant so much to both of us."

"How long did you date before your commitment ceremony?"

"Ten years. We met on our first day of college at The Ohio State University."

"Wow, you were together twenty years," Julius said softly, briefly breaking eye contact.

"Jules," I said softly, pulling his eyes back to mine. "I wouldn't have asked you to dinner if I wasn't ready. My reason for not dating until now was because I hadn't met a man who interested me enough to…" What? Put forth the effort? Risk the heartbreak? None of those sounded right. They either made me sound juvenile, lazy, or afraid. I was none of those things. I decided to go with another approach. "I'm not the kind of man who wants to use a dating app or pick up strangers in a bar. That's just not me. I am a man who knows what it's like to have a loving relationship, and that's what I'm looking for now. I'm not assuming you want the same thing, but you make me want to put myself out there to find out. I loved Peter with every fiber of my being, and I am grateful for the time we shared because he made me a better man. Peter wouldn't want me to live the rest of my life alone. He'd want me to fill my days with laughter and love. I know this because I would've felt the same way had the situation been reversed. I can't erase his existence, nor would you want me to."

Julius nodded and vehemently said, "I would never want to deny you the memories you have of Peter. Oddly, this reminds me of a conversation I had with my mother on the way over here. I told her about our date then gave her a hard time when she started giving me dating advice and telling me to wear good underwear. I told her to go find her own silver fox and stop obsessing about mine." I just blinked at him. His silver fox? That was how he thought of me. "Um…"

"Oh no. You're not walking that back now, Jules." My smile was so big it made my face hurt.

"Anyway," he said, spearing a forkful of salad, "I used the same reasoning with her as you gave for Peter. My dad wouldn't want her sitting home alone each night, especially now that Marcus and I are both gone."

"I'm sorry to hear your dad passed away," I said gently.

"Thank you. Eight years ago, he kissed my mother goodbye then dropped my brother off at school on his way to work. He had a ruptured aneurysm on the job and died suddenly. To say it blew our world apart was putting it mildly, so I understand why it takes a person a long time to recover and put themselves out there again. My mom will know when the time is right for her, just like you know the time is right for you now."

"You have an old soul, Jules. Wise way beyond your years."

"That's what my grandmother says too. Maybe I've always been mature for my age, but I know a lot shifted in my brain after my dad died. I felt like I needed to step up and be a rock for my family to lean on." I wondered who he had turned to when the burden became too heavy for him to shoulder alone. Jules ate the bite of salad then took another sip of wine. "Even though I don't know you well, I trust you to know how you feel and what you want. I'm not going to waste precious time second-guessing your motives."

"Thank you." I decided to steer us away from heavier topics and asked, "When did you start playing music?"

"My father taught me how to play the piano when I was five years old then I moved on to the cello, violin, and guitar when I was older. If the instrument has strings, then I can play it. Well, except for the harp. I'm just not a big fan of its sound."

"What about writing music? When did that start?"

Jules snorted. "Angsty teen years, of course. Man, I had a notebook full of tragic melodies." After another bite of chicken, he asked, "When did you start theater?"

"I was probably seven years old. I auditioned for a part in Charlie and the Chocolate Factory at the kids' theater. My mom said I was too dramatic and needed a healthy outlet for it."

"Did you get a part right out of the gate?"

"Sure did. I was cast as Charlie, and let me tell you, it didn't go over well with the parents of the kids who'd been acting for a while. Here came this upstart taking the lead role. It was the first time I realized I performed best when people didn't think I was capable."

"It was the same for me while auditioning for spots on the children's orchestra. I grew up in a predominantly black neighborhood, and there weren't many opportunities to play classical music, so my parents took me to a wealthier, whiter neighborhood. I'm not sure anyone took me as a serious threat when I walked in with my second-hand cello. I already stuck out because I was taller than most of the kids, but then my skin was darker and my instrument not as shiny."

"Then you began to play, and everyone took notice."

"Yes, they did. Being part of an orchestra was heavenly to me. All of those different instruments coming together to create magic." Jules closed his eyes and smiled contentedly. I wondered where his mind had taken him, but I wouldn't interrupt the serenity of the moment by asking. Then he reopened his eyes and I fell into their hazel depths. "Music transcends all the labels people want to slap on us like race, religion, gender, and orientation. People might not always rise above the fray, but music does."

"I think you're beautiful," I said then immediately felt myself blush. "Um…"

"Oh no. You're not walking that back now, Rome," he said, echoing my words from earlier. "I think you're beautiful too, and I'd love to explore your music collection more. I was too busy admiring the unit Pete built for you and didn't look at the titles on the albums or CDs."

"That's not my entire collection," I confessed.

"It's not?" he asked, eyebrow lifting.

"That's a small part of what I own. Peter had planned to make additional units, but he never got around to it. I'll show you the rest after you eat."

Our conversation for the rest of the meal turned to the play and the plans we had for the next part in the production. I told Julius my concerns about allowing the playwrights to audition for parts they created because I felt it would be unfair on many levels. First, they knew the parts better than anyone else because they created them. While reading the play, I could see the three kids created characters in their spitting images, and I wondered how much of the story was about their lives. Second, if they did try out and land the parts, I would be accused of favoritism. Lastly, I wasn't sure how they would handle me directing them. They saw the characters one way, but I might see them in a different light. I didn't want to spend countless hours arguing with them. The most prevailing thought in my mind though was that no one other than them could play those roles as well. They were tailor fit for them. How could I even think about giving those roles out to anyone else?

Jules nodded when I shared my concerns with him. He said he had felt the same way about the music. He wanted to hold auditions for solo parts but felt in his heart that no one but Curtis could sing the songs he wrote with as much emotion. They were so personal to him. In the end, we decided to sit down with Ellie, Clara, and Curtis to have a discussion about auditions and find out how they would feel about someone other than them performing roles and singing songs that meant so much to them.

After dinner, Jules tried to insist on cleaning up and doing dishes, but I wouldn't allow it. I didn't want to waste a minute cleaning when we could listen to music and drink more wine. "Are you sure you're ready to see what's hidden behind this door?" I asked, standing outside the largest of the spare bedrooms.

"Unless it's a headless doll collection then yes."

I opened the door before I could talk myself out of it. The rest of my house was tidy and orderly, but this was the room I retreated to when I needed things to be comfortable and messy.

"Whoa," Jules said when I opened the door. He walked into the center of the room and turned in a slow circle, taking it all in.

I'd chosen a deep shade of amethyst paint color for the walls, but it was hard to see it behind the rows of shelves filled with books, albums, and CDs wrapping around three walls of the room. I'd pushed my worn-out, brown leather loveseat against the fourth wall and covered the walls above it with framed playbills from my favorite productions. On either side of the loveseat were battered, antique end tables big enough to hold reading lamps and wine. The main focus of the room was my pride and joy. I'd carefully hung the shelves on one wall to direct the eye's focus on the RCA Victor Victrola record player I'd found at a yard sale when I was foraging for vinyl records. I'd later had it appraised and was shocked that the player I paid a hundred bucks for was worth over three thousand dollars.

Jules turned and looked at me. "I love this room. Thank you for sharing it with me."

"Find us some music," I urged, and he complied.

I sat on the loveseat and propped my feet on the ottoman big enough for two while Jules perused the records. He was so enamored with the selection that he seemingly forgot I was there, but I wasn't upset. I just loved seeing him in my space. He looked like he belonged, and I could picture endless nights of listening to music and reading on the loveseat together. Julius pulled a few records off the shelf as if he couldn't quite decide which one he wanted to hear the most. I wanted to tell him he didn't have to choose just one because we had all night, but I was too busy enjoying the smile on his face when he found an album that surprised him.

In the end, he chose Billie Holiday. Jules refilled our wine glasses while I put the record on. I wasn't sure how close he wanted me to sit and was prepared to curl up in the corner opposite him, but he patted the cushion beside him. There in the dim light, with the soulful voice of Billie Holiday playing in the background, Jules took my face in his hands and kissed me. He was tentative at first, his tongue gently seeking mine but grew bolder when I gripped the front of his light blue cashmere sweater. Our hands never explored each other, even though our bodies hummed with need and want. He kissed me long after the last song on the record ended, and the only word I could speak was his name.

Chapter Eight

"Probability is expectation founded upon partial knowledge."
~George Boole

*"Don't make assumptions and predictions when you only
know half of the story."*
~Julius Shepherd

"I'M NOT LISTENING TO ANY CLASSICAL CRAP FOR TEN HOURS," Marcus said after getting in my car late Sunday morning. I'd stopped by to pick him up for the drive to Lexington, Kentucky, to see our paternal grandparents.

"It's only an hour and twenty minutes from here each way. That's nowhere near ten hours."

"It feels like it," he groused, sounding grouchier than normal.

"What's wrong with you?"

"Nothing."

"Liar."

"Nothing I feel like talking about anyway." Marcus released a frustrated groan. "I've met a girl, and I care about her a lot."

"That's great, bro. Why do you sound like it's such a bad thing? Does she not return your feelings?"

Marcus scoffed. "Return my feelings? You sound older than Gram and Gramps. She's into me too, that's not the problem."

"Than what is the problem, Marc?"

"I'm getting a lot of blowback from the team and coach, okay? They think I'm getting in over my head."

"I'm confused," I said. "Coach isn't in a relationship, and no other players have girlfriends or boyfriends?"

"Coach is married and most of the guys on the team are dating."

"Then why are you being held to a higher standard?"

"Things with Camilla are complicated," Marc said with a shrug. Talking to him was like pulling teeth sometimes. He preferred to work through things on his own, and I knew he'd come to me if he needed me, so I was prepared to let the subject drop. "She has a kid."

"Camilla does?"

"Yeah." His voice had gone soft, and I could hear the smile in his voice. "He's named Manuel after Camilla's dad, but they all call him Manny. I call him my little man. I love her, J. I love Manny too. They make me happy."

"Bro, I consider myself to have an analytical mind, but I'm just not computing here. She loves you too?" I asked. From the corner of my eyes, I saw Marc nod. "And you love her. What is the problem? Why does anyone care about you dating Camilla?"

"They said Camilla's just using me for a free ride out of poverty. That's not true, J. I met her at the diner where she works. Camilla had no idea who I was. She just called me peanut butter pie guy. I'm a good judge of character, right?" he asked.

"You are, Marc. If you say that Camilla cares about you, then I believe you."

He blew out a relieved breath. "I haven't told Mom about Camilla and Manny yet. How do you think she'll react?"

"Mom loves who we love; no questions asked. She'd told us both that a thousand times at least. Tell her when you're ready."

"Yeah, you're right. I'm letting outside influences mess with my mind. I've never caved to that kind of pressure, and now isn't the time to start." He turned his head and studied me silently for a few seconds. "What's different about you? You look more relaxed than the last time I saw you."

"Nothing," I said with a casual shrug.

He sucked in a quick breath, almost gasping. "You got laid."

"No, I didn't." Well, not the way he was thinking. I spent hours making out with a gorgeous man with an equally beautiful soul until my body throbbed and my cock ached. I'd gone home and relieved the tension while reliving the feel of Rome's lips on mine and imagining other places on my body he could kiss.

"You've met someone then," Marcus persisted.

"Why don't we talk about your stellar football game yesterday," I suggested. "I didn't find you afterward to talk since we had plans today."

"Bullshit. That's never stopped you. You didn't find me because you had plans with some dude. What's his name? Where'd you meet?"

"You sound as bad as Mom," I chided my younger brother, but I couldn't keep the goofy grin off my face. "I have met a guy, and he's really special." A kaleidoscope of images crossed my mind. Rome listening to the music I wrote for the play with so much awe in his expression, his awkward attempts at conversation the nights before, and the way he melted in my arms on the sofa in his library.

"Where'd you meet?"

"He's the superintendent of schools."

"In Whereville?" Marcus asked, making fun of the town I'd chosen to teach and live in.

"You know damn well the town is called Blissville, and yes, Rome is the superintendent of schools there." I could see Marcus fiddling around with his phone and knew he was doing the same thing Mom did when I told her about Rome.

"Dr. Romeo Bradley," Marcus said then blew out a whistle. "His mother must've been a fan of Shakespeare."

"I didn't ask." I might the next time we chatted though.

"He looks like he's quite a bit older than you."

"I think he probably started to turn silver early like a lot of dark-haired men do. He's only forty-five."

"Our mother is fifty," Marcus pointed out. "That doesn't bother you?"

My kneejerk response would've been "of course not" but I gave it some thought. Julius's age didn't bother me, but I was acutely aware that his experiences were vastly different than mine. I didn't think experience was necessarily a bad thing though. Before I could answer, Marcus was speaking again.

"And why is a handsome, successful guy like him still single? Is he divorced or just a player? You're not the one-and-done kind of guy, Jules. You practically live like a monk."

"He's not a player," I responded, or at least I didn't get the impression he was by the clumsy way he handled the beginning of our date. "He's a widower."

"Oh," Marcus said then got quiet as he thought about that. "Is that weird?"

"I wouldn't say it's weird, but it's different dating a man who shared an entire lifetime with someone else."

"Someone they'd still be with if given a choice," Marcus added, earning a glare from me. "Sorry."

I recalled the conversation I had with Rome the previous night. I'd told him I trusted him to know his heart and mind. Only time would tell if I was making a mistake.

"Have you been dating long?"

"Last night was our first official date."

"I hope it works out for you, Jules. No one deserves happiness like you do."

"Thanks, bub," I said, reaching over to mess up his hair. "Rome told me to pass along his congratulations for breaking the school record in career interceptions."

"Are we back to football again?" Marcus asked, sounding hesitant to discuss something he used to love so much.

"We don't have to talk about football, but we usually do. What's going on?"

"Just tired, I guess," he replied, sliding down lower in his seat. "There are just a lot of expectations and people wanting me to make some tough decisions."

"Such as?"

"Whether or not I plan to enter the draft."

He meant the NFL draft. "What's the deadline?"

"I have to commit by January fifteenth."

"It's only September and the season has just begun," I reminded him. "The first response that comes to my mind is that you tell people you're focused on winning football games and the conference championship. Anything beyond this season isn't relevant right now."

"That's the approach I've taken with coaches and reporters, but I can't seem to get my brain to agree with that logic."

"Marc, what do your coaches think?"

"Let's put it this way," he said, turning to look out the window, "my coaches have already been contacted by scouts who are interested in seeing what I can do at the combines in February."

"There's obvious interest on their part, but are *you* interested in playing football professionally?"

"Depends on the day of the week," Marcus said with a snort. "When I'm playing, I can't see myself doing anything else. When I'm tired and sore after a grueling practice or physical game, I can't imagine putting my body through this for any longer than I have to. It just depends which Marcus Shepherd shows up."

"You have plenty of time," I told him. "I have every confidence you'll make the best decision for yourself."

"Thanks, J. It means a lot to hear you say that. Can we talk about *you* now?"

"I composed music for the school play the drama club is going to put on next spring. The play and songs were written by three of the kids in the school. It's called *Inside Out,* and it's similar to *The Outsiders,* except the students don't just explore the difference between social classes. They look at race, gender, and orientation. I'm telling you, Marc, these kids are so ahead of their time. The lyrics this boy started writing in eighth grade are just…stunning and heartbreaking at the same time. No kid should know that kind of hurt and rejection."

"He's in a good place now?" Marcus asked. I liked that he cared about a kid he didn't even know. Maybe it was because of the shit we heard growing up. We were too black, not black enough, too white, or not white enough. We didn't fit in any of the molds people wanted to shove us in. Or maybe it was because our parents taught us to be compassionate and giving people, even when we weren't on the receiving end of it ourselves.

"It seems that way. I haven't met his parents yet, but he seems happy unless it's time to take a test. I'm sure I'll get to know him better once the play gets started. I'm nervous for him to hear the music, but I'm going to play it for him during his lunch period tomorrow."

"I bet he's going to be blown away by your talent. Is the music on your phone? I want to listen to it."

"I thought you didn't like that classical crap?"

"I do when it's something you play, bro," Marcus said.

I handed my phone to Marcus and instructed him where to find it so I could keep my attention on the road. It wasn't long before the first song with its haunting melody began to play. When the songs finished, I glanced over to see Marcus wiping his eyes.

"I don't even know the lyrics to these songs and I'm moved to tears. That's so powerful and beautiful."

"I hope Curtis likes it."

"How could he not?" Marcus asked.

"It might not be what he had in mind, but I'll find out soon enough."

Marcus replayed the songs a few more times before we reached Gram and Gramp's house. Our father's parents wouldn't be considered wealthy, but they were a bracket or two higher than middle class. The lived in an older neighborhood with bigger yards and well-maintained brick homes, unlike the new subdivisions where the houses were practically built on top of one another and you could mow the back yard in three passes. It was a lovely, safe neighborhood to raise a kid, and the photos adorning the walls showed our dad had a happy childhood. He carried that same infectious smile into adulthood, and it was often followed by a booming laugh. God, how I missed his smile, his laughter, and his hugs.

"You okay?" Marcus asked.

"Yeah, bub. I'm good."

Gram was already waiting for us on the front porch by the time we got out and rounded the hood. Marcus reached the porch first and scooped her up in a hug. "Hello, Gram."

Gram held Marcus tight then pulled back to look into his eyes. "How's school going?" I gave her credit. She didn't start every conversation with football like everyone else did with Marcus. She was more interested in his grades and the things going on in his personal life. Later, she'd get around to talking about football, but not until she established that Marcus was more to her than a standout athlete.

"It's going pretty good so far. I'm going to have some tough classes this year, but I'm looking forward to the challenge."

"You sound just like your father. He never shied away from something because it was tough."

"We learned it from our mother too," I said softly.

"Of course you did," Gram said. "How is Sherice?"

"Mama is doing well." I stepped forward and reached for her, opening my arms.

She smile warmly and closed the distance between us, resting her forehead on my shoulder as I hugged her gently. "I'm so happy when you boys come for a visit. It's like having your father alive all over again."

"We'll try to get here more often once Marcus's season is over."

"Quit hogging the boys," Gramps said from the doorway. I lifted my head and met his joyful gaze.

"Hi, Gramps," I said, stepping back from Gram's embrace. "It's good to see you." I hugged him too.

"It's been too long. I hope you guys are in the mood for smoked beef brisket, potato salad, macaroni and cheese, and homemade peach cobbler," Gramps said eagerly.

"I thought I smelled smoked meat when we got out of the car," Marcus said, rubbing his hands together gleefully.

"I got a smoker for my birthday," Gramps responded excitedly. "This is his maiden voyage."

"Smells delicious," I said, following him inside with Marcus and Gram behind me.

"We'll have every stray cat and dog in a five-mile radius prowling and howling in our back yard before the day is through," Gram teased.

"It'll be worth it," Gramps said.

His smoked brisket was every bit as good as it smelled, and the side dishes Gram made were delicious. During the meal, Marcus talked about the game from the day before and was pleased to hear they had watched the game online. I noticed he didn't discuss the turmoil he felt about committing to the draft nor did he bring up Camilla or Manny. I told our grandparents I loved my new town and job but didn't say anything about Rome. It was still too new.

I offered to help Gram clean up just as I had with Rome the night before, but unlike him, she didn't refuse. Gramps and Marcus went into the living room to watch the Bengals game while I followed Gram into the kitchen. I could tell she had a system down. Her movements were fluid and graceful as she pulled down the plastic containers and lids from the cabinets. I started rinsing dishes and stacking them in the dishwasher while Gram stored the leftovers in the refrigerator. We worked quietly until we finished our tasks and the only dishes left to wash were the ones that wouldn't fit in the dishwasher.

"I'll wash, and you dry?" she suggested.

"Sure," I agreed then watched as she filled the sink with soapy water. I wouldn't say she was stiff and uncomfortable, but I could tell something was on her mind. She sank her hands in the sink and silently looked out the window for at least a minute or maybe two. "Something wrong?" I asked her.

"Wrong? No. I do my best thinking when I have my hands down in the soapy water washing dishes. I start mentally planning for things I need to do the next day, but I don't want to waste our precious moments together. It sounds like you're having a great season coaching tennis. I saw where Blissville is in line to win their league title for the first time. You must be so proud of the kids."

I nodded. "I certainly am. I had no clue what to expect when I accepted the job. I just knew they had one hell of a science program that I wanted to be a part of. There were some things I didn't plan for."

"Such as?" she gently prodded while washing a serving dish.

"I was asked to compose music for the school play this year."

"Oh, that's wonderful. What production will they perform?"

"It's called *Inside Out*, and it was written by three of the senior kids. They began writing it when they were in eighth grade. Over time, they've updated and fine-tuned it. One of the kids, his name is Curtis, wrote the lyrics for the songs, but needed help coming up with the melodies. These kids are really special, Gram."

"What's the play about?" She listened as I gave her the overview, shared parts of scenes, and even quoted some of the lyrics. "Oh my," she tearfully said, placing a soapy hand over her heart. "It sounds so powerful and to think kids wrote it."

"I have a feeling it's going to be an amazing production."

We rejoined Marcus and Gramps in the living room after the kitchen was spotless once more, but we didn't stay long. Marcus had studying to do, and I needed to do laundry and grade papers. We hugged our grandparents goodbye and promised we would be back soon.

We kept our conversation light on the way home and even sang along with the radio. I'd had enough thinking for one day and just wanted to enjoy the time with my little brother. Instead of driving him back to his dorm, he asked if I would drop him off at the diner where Camilla was working.

"I want you to meet her," Marc said. "Her shift ends soon, and if you're lucky, her mom will be there with Manny and you can meet them too."

My brother was over the moon for this girl and her kid. The logical part of my brain that focused on equations, formulas, and problem-solving worried Marc was taking on too much for his age. He had big decisions he had to make about his future. He'd already applied and was accepted to several law schools, and there was the allure of playing professional football. On top of that, there was his obvious affection for this young lady and her little boy. I feared it was just too much all at once.

Then we walked into the diner, and I saw the way Camilla looked at my brother. I didn't need to read the name tag on her uniform to know which of the waitresses had snagged Marc's heart because the huge smile on her face told me everything I needed to know. She wasn't looking at a meal ticket or an escape from an unhappy life; she was looking at the man she loved. Her heart was in her dark, shining eyes. And Marc? His entire demeanor changed right before my very eyes. He wasn't the swaggering football hero or the smart-ass kid brother I knew and adored, he was a man who was in love. It softened his edges and gave him a completely different kind of confidence than playing football did. He was wise beyond his years because he had already realized what was important in life.

Camilla came around the counter, and Marc picked her up and twirled her around like some rom-com movie I'd never admit to watching on Hallmark. The gesture was more poignant when Marc did it instead of some movie heartthrob because it was a move we'd seen our dad make with our mom. Our life hadn't always been easy, but we'd had each other.

"I've missed you, love," Dad said after he set Mom down.

"I just went to the grocery store for ice cream and Chips Ahoy," Mom countered, blushing happily. "I was gone twenty minutes tops."

"Twenty minutes too long."

My musician's soul saw what my logical brain struggled to comprehend. Marc had found harmony in his life, even if it wasn't what any of us had imagined for him.

"Mar! Mar!"

Marcus set Camilla down and turned in time to catch the toddler who ran by me as fast as his little legs could carry him. Manny had a head full of dark, black curls that bounced when Marc hoisted him in the air. I guessed he was two years old.

"How's my little man today?" Marc asked. "Did you miss me as much as I missed you?"

"Mar! Mar!" It almost sounded like he said more instead of Mar.

Marcus kissed Manny's forehead then lifted his head to look at me. I saw it then, his need for my approval. After we lost Dad, my role as his big brother shifted a bit. I felt even more pressure to set a good example for Marc. I tried to be the guy who never let my little brother down, and I asked myself what our father would do in any given situation. I didn't have to think very hard that day in the diner; the answer was as obvious as the love in front of me.

I gave Marcus the smile I reserved for big moments in his life, the one that said I love you and I'm incredibly proud of you. He visibly relaxed then nestled Manny closer while slipping his free arm around Camilla.

"Jules, this is my best girl, Camilla," he said. "Kitten, this is my big brother. He's the best man I know. It's past time I introduced the two of you. And this little guy is Manny."

"I'm so happy to meet you, Camilla." She was as tiny and delicate as a bird, so I tried not to crush her when I hugged her. "It's good to see Marcus so happy."

"I'm the happy one," she said, smiling up at me. "Let me introduce you to my mother. We've heard so many stories about you from Marc. Mama," Camilla said, waving her hand for her mother to come over. "This is Julius, Mama." I smiled at the shy woman and extended my hand. "This is my mother, Isabella Álvarez."

She took both my hands between hers. "Nice to meet you." She rose on her tiptoes which was my cue to lower my head so she could kiss my cheek. "Marcus is a good boy."

"The best," I agreed. "Introduce me to your little man."

"Manny, can you say hello to Julius?"

Manny turned and watched me with cautious eyes as I approached him. "Hello, Manny."

"Hi." Manny opened and closed his chubby fist in the toddler's wave. "Manny," he said, patting his chest.

"Julius," I said, patting mine.

Instead of rushing off like I'd planned, I sat with Marcus for a while and got to know Mrs. Álvarez and Manny while Camilla finished her shift. She treated all of us with a piece of Marc's favorite peanut butter pie. Well, Manny didn't get his own piece, but he sure got plenty of Marcus's, which told me just how much he loved the little boy. Marc didn't share his peanut butter pie with anyone.

"I need to get home and get some things done," I told them. "It was lovely meeting you all." I ruffled Manny's hair, making him laugh. "Especially you, cutie." Manny giggled and buried his head in Marc's neck. I hugged the ladies then turned to my brother. "Walk me out?"

"Sure." He handed Manny to Mrs. Álvarez and followed me outside to my car. I caught Camilla's nervous expression through the big window and winked to let her know everything was good.

"Marc," I said, placing my hands on his shoulders, "I think you know what path you really want to choose for your future. There's really not much of a decision to make, is there?"

"No, there isn't."

"You've already been accepted to some wonderful law schools, including the University of Cincinnati. It won't be easy going to law school while working to support a young family, but you can do it. Camilla's family is here, Gram and Gramps are close, and I'm only forty-five minutes away. You're not alone. Choose *your* dreams, Marc. Follow *your* heart."

"I love you, Jules," Marc said, throwing his arms around me.

"I love you too, little brother. Now turn loose of me and get back in the diner so I can leave before we both become blubbering messes."

"Okay," Marc said, grinning broadly as he wiped tears from his eyes. "I'm going to ask you to follow your heart too, big brother. And don't look at me like I'm clueless either. You want something then you go get it. Or should I say someone?" he asked, walking backwards. "Drive safe."

"Always."

My thoughts turned to Rome as soon as I drove away. I knew he had a family dinner in Columbus and wouldn't be home for a few more hours, which gave me plenty of time to do laundry, grade papers, and maybe lure my silver fox over for a drink.

Once I got home, I typed out a text message to Rome. *I miss your lips. How about a drink at my place when you get back to town?* I felt dizzy and realized I'd been holding my breath while staring at my screen. My finger hovered over the send arrow. To send or not to send? *That* was the question. I could analyze everything I knew about Rome and myself and try to determine whether a relationship could succeed between us, or I could just hit send and see what happened. The scientist in me wanted more data to make a decision, but the musician wanted more of the melody I heard when I'd held the man in my arms the previous night.

I took a deep breath and hit send.

Chapter Nine

"Parting is such sweet sorrow, that I shall say goodnight till it be morrow."
~William Shakespeare

"Tomorrow can't come quick enough."
~Romeo Bradley

I'D JUST STEPPED OUT OF THE CAR IN MY SISTER'S DRIVEWAY WHEN MY phone buzzed. Tucking the bottle of rosé under my left arm, I pulled my phone out of my pocket. Seeing I had a text message from Julius made me laugh because it was a miracle we'd remembered to exchange phone numbers after the make out session the previous night. Smiling like a loon, I opened the message to read what he had to say.

I miss your lips. How about a drink at my place when you get back to town?

It took everything I had not to get in the car and drive straight back to Blissville from Columbus without saying so much as hello to my family. I wanted to tell Julius I'd be back in a little over an hour, but I managed to get a grip on myself and replied:

God, yes! My lips are still tingling. I'll text you when I leave my sister's house.

I can kiss other places if you're too sore.

I'm getting in the car right now and driving back to Blissville.

No, no. Visit with your family. These lips aren't going anywhere.

Better not, I sent back. *I'll text you soon.*

A sharp, judgmental bark came from the back seat of my car. "Fuck!" I said, rushing to open the door behind mine. "I'm so sorry, Dolly. I wasn't going to leave you back here." Her reproachful look said she didn't believe me. I slid my phone back in my pocket and reached for her leash. "Let's get you inside."

I waited for Dolly to sniff Ashley and Ben's perfectly manicured lawn until she found the perfect spot to pee before we headed into my sister and brother in-law's two-story, contemporary home. The place was massive and much bigger than four people could ever use, but my two nieces, Laurel and Michele, loved the friends they'd already made in the few weeks they'd lived there. I was happy to see the girls smiling joyfully in the pictures they posted on Facebook, and happier to see that their affluent neighborhood was also diverse.

"Hello," I yelled when I let myself in the front door. "Anybody home?"

"Uncle Rome!" I heard two teenage girls yell before the sound of thundering feet reached my ears. How did two petite girls make so much noise? Beside me, Dolly barked and twirled in circles.

"Pizza delivery," I teased.

"Oh, how I wish that were true," Michele said. At sixteen, she was the spitting image of her mother. Long, jet-black hair, the same light blue eyes similar to mine, and a tall, wispy frame. "Mom's serving vegan lasagna," she said in mock horror.

"Don't be so dramatic, Mimi," Laurel said, rolling her eyes. "She has one for the carnivores too." The fourteen-year-old was the opposite of her sister in looks and demeanor, inheriting Ben's blond looks and serious temperament. Laurel might've been younger, but she had an old soul.

"I like vegan lasagna," I said, earning Laurel's approval.

"Is that a wine bottle tucked under your left arm?" Michele asked.

"Nope. Rocket launcher."

A noise that was part snort and part giggle escaped from Michele. "Allow me to take the rocket launcher then. What do you think about this house?"

"Well, I've only seen the outside and the grand entry. So far, it's a gorgeous display of…"

"Wealth?" Laurel suggested.

"I was going to say modern architecture and design."

"I much prefer your smaller house in Whoville," Laurel said.

"Blissville," Michele said after she burst out giggling. "You're such a brat."

"This place is ginormous," Laurel said, finally sounding like a teenager. "We could fit three more families in here."

"Well, yeah," I said. "Haven't you heard your mother's latest plan?"

"What?" Michele and Laurel simultaneously asked.

"Don't listen to him," Ashley said, approaching us from the rear of the house. My sister still looked like a supermodel who just stepped off the runway, but her brain was sharper than her looks. Ashley worked for one of the most prestigious law firms in the state of Ohio where she managed a team of lawyers specializing in civil rights. You wouldn't know it by her outfit of distressed denim and a light gray, cold shoulder T-shirt. "I was going to invite you in to see the rest of the house, but I'm not so sure now." She flipped her black hair over her shoulder dramatically. She had either missed the premature-gray gene or she spent a lot of time at the hair salon. "Must you rile them up with ridiculous stories."

"What?" I asked, playing dumb. "You and Ben aren't adopting four little boys ranging in age from two to twelve?"

"Mom!" Michele gasped. "Is that true? There *are* a lot of bedrooms in this house."

"He's joking, right?" Laurel asked, folding her arms across her chest.

Leaning toward me and lowering her voice so only I could hear,

Ashley said, "I'm going to murder you." Then she faced her daughters with a sweet smile. "Don't listen to him. We're not adopting a family of four brothers. We're not adopting *any* children," she added to clarify. "We bought this house because we apparently have more money than sense."

I looked up at the ceiling that opened up to the second-story landing and admired the way the dark wood beams looked against the light ceiling. From the center of one of the beams hung an ornate crystal chandelier that probably cost as much as my car. I didn't begrudge them their success, but as beautiful as this house was, it wasn't my style. I would've chosen to take the girls and travel the world during their summer breaks instead.

"It's not crystal," Ashley said, reading my thoughts. "Those are actually plastic pieces cut to look like crystal."

"There had to be at least a thousand pieces to that chandelier," Ben said, striding toward us. I'm sure he was wondering what was taking us so long to join the group.

Like my sister, Ben looked like a distinguished model you expected to find gracing the cover of a magazine about men's health in their fifties. He had always been a stunning guy, but he got even better looking with age. As an environmental engineer, he traveled a lot, and I admired the confidence Ash had in her marriage. I'd even asked her about it once. She replied that she knew Ben could have any woman he wanted, and she was grateful she was who he'd chosen. It was obvious in the way he constantly reached for her that he was still as enraptured with Ash as he was on their wedding day.

Ben slipped his hand around her waist and pulled her into him when he reached the group. "We got a really great deal on this house. The sellers were motivated, and we fell in love with it."

"We still have money left in our college funds, right?" Laurel asked. God, this girl cracked me up.

"Mom and I are paying for part of your college, but not all," Ben said. "We've had this discussion already. Mom and I paid our way through life by taking out loans and working hard to pay them off. We've been very frank about this." They had always strived to achieve balance with the girls. I'd heard them say on more than one occasion that just because they could afford to do something for the girls didn't mean they would.

"Dad is making me get a job," Michele said, turning to face me. "None of my friends work."

"None of your friends are probably as grounded as you and your sister either," I told her. "There's nothing wrong with hard work and respecting how difficult it is to make money. Wait until you see how much of your check goes to taxes." I reached out and cupped her cheek. "You're going to be so much better off in life because your parents could've made you both spoiled brats, not the loving, responsible young ladies you are today."

"You're forgiven for traumatizing the girls," Ash said.

"Traumatizing?" Ben asked with a quirked brow.

"He told us you and Mom bought the house because we needed more room for the four brothers you planned to adopt."

"Huh," Ben said, tipping his head to the side as if he was considering it. He and Ashley had always said they wanted a large family, but Ash had required a hysterectomy before they could realize that dream. "We do have plenty of room."

Laurel and Michele glared daggers at me while Ash studied Ben to gauge his seriousness. The smile he gave his wife said they'd talk about it privately.

"What's taking so long?" yelled a voice from the rear of the house. "Is that my Romeo?"

"Coming, Aunt Astrid," I said, pulling free from the group and following the sounds of her delighted clapping.

Astrid Abbot was actually our late grandmother's twin sister which made her my great-aunt. The last time I saw her was two months ago when we celebrated her ninety-fifth birthday. She wasn't as mobile as she used to be, but sharp as a tack. Arthritis didn't cripple her fingers like it did many her age, which meant she could still knit. While that was great for Aunt Astrid, it was horrible for me—her favorite nephew. If she wasn't knitting me sweaters and caps, she was buying the weirdest things she saw on television. One year for Christmas, she bought my sister a coat that looked like it was made from strips of those air pillows they stuff in packages to keep items from breaking during shipping. At least I got crooked sweaters and hats.

I stepped into the enormous room on the back of the house overlooking the inground pool. Three of the four walls were made of windows and doors that opened to the outdoor living area. Part of the room was a comfortable sitting area and the other was the most beautiful kitchen I'd ever seen. It was equal parts contemporary and French country which shouldn't have worked but did. The modern touches were the commercial grade stainless steel appliances and the white and gray marble countertops, including the one on the kitchen island the size of a double bed. One side of the island had a sink and a glass stove insert along with a generous area for prepping the food. The other side was elevated and acted as an eating area. The cabinets were antique white, distressed, and looked like something that came from the French countryside. I was in love with the space.

Ash came up beside me and tucked herself beneath my arm when I raised it for her. "'It's a beaut, Clark.'" She giggled when I quoted our favorite line from *National Lampoon's Christmas Vacation.*

"I knew you'd love the kitchen. To be honest, it was all I could see when we toured the house. It was a good thing Ben stayed grounded and paid attention."

"It was a good thing I didn't see the man cave in the basement first, or we would've both been in trouble."

"True," Ash said, smiling at her husband. "I haven't seen your eyes glaze over like that since the first time—"

"Ewww. No," Laurel and Michele both said, making their parents laugh with evil glee.

"I was going to say the first time he drove his father's classic Mustang before you so rudely interrupted."

"Yeah, I bet," Michele said.

"Nice save, sis."

"No way I looked hungrier at the Mustang than—"

"I'm out," I said, cutting off Ben. I walked over to the sitting area where my parents and Aunt Astrid waited. "Hello, Mom," I said, hugging her tight. "I've missed you."

"I miss you too, Rome," she said, pulling back and cupping my face. Amelia Bradley narrowed her eyes as she studied me. "Something is different than the last time I saw you."

"I didn't have any cosmetic work done, Mom."

"Not that," she said, shaking her head. "It's internal."

"Don't start with that aura crap, Amelia," my dad said. He was slower to get up because of his arthritic knees, but at seventy years old, he still towered over me.

"It's not crap, Dan," she chided. "See for yourself. Our boy looks happier than I've seen him look in years."

I leaned forward and kissed her forehead. "I am happy. I love my job and new town. I'm even directing the school play this year. It was written by three students, and I'm going to make sure you all have tickets because I know it's going to be spectacular."

"Even me?" Aunt Astrid asked from her wheelchair.

I pulled free of my mom and walked over to kneel in front of my favorite aunt. Despite her weird gifts, I loved this woman immeasurably. She'd never married nor had children of her own, so she had claimed me when I was a boy. I owed my love of theater and fine arts to Aunt Astrid because she took me to countless shows and museums during my childhood. She was the one who encouraged me to try out for my first play, and she never missed a performance since. Astrid was a dancer and a model in her youth and had never seen herself settling down. She had always doted on us and was an honorary aunt to many of her friends' children. I was always her favorite.

"Especially you," I said sincerely. "I'll have a front row seat for you."

"I'm glad I brought you a new scarf then," she said then tipped her head toward her cavernous handbag on the floor. It reminded me a lot of Mary Poppins's carpetbag. "Hand that to me, will you?"

I didn't want to, but I couldn't say no to her. I picked the bag up and was surprised it was so heavy. "What in the world do you have in here?"

"I think she stole the toaster from 'the home' again," Dad said in a mock whisper.

"Amelia," Aunt Astrid said shrilly, "I still think you could've done better than this guy. It's not too late you know. You're still young enough to snag you a good one." Astrid cackled gleefully. "I still get plenty of action at my age." The rest of us groaned because we didn't want to think about Astrid getting it on with her geriatric guys. "What? A woman has needs."

"Kindly remember there are children in the room," my mother admonished, but she couldn't keep the laughter out of her voice.

"Ashley," Astrid said, mimicking Scarlet O'Hara, "I have a house-warming gift for you, and I contributed to dinner."

"Oh, Aunt Astrid, you shouldn't have," my sister said, and I had to bite my lip to keep from grinning.

"It's rude to show up without gifts. I have limited access, you see, since they took my computer away for watching my favorite sites for p—"

"Astrid!" Mother shrieked. Michele and Laurel giggled, but I figured it was more from their grandmother's outburst than them knowing what Astrid had been about to say. At least I hoped.

Astrid stuck a finger in her ear and wiggled it around like perhaps her ears were ringing. "I was going to say programs, Amelia."

She was going to say porn, and we all knew it. Astrid had fallen asleep while watching gay porn on her laptop one time too many and lost the privilege. She'd told me it was research to make sure I was doing things properly. I had died from mortification but thanked her for her thoughtfulness anyway. Just remembering the conversation made my face flush with embarrassment.

"You do look different," Astrid said, searching my face.

"That's your cataracts," my dad said from behind me. "Rome looks the same as he always does."

"No, he doesn't," all the ladies, including my nieces, chimed in.

"He looks more relaxed," Michele said.

"Yeah, less tense," Laurel agreed.

"He looks like he got laid," Astrid said.

"I'm going to need Rome's help in the kitchen," Ashley said. "Girls, take Dolly outside. Let her off the leash so she can run around and play in the grass. Keep her away from the pool, okay?"

"Mom," they both protested. One quirked brow from Ash and they took Dolly's leash from my hands.

"We miss all the good stuff," Michele grumbled.

"They think we're still little kids," Laurel agreed.

"Before you steal Romeo to gossip away from my prying ear," Astrid said, "let me give you the gifts I brought you."

"Okay, Aunt Astrid," Ashley said with a forced smile while she braced herself for only God knew what.

"First, my dinner contribution." She pulled out an industrial-size can of sweet corn that she must have pilfered from the kitchen of her nursing home. "That should be enough to feed us all."

"I'll say," Ashley agreed. "Thank you."

"And I made you these to use in your lovely kitchen." Astrid pulled out misshapen knitted objects that I believed were potholders, but I couldn't be sure. If so, the holes between the knit were too big to afford any protection from a hot pan or baking dish. "I went with a neutral yarn because I didn't know what color scheme your kitchen was." Chartreuse was considered neutral? I couldn't keep the wicked smile off my face when I looked at Ashley after she accepted the gifts. Luckily, Astrid couldn't see the evil lurking on my face.

"They're lovely, Aunt Astrid. Thank you so much."

"You're so welcome, my lovely girl. And for you, Rome," she said, pulling my attention back to her. "I thought this would keep you warm this winter." Astrid pulled out a gorgeously knitted, rainbow scarf from her bag. "Every day can be pride day with this bad boy."

"It's gorgeous," I said, unable to keep the shock from my voice. "You made this for me?" Where were all the crooked lines and gaping holes.

"Don't be silly. I couldn't knit this well if my life depended on it. I hired that handsome nurse, Kurt, to make it for you. I was going to try and fix you up on a date with him, but I can see I waited too long."

"Rome, can I please get your help in the kitchen?" Ashley asked.

"Just because the man is gay doesn't mean he can cook," Astrid told my sister.

"That's true, Astrid," Ashley replied as she headed to the kitchen with the huge can of corn and her potholders, "but this is one gay man who can cook very well."

I set my scarf on the arm of the couch and leaned forward to kiss Aunt Astrid's cheek. "This is a lovely scarf, and I'll wear it proudly."

"I love you, and I'm so relieved to see you happy again. I can die in peace now." Most people would've been alarmed by such a comment, but Astrid had been saying it for at least fifteen years.

"You'll outlive us all," I told her then joined Ashley in the kitchen. Of course, my mother was right on my heels.

"Who is he?" Mom asked before Ashley could.

"How long has this been going on without us knowing?" Ashley followed.

"Whoa, ladies," I said, holding up my hands. "It's all too new to really get into right now. Yes, I've met someone special, but we've only had one date." And hours of kissing, but they didn't need to know that.

"You look so relaxed, Rome," Ashely said softly. "I only want you to be happy. I didn't mean to pry."

"I did," Mom said.

"Make sure you get all the juicy details," Astrid yelled from the living room.

"Sure thing," Mom replied. She looked at me and shrugged. "Get talking while we work, or I'll make things up for Astrid. You choose."

So, I caught them up on everything that had happened since the beginning of school. I told them all about the play, the amazing staff at the schools, and lastly, I told them about my Julius, as I was already starting to think of him. It was too soon, I knew that, but I was also a man who recognized something special when it happened.

I didn't linger as late as I usually did because Julius was waiting for me, and I wanted to make a quick stop before it got dark. I pulled into Green Lawn Cemetery and drove the winding road I'd traveled so many times over the past seven years. I parked my car but left Dolly inside with the windows rolled down. I knew she'd be watching me from the window in the back seat.

I knelt in front of the beautiful tombstone and traced my fingers over the letters that spelled Peter Chastain. "Hi, Peter," I said. "It's been a while since I stopped by, but you know that already." After Peter first died, I visited several times a week, but over the years that had changed to special occasions like holidays, birthdays, and anniversaries. Peter's soul wasn't in the ground; he lived in my heart. "I couldn't imagine life without you. I've muddled through somehow, but I was just going through the motions. And now, well, I want to do more than stumble and scrape by. I want to dance again and embrace life to the fullest. I can only do that because I know it's what you would want for me. I loved you so much, Peter." Hot tears rushed down my face. "Loving someone else won't diminish what I felt for you. I finally understand that now."

I sat there in the serene setting for a while, reminiscing on some of the happiest times in my life and realizing there was still so much joy ahead of me. Then I got in my car and drove toward the man whose smile and laughter filled me with warmth, whose music stirred my soul, and whose kisses made my toes curl.

Chapter Ten

"When gravitational waves reach the earth, the waves stretch and squeeze space. This is a tiny stretch and squeeze. Far too small to detect with ordinary human senses."
~Kip Thorne

"The gravitational pull of the human heart surpasses any scientific explanation."
~Julius Shepherd

IT WAS NEARLY IMPOSSIBLE TO KEEP FROM CHECKING THE CLOCK AFTER receiving the text from Rome that he was on his way back to Blissville. I tried watching the football games on TV, but I couldn't tell you the score or even who was playing. I also kept my ears tuned for the sound of his car pulling up outside.

The apartment I rented was above a garage and could only be accessed by walking through it, which might make many feel like they were trespassing. Wren did keep a classic car in the garage below and a ton of tools, so I was always cautious to keep the door locked. When I finally heard Rome's car pull into the driveway and stop beside my car, I jogged down the steps and opened the outside door.

"Hey," I said when he and Dolly reached me.

"Hey yourself," he said warmly. I could see how badly he wanted to kiss me, so I stepped closer and met him halfway. I didn't want there to be any hesitation between us unless we were in a place where PDA wouldn't be appreciated.

"I wasn't sure if I should kiss you in open view of Dare and Wren's house," he said, staring at my lips.

"They might not be watching." I moved until my lips were just a breath away. If he wanted me, he would need to come and get me. "Then again, they could have the binoculars out."

A seductive smile spread across his handsome face and he said, "Let's give them something to gawk at then." Rome cupped the back of my neck and pressed his lips to mine. Soft and teasing at first, but the happy sigh that escaped my parted lips spurred him on to deepen the kiss. I braced one hand on the door to hold myself up and fisted my other in his lightweight sweater. God, the man could kiss. There was something to be said about a man with more experience than me. Kissing Rome didn't just involve my tongue and lips; every part of my body was in on the action. My heart raced, my dick throbbed, and something deeper yearned to learn everything there was to know about the man, including all the ways I could please him in bed. The last thought had me pulling back and looking at him through half-lidded eyes.

A sharply whistled catcall ripped through the silent back yard followed by clapping. Rome stepped aside, and I could see Dare looking at us through an open window. "Encore! Encore!"

Laughing, I pulled an equally amused Rome along with Dolly into the garage and closed the door behind them. "He's a nut, but I couldn't ask for a better landlord. Come on up," I said, nodding toward the stairs. "You might want to carry Dolly because her little legs might have a hard time navigating the steps."

"I was just thinking the same thing." Rome scooped Dolly up and she licked his chin. Was it ridiculous to be jealous over a dog? He caught me watching him and grinned wickedly like he knew what I was thinking.

"Right. Follow me."

I felt his eyes appraising my ass as I walked up the steps to the apartment, and I liked knowing I wasn't the only one feeling the chemistry between us. I had resisted him for as long as I could, but I was no longer interested in fighting his gravitational pull. I wanted to be in his orbit, not circling it. Wow. That kind of sounded dirty. Didn't make it less true.

"Can I get you something to drink?" I asked once we were inside my apartment. "I don't have wine, but I have several different types of IPA from my favorite brewery."

"Who's your favorite?" I knew he would file the information away so he could have it on hand the next time I was at his house, just as I made a note in my phone about the cabernet he'd enjoyed the previous night.

"Four Brothers Brewery from—" Rome's laughter interrupted me before I could finish. "What's so funny?"

"It reminded me of the trouble I stirred at my sister's house tonight. You wouldn't believe the evening I had."

"I want to hear all about it. Would you like to try one of my beers or would you prefer soda or water? Milk and cookies?"

"Is the last one an option?" Rome asked.

"If you want it to be."

"I'd like to try your favorite beer," he replied.

I grabbed two of the pale ales from the refrigerator and two frosty mugs from the freezer.

"I really like your apartment, Jules. It's much bigger than I thought it would be from the outside."

"Thanks. Dare and Wren said it had undergone a massive remodel before I rented it. Wren said it was a throwback to the seventies, but I don't even know how bad that was."

"Bad," Rome said with an exaggerated shrug. "We're talking burnt orange, avocado green, yellow, and brown. It was like the whole decade was on an acid trip. It probably had shaggy carpets too."

I laughed at his description. "Sounds like a nightmare."

"One that no one wants to relive."

"Tell me about your evening," I urged when I handed him the mug.

I wedged myself in the corner of the couch and folded my legs so I could watch him as he spoke. Rome struck the exact same pose in the opposite corner while Dolly lay on the floor beside the couch chewing the toy he'd brought along.

"Dolly is welcome on the couch," I said, gesturing to the empty cushion between us.

Rome shook his head. "I don't want anyone or anything between us." Then he sipped his beer and licked his lips. "Oh, that's good," he said, studying the glass. "Light, crisp, with a hint of citrus." I had a hard time looking away from his lips. "Oh, about the four brothers thing. I told my nieces, ages sixteen and fourteen, their parents were going to adopt a family of four brothers. I can't remember what I said their ages were because I was just throwing bullshit out there hoping it would stick, but I think I said between two and twelve."

"I take it they weren't happy about the idea?"

"Not in the least." Rome started laughing some more. "I have to tell you about my aunt Astrid." He then proceeded to give me some background about the lady before he got to their conversation. His aunt Astrid sounded like a real firecracker. "I know damn well she was going to say porn. We all did. My mom is her medical power of attorney and the person the nursing home calls when she acts up. Imagine how embarrassed my mom was when she raised hell with the administration for taking her laptop away only to find out what had been going on."

"I don't understand why they couldn't let the little lady indulge."

"They gave her a warning when they caught her watching it in the community rooms." I snorted. "She wasn't wearing headphones. The final straw was when she fell asleep watching it with the sounds of grunts and groans filling the room she shared with another woman. Her roommate was so hard of hearing she didn't know what was going on, but her family sure recognized the sounds."

"Oh shit." I laughed until I cried.

"There was one comment everyone except my oblivious father said to me tonight."

"What's that?"

"The remarked about how happy and relaxed I looked." Rome unfolded his legs and leaned over to set his mug down on the coffee table before crawling across the couch to reach me. "Guess what they accredited the changes to?" Rome took my mug from my hand and set it on the table beside his.

"A good night's rest?"

Rome shook his head and whispered, "They said it must be a man."

"Should I be jealous?"

Rome caressed my bottom lip with his thumb. "Huh-uh. I think you should kiss me."

"Yeah?" I asked, unfolding my legs to make room for Rome. "You've been thinking about my lips on yours?"

"And other places."

"Me too," I admitted.

"I feel so damn clumsy and out of practice. I think I look and sound suave, but I worry that I'm more Gilligan than James Bond."

I couldn't help laughing at the two choices he presented. "You're nowhere near as clumsy as Gilligan, and I love that you're not a player like Bond."

"Yeah?" he asked, removing his thumb and lowering his head until his lips hovered a hairsbreadth away from mine.

"Hell yeah." I cupped the back of his neck and pulled him the rest of the way.

Rome's mouth against mine was like setting a lit match to a piece of dry paper, burning so hot there wouldn't be anything left of me, not even ashes. There wasn't anything gentle about the way we kissed each other this time—teeth clacked and tongues rasped and swirled in an erotic dance. Our bodies moved in unspoken accord to slide lower on the couch until I was on my back and Rome was between my spread thighs.

I wrapped my arms around Rome, loving the weight of him against me but needing more. I slid my hands beneath his sweater and trailed my fingers down the center of his back until I reached the waistband of his jeans. I ached to slide my hands beneath his jeans but settled for gripping his firm ass through the denim instead. Rome took my cue and began rocking his pelvis forward and back, eliciting a groan from me because the friction of our erections grinding against each other was out of this world, even if we were separated by sweatpants and jeans.

Rome stilled his hips and pulled his mouth away from mine. We were both breathing hard, sucking air into our lungs. "Is this okay?" I loved that I could make him sound so breathless. Rome's pupils were blown, and his face was flushed with acute arousal, but he still stopped to make sure he wasn't moving too fast for me. It only made me want him that much more.

"Those were moans for more, sexy," I said. And if my words weren't enough, I lifted my hips to grind my erection against his, encouraging him to start moving again. "Take this off," I said tugging at his sweater. "I want to touch you."

Rome rose up and whipped his sweater over his head, baring his chest to me for the first time. The man spent a lot of time in the gym to maintain his lean, muscular frame and his cut abdomen. I traced my finger over the pulse in his neck and his collarbone before flattening my palm against his chest and sliding it down over smooth skin and rigid muscle. I loved the way his happy trail tickled my palm and was eager to follow it beneath the fly of his low-riding jeans.

"Your turn," Rome said huskily. "I need to touch you too."

I reluctantly dropped my hand from his body but did what he asked. Rome placed both of his palms flat against my pecs and licked his lips in appreciation. My commitment to the gym had always been about my health and having energy, but the lust in his eyes made me appreciate my efforts for a whole other reason. I raised my arms and tucked my hands under my head, completely turning myself over to him.

"God, you're beautiful," Rome said, touching me everywhere. I gasped when his palms brushed over my nipples. I'd never realized how sensitive they were until that moment with Rome. They'd always just been there. It looked like kissing wasn't the only thing my silver fox excelled at. Rome, hearing my sharp intake of breath, jerked his eyes up to meet mine, gauging to see if my reaction was good or bad. Liking what he saw, he returned his hands to my pecs and circled my nipples until they were painfully erect then pinched and rolled them between his thumb and forefinger.

"Unh," I groaned, arching my back off the couch. I could feel my cock leaking and was desperate for friction or anything that would put me out of my misery and calm the surging tide of arousal. I'd had sex before, but this was…this didn't feel like the same solar system as sex. Rome was an unknown, undiscovered planet pulling me into his orbit until being with him was all I could think about or feel. I. Needed. Him. Not just an orgasm, but one that *he* gave me. "More."

A wicked smile tugged at his lips. "More what? This?" He pinched my nipples tighter. "Do you want my hands lower? Or…" Rome paused to lower his body so his head hovered over my chest. "Do you want my mouth on you instead?"

"Y-yes," I moaned, pulling a dark chuckle from my tormentor.

"It wasn't a yes-or-no question." How was he even thinking? What had happened to the man who practically stuttered and stumbled when I was near. How had the roles reversed so quickly? "Which leaves me to interpret your needs."

Rome lowered his head and made a wet pass over one nipple then the other while I fisted my hand in his hair, moaning and writhing. He continued with the little licks when what I really wanted was him to wrap his lips around my nipples and suck hard. "Rome, please?" I begged, finding my voice.

Rome's dark chuckle created a vibration against my skin. Then he stopped teasing me and sucked one aching nipple into his mouth while rolling his tongue over the distended nub.

"God yes! More!" Rome answered by moving his mouth over to the neglected nipple and repeated the toe-curling suction slash licking maneuver. Unable to lie still beneath him a second longer, I undulated my hips, rocking my erection against his rock-hard abs. "I need... I need..."

Rome slowly released my nipple, letting his teeth lightly rasp over the sensitive nub. He repositioned his body until we were chest to chest and dick to dick. "I know, baby."

"Less clothes."

I saw doubt in his eyes like maybe we were moving too quick too soon, but he didn't have to worry I would wake with regret. I'd only kick myself in the ass if I let him walk away without knowing what his face looked like during an orgasm. I'd pictured it many times, but I knew the flesh and blood reality would be so much better than any fantasy. So, I reached between our bodies and shoved my sweats and briefs below my ass to release my cock. It slapped hot, hard, and sticky against my abdomen, gaining Rome's full attention.

"Mercy," he said lustfully as he rose to his knees and reached for his button fly.

I placed my hands over his, halting him. "Let me."

Ignoring my throbbing dick, I took my time sliding each button through the hole until I revealed his light gray underwear and the wet circle that said he wanted me as much as I wanted him. The smell of arousal and cum was far sexier than any cologne or body wash you could buy. I glanced up at Rome's face and saw that he was biting his lip in anticipation. I lifted my hands to tease his nipples just as he'd teased mine, noting how rigid his body was from tension.

"I'm about to combust, Jules," he whispered, pulling my gaze back up to meet his. "Play time is over, yeah?"

"Hell yeah."

I tugged his jeans and underwear down over his straining erection to rest at mid-thigh, then fisted his leaking cock, stroking him as he did the same for me. I loved having his hand wrapped around my dick, working me up and down, but it wasn't enough.

"C'mere," I said, sounding drunk.

Rome lowered his body once more, lining up our dicks and recapturing my lips in a devastating kiss as he began shuttling his cock back and forth over mine. Our combined precum coated our dicks, making the grinding flesh sticky but oh so fucking sexy. I wouldn't last long, but I was too far gone in lust to worry about shooting too quick.

"Ride me," I groaned against his lips, gripping his ass to urge him to move faster and harder.

Rome shifted his body and shoved his jeans and underwear completely off, and I pushed my thighs together. Rome straddled my hips and aligned our cocks once more. He placed his arms on my shoulders for leverage while I gripped his ass to keep him close. He began to move again—faster and harder. I'd seen frotting in porn, but I'd never done it myself. I didn't know how much I had missed out on, but then again, maybe not. Maybe Rome was the reason why all my senses were heightened.

"Almost…" I said, arching my neck as I felt my balls draw tighter against my body.

"Me too."

Rome dropped his right hand down to pinch my nipple at the same time I slid a finger between his spread ass cheeks to circle his pucker. We went off at the same time, grunting, groaning, and covering my stomach with our combined cum. My silver fox collapsed in my arms, panting hot air against my neck while I held him tight.

"I may never recover," he teased. "That was…" His words trailed off as his blood-deprived brain searched for the right words.

"Amazing."

"Yep! That's it."

I chuckled then rolled until we lay side by side, looking into each other's drowsy eyes. "It was better than I ever dreamed it would be," I told him, tracing a finger over his swollen lips.

"You thought about it a lot?"

"At least twice a day."

"Every day?"

"At least five or six days a week."

"I'm going to research a diet that will allow me to keep up with your...um...insatiable appetites," Rome said, but he didn't look the least bit worried he couldn't hang with me.

"I have a feeling you're going to do just fine without any help from super foods." I ran my fingers through his hair. "In all my fantasies, I never imagined one thing I learned about you tonight."

"Uh-oh," he said ominously. "Do I want to know?"

I tweaked his nipple playfully. "I didn't know you matched your underwear to your shirt."

Rome threw his head back and laughed. "I don't. It was pure coincidence."

I snatched my T-shirt off the floor and wiped both of our chests off before I grabbed the blanket off the back of my couch and covered us. "I want to hear about the rest of your day," I said.

"I want to hear about yours too."

"There were some huge revelations today," I told him while stroking my fingers over his smooth skin. "My brother has grappled with some big decisions lately, but he finally knows what he wants for his life." I told Rome about the conversation we'd had on the way to our grandparents' house and then meeting Camilla and Manny. "He wasn't just my kid brother anymore; he was this grown-ass man with a family. I've never seen him look so happy. That little boy has him wrapped around his chubby little finger too."

"What about you?" Rome asked, tracing a heart on my chest. "Were you wrapped around Manny's finger too?"

"Completely," I admitted. Rome hummed happily in my arms. "Besides traumatizing your nieces, what else happened at dinner?"

I listened as Rome told me about the day with his family and was blown away by his openness when he talked about stopping by Peter's grave. We talked, and we kissed long past the time we should've called it a night, considering we both had to be at the school by seven in the morning. I knew I wouldn't regret the lack of sleep, and I wouldn't even need to get a caffeine buzz first thing in the morning, because I would be high on the promise I saw in Romeo Bradley's eyes when he kissed me goodnight.

Chapter Eleven

"I would challenge you to a battle of wits, but I see you are unarmed."
~William Shakespeare

"You can't fix stupid."
~Romeo Bradley

THERE WAS NO DENYING I WALKED WITH EXTRA PEP IN MY STEP THAT morning nor was there doubt as to why it felt like I was floating instead of walking. *Julius.* I'd earned a quirked brow from Lily when I dropped Dolly off, but she didn't ask any questions.

"By the way, your marinara sauce was the best I've ever had," I said when I released Dolly from the leash before handing it to Lily.

"I'm so happy you enjoyed it. Would you like another jar? I have plenty."

"I will graciously accept your generosity when I pick Dolly up tonight. I'd really like you to teach me how to grow the right tomatoes and make the sauce myself. I'm ruined for jarred spaghetti sauce from the store."

"Really?" Lily asked. "I'd love to teach you this summer if that's really what you want."

"I do."

After dropping off Dolly, I stopped at Books and Brew to pick up a cup of coffee and a pastry for both myself and Priscilla. She was partial to their blueberry and cream cheese Danish, and I wanted to bring her a treat to get her week started off on the right foot. Milo was working the counter and eyeing me speculatively. I gave him my order and paid for it while Maegan started making our drinks.

"That looks really good on you, Rome."

"Thanks, this tie is my favorite," I told Milo, although I suspected he meant the sappy grin I couldn't wipe off my face.

"You know darn well I wasn't talking about your yellow paisley tie." It was said with so much derision I had to study my choice to see if it looked as bad as he implied. I loved the pastel colors in the paisley print and thought it looked sharp against the lavender shirt I'd chosen.

"What's wrong with my tie?" I asked, scowling at him.

"Milo, we don't insult our patrons' clothes," Maegan said from the espresso machine. She turned and faced me. "Your tie looks as lovely as the glow you're wearing."

"Mae, he was being deliberately obtuse," Milo countered. "I guess we'll let the man keep his secrets."

"In this town?" Mae snorted. "Good luck with that, Rome."

I hadn't planned on keeping my relationship with Julius a secret; I just wasn't willing to reveal my feelings to people I hardly knew. Did Julius want us to keep our relationship a secret? If he did, we'd have to be extraordinarily careful and have all our dates away from Blissville, and there could be no overnight stays at either of our houses. That sounded horrible to me, but I would try if it's what he wanted. *If he had a valid reason for denying us.* I just wasn't sure how long I could pull it off. It wasn't like I expected him to hold my hand or kiss me at the school, but the thought of not being able to smile at him in the hallway or share lunch with him during our break bothered me more than it should.

"Uh-oh," Milo said. "Mae didn't mean to diminish your sunny disposition."

"Me?" Maegan said, placing her hands on her hips. "You're the one insulting his tie, so you started it."

That quickly, the clouds parted and allowed the sun to shine bright again. I clutched my stomach and laughed at their antics. "Oh, you two are something else. I bet you kept your folks on their toes."

"Kept?" asked an amused voice from behind me. I turned and saw a smiling older version of Maegan. "I'm Jackie Miracle, and the mother of these two hooligans. There is never a dull moment with Milo and Maegan."

"I'm Romeo Bradley," I said, offering my hand.

"I know who you are, Dr. Bradley," she replied, firmly shaking my hand. "It's nice to finally meet you."

"Likewise."

Maegan placed a carrier with my drinks and a bag with the pastries on the counter. "Have a great day. Sorry again that we hijacked your good mood the minute you crossed the threshold."

"You did no such thing, guys. I always feel like I'm getting free entertainment with my coffee and pastries when both of you are working behind the counter. I'll be back for more tomorrow."

"See you tomorrow then," Milo said with a devious smile. It looked like he was already coming up with a scheme to irritate his sister and entertain me at the same time. I had every faith he could pull it off.

"Good luck with them, Mrs. Miracle."

"Please call me Jackie, and thank you. I'll take all the luck I can get."

My phone rang as soon as I settled in my car. I hadn't started my engine yet, so the call didn't show up on my display or ring through my speakers. I fished my phone out of my pocket and saw that Priscilla was calling me. I wasn't late, so there was no reason for her to be busting my balls so early on a Monday morning.

"Good morning, sunshine," I said, knowing it would rile her up.

She ignored my greeting and didn't offer one in returned. "You better get your ass over here. We have big trouble brewing."

"How can there be big trouble brewing already. The day hasn't started yet."

"Evil waits for no one." Click. She hung up without another word.

My mood soured quickly as I made the short drive to my office. I shared a space with the school board officers: president, vice president, treasurer, and secretary; the assistant the four of them had to share; and my secretary, Priscilla. When I walked through the door, I was surprised to find all the school board members present, not just the officers, along with their assistant.

"Surprise," Priscilla said drolly.

"You shouldn't have. It's not my birthday," I replied, trying to inject a sense of humor to lighten the mood of the room. Whatever they had to say couldn't be that bad. My optimism faded when it occurred to me someone might've seen Julius walk me to my car at one o'clock that morning and kiss me goodbye. We weren't talking about a quick peck either. Julius gave me a why-don't-we-take-this-back-inside kiss.

"Dr. Bradley, could we have a private word in the boardroom?" Caitlyn Simpson posed it as a question, but the look on her face told me she expected me to follow without hesitation.

"After you," I said to all of them. I stopped by Priscilla's desk and handed her the coffee carrier and bag of pastries. "Go ahead and enjoy your treat."

"You're too good to me," she said tearfully.

"It's going to be okay," I consoled her, wishing I felt as certain as I sounded. "I haven't done anything wrong."

She snorted. "That evil bastard doesn't care who he destroys."

I wanted to ask who she meant but knew I'd find out soon enough. The school board looked pissed enough as it was, so I didn't want to keep them waiting. Each of the board members had daytime jobs they were missing to host this impromptu meeting with me.

"Dr. Bradley, won't you have a seat?" Caitlyn asked, gesturing to an open chair across from her. "We won't keep you long, but an issue was brought to our attention late yesterday evening that impacts all of us and our students. We decided it was best to get this out in the open so we can devise a plan."

"Why didn't you just call me last night, Cait?" I asked. "Maybe it would've saved you all the hassle of being late to your jobs."

"This is too important to handle over the phone," she replied. I noticed both her posture and tone of voice had softened. "Dr. Bradley, we"—she circled her forefinger in the air to encompass everyone in the room—"really like you and the positivity and experience you bring to our school. We respect all the measures you've taken to re-build the relationship between the faculty and the school board. I cannot express how happy that makes me—us."

I glanced around the room to see everyone nodding solemnly. "But…"

"There are no buts," Earl Jenner, the vice president said. "We just want you to know how much we appreciate you before we discuss the matter at hand."

"Which is?" I prompted.

"You have the board's full support, Dr. Bradley," Cheryl Highlander said. "We truly admire you."

"Thank you," I told her. If they were so happy with my job performance, then why did it look like they were attending my funeral? "I have to admit, I've never received praise like this delivered in gloomy monotones. It kind of feels like I entered *The Twilight Zone*."

"It's because none of us want to be the one to repeat mean, hurt-ful things to a person who's done nothing to deserve them," Cait said.

"Clearly a complaint was filed against me. Can I ask by whom and what their grievances were?"

"Apparently, word has filtered around the county about the play we plan to perform in January," Cait told me.

"The play the board voted on before I was hired?"

"Yes, that play. The school board has received a signed petition asking us to terminate the production of *Inside Out*." Then I realized that most of Caitlyn's hurt came from the idea of disappointing her daughter. She had to know how much *Inside Out* meant to Clara.

"No," I said firmly. "There's not a single line in that play that is inappropriate for the student body to speak or an audience to hear."

"I agree with you wholeheartedly, Dr. Bradley," Cait said. "You have to know how personal this is for me, but I have to think like a mature adult and not the mother of one of the creators."

"What's that mean?" I asked her. "Are you even considering honoring the petition?"

"We have to take these things seriously, Rome," Earl said. "None of us want cancel the play."

"Okay, then why the gloom and doom?"

"We think it's best to at least hold a public meeting to allow the parents to speak their minds and let them hear our thoughts in return."

"Okay," I said, nodding. "I agree that's fair, but are there really that many parents upset about the play? How many signatures did they collect?"

"Seven hundred and fifty," Cait said.

"We only have six hundred and thirty-two students registered at Blissville High School," I stated. Cait snorted, Earl chuckled, and a few others snickered in the room. "I'm sorry. I didn't mean to imply you weren't aware of enrollment numbers."

"It's okay, Dr. Bradley. We understand why you're upset. We are too."

"I think we need to cross reference the names on the petition to the names of our high school student body," I recommended.

"Why?" Betsy Jones asked.

"Because I'm not willing to listen to any complaints from anyone outside our school district or anyone who doesn't have a child enrolled in the high school. If parents of a kindergartner don't want their kid to attend the play, then they don't have to drive them to Goodville to attend any of the performances. It isn't like they can accidentally stumble across the play."

"You make a valid point," Cait said. "I'm so irritated I didn't think of that."

"I'm plenty fired up about it, but that only makes my thoughts sharper."

"I'll ask Sandra to compare names on the petitions to our roster," Cait said. Sandra was the assistant assigned to the board members.

"Or you can have Priscilla look at it," I suggested. "She knows everybody in this town. Hell, she's worked in this district for fifty years."

"True," Earl said. "Her mind is quicker than any computer."

"That's what she keeps telling me," I replied. "Who drew up the petition in the first place?"

"Roy Halifax," Cait replied, disdain dripping from her tongue. "There has never been a more grotesque man to walk this earth."

"He founded the Preserving Our Society group, and they hold meetings each month to discuss ways they can run off the gays and other minorities who they feel are ruining our way of life."

"You don't say?" I asked, sitting back in my chair. My mood had improved for the first time since I arrived.

"Why are you smirking?" Cait asked suspiciously.

"I refuse to fear any group with an acronym of POS."

"He is a piece of shit!" Cait declared then covered her mouth and burst into laughter.

The rest of us followed her until we were practically crying from laughing so hard at her outburst. I knew in that moment we would take on the piece of shits together and come out the victor.

"We're set to have the auditions next week," I reminded Cait. "Do you want me to slide them back a week?"

"No," she replied firmly. "We'll schedule a public meeting for Friday and take it from there. Emails will go out to high school parents, and I'll make sure it gets announced in the Blissville Daily News."

"Do you think it's wise to encourage more people to show up?" Earl asked.

"First of all, we don't do things in secret," Cait said firmly. "The previous school board, along with the former superintendent who is serving time in jail, operated on corruption and deceit. I promised transparency, and that's what I'm going to deliver. Besides, if we don't tell our students and their parents, only the people who want to stop the play will show up. Is that what we want?"

"Not at all," Cheryl said.

"We'll need to include the overview of the play in the newsletter and inform the parents that three of Blissville High's students wrote the play and lyrics for the songs. I would think that most parents would be impressed," I suggested.

"Agreed," Cait said. "I'll also let them know the full board, not just the parent of one of the playwrights, read the play and approved it. I plan to objectively listen to valid complaints, not hateful rhetoric, and hold a public vote in front of those who attend." The look in her eye said she wouldn't be swayed to cancel the play because of some ignorant bigot, so I released a grateful sigh.

"Well, I guess that concludes this meeting then?" I asked. "Or was there anything else we needed to discuss?"

Cait looked around the room to see if anyone else had something they wished to bring up, but everyone shook their heads. "Meeting adjourned then. I will email everyone in the next day or so to confirm a time for Friday's meeting."

I shook the hands of each member as they left the boardroom then went in search of Priscilla and found her in Sandra's office. Both of them were sitting behind Sandra's desk looking at the computer, and I had no doubt they were already scrutinizing the names on the petition list.

"This is ridiculous," Priscilla said, shaking her head. "It would be easier to point out the legitimate names on this list since there are so few of them. Ha! Gresham Powell died in 2015. Who the hell are they trying to fool with this bullshit list? I'm going to nail their balls to the wall." Uh-oh! Someone woke up "The Dragon" and they would pay dearly.

"Let me know if I can help in any way," I said, eliciting a startled gasp from the ladies. They'd been too enthralled with the list to notice I was standing inside the doorway.

"You can help by not giving an old woman a heart attack," Priscilla told me. "Why are you sneaking around here? It's unsettling."

"I'm not sneaking around. You were just so absorbed by your mission you didn't notice."

Priscilla conceded with a shrug of her bony shoulders. "Your handsome fella dropped something off at your desk. He looked disappointed you weren't available." Just like that, the sun was shining and birds were singing once more. "It's a good thing he stopped by because I gave your muffin to Sandra."

"That's okay. Had I known Sandra would be in today, I would've brought her a coffee and pastry too."

"I know that," Priscilla said. "You're a damn good man. Now get out of here so we can save the school play."

"Yes, ma'am," I said, quickly retreating toward my office.

On my desk sat a bouquet of sunflowers, a cup of coffee, and a Styrofoam carryout container that filled my room with a delicious fragrance. I smelled cinnamon, butter, sugar, and yeast. I crossed to my desk and opened the container and saw the fattest, gooiest cinnamon roll I had ever seen. The icing dripping down the sides of the pastry made me think of the mess we made on Julius's stomach. I had to steer my mind away from that image before my body started to react to it.

Beside the coffee was a message written on a Post-it note. *Sorry I missed you. Available for lunch? J*

I didn't bother checking my calendar because I never scheduled appointments during my lunchtime. I checked the time and saw classes hadn't started yet, so I typed out a quick message. *Thank you for my lovely surprise. Your place or mine?*

Mine.

Great. You want me to bring you lunch from the cafeteria or do you want me to run to the diner? I had a lot more freedom than Jules did.

His reply came back quick. *It's chicken nuggets and macaroni and cheese day. Some things a guy just never outgrows.*

I laughed at his reply. *I'll be there at eleven fifteen sharp.*

I dug into my cinnamon roll while tracing a finger over the petals of my beautiful flowers, vowing not to allow ignorance to ruin my day.

Chapter Twelve

"There is always some madness in love. But there is also always some reason in madness."
~Friedrich Nietzsche

"There's no logic in love, but sometimes the chaos just makes sense."
~Julius Shepherd

THE ANTICIPATION AND EXCITEMENT OF SEEING ROME AGAIN WAS greater than I had ever experienced before in my life which felt both strange and right at the same time. I thought it was odd I was more antsy over a simple lunch date than I was during my first solo cello performance as a kid or the first time I stood in front of a class of high school kids as their teacher. Those were moments when things could either go really good or really bad for me, and my blossoming relationship with Rome was no different. There was no way to know things wouldn't blow up in my face, but it just felt right. I couldn't turn back now if someone offered me money.

I gave myself a mental shake to get my head back in my classroom where it belonged. There was no room for that kind of distraction, any distraction, with twenty-five kids needing my best. I had exciting news to share with the class, and that's where my focus was required.

"I have a special announcement to make," I said. The students looked up from the homework assignments they'd already started. "Have any of you ever heard of the Ohio Science Olympiad hosted at The Ohio State University in August of each year?" A few students nodded but most shook their head. "It's the state's premier science competition that allows us to show what skills Blissville is teaching in science, technology, engineering, and math. I can only take fifteen students, and there will be twenty-three events we can compete in. I've coached teams in a similar competition in Philadelphia, so I'm familiar with the structure and rules. The maximum number of seniors I can take for our division is five, and I must pick the remaining members from the other three classes. Because this contest won't be held until the next school year, this year's seniors aren't eligible. I truly wish I started teaching here a year earlier because you are some of the brightest, inquisitive minds I've taught."

"That is a bummer," Clara said. "I would've loved to compete in the Science Olympiad."

"I'm sorry to disappoint you, and I wouldn't have brought it up, but there aren't just seniors in this class." My classes had a mixture of seniors, juniors, sophomores, and a few freshmen.

"I hope there is more interest than there are slots because it shows how much you all love science and math. I'm going to pass around a clipboard with a signup sheet. Once I know how many people are interested, I will form a game plan."

"Does that mean you're going to have some kind of competition and the winners make the team?" Mark Vaughn asked.

"That's the only fair way to do it," I told him. "The contest will be threefold. You will submit a concept for approval; once approved, you will document the building of your project with detailed notes, photos, or videos; and the final phase will be the demonstration. I must complete the paperwork in November if we're to take a team to the competition in August."

"That's a lot of planning," Bobby said from the back row. "This must be a big deal."

"OSU is a highly respected school in the fields of science, medicine, and engineering, Bobby. Placing well at this competition will look amazing on college applications."

"I bet," he replied.

"As you can imagine, this won't be cheap, so we will try to offset some of the cost by hosting fundraisers throughout the year."

"Not more cookie dough," one of the boys in the far-right corner said.

"No, I thought we'd try to do something a little more entertaining, but I'm going to need school board approval." Clara perked up in her seat, eager to help. "I will take this to the board on my own."

"Fair enough, Mr. S."

"I'm going to pass this clipboard around, and the only thing you're indicating today is if you're interested in being on the team. I will put together a packet of information to share with your parents which will include dates, costs, and the things required of you and therefore them."

I started with the table on the far left and handed the clipboard to Mark, who eagerly wrote in his name before handing it to his partner, Daniel. I knew the boys were an inseparable duo and did almost everything together, so I wasn't surprised when Daniel wrote his name down too before passing it to the table behind them.

I returned to my desk and started looking over the notes I'd made about the competition and ways to defer cost so the parents wouldn't be facing a steep fee. I looked up when Bobby set the clipboard on my desk.

"Here you go, Mr. S."

"Thanks, Bobby."

I glanced over the list and saw every eligible student had declared their interest just like the four classes before them had. I was deliriously happy to see so many kids sign up, but that meant I was going to face a hard task of eliminating some of them. I realized it was something I couldn't do alone and decided to ask my fellow science teachers if they wanted to help choose and coach the team.

When the bell rang, the students were quick to their feet and shuffled out the door. My pulse leapt because I knew Rome would be waiting in the hallway to enter my room. He stepped inside as soon as the last kid walked through the door. I rose to my feet, unable to stay still. My hands were suddenly damp and nervous energy buzzed through my body until he smiled at me. Then all the noise and chaos went away until it was the two of us alone in my room.

"Hi," I said lamely.

"Hello."

"Um," I said, looking around. "Do you want to eat at one of the tables or scoot a chair over and eat across the desk from me?"

"We should probably keep the desk between us, Jules." The deep timbre of his voice made me shiver. I nodded because the things I wanted to do weren't appropriate for my classroom. "I didn't know what kind of beverage you wanted, so I bought white, chocolate, and strawberry milk and an apple juice."

"Do I see cookies on the trays?" I asked.

Rome nodded. "Snickerdoodles."

"Those are my favorite," I said, eyeing them appreciatively. I could tell Rome was filing the information away for future use. "What are your favorite cookies?"

"Oatmeal raisin," he replied, setting the trays on my desk then walking over to snag a chair from the closest table. "Everyone else hates them, but I love them. My aunt Astrid made the best."

"I'll take your word for it."

"Not a fan of oatmeal raisin cookies, huh?"

"It's one of the few times I'm in the majority," I quipped. "Why does my portion of macaroni and cheese look so much bigger than yours?"

"I had Stella give you a little extra since you're such a big fan."

I chose the strawberry milk, making Rome smile. "Some things just bring out the kid in me."

"Nuggets, macaroni and cheese, and strawberry milk do that to you, huh?"

"Snickerdoodles too. They're my mom's specialty. All the other kids wanted chocolate this and chocolate that, but I just wanted Mama's snickerdoodles."

"So, I have some news to share with you, and it's not necessarily good news." Rome's words made my heart sink, and it must've been written all over my face. "I think everything is going to work out, but since you're involved, it's only fair that you hear this from me and not through the rumor mill."

I set my fork down and forgot all about the cheesy pasta I loved so much. "Go ahead." My voice sounded dry and brittle.

"Oh no," Rome said, reaching across the desk to cover my hands. "This isn't about us, Jules. Some local bigot started a petition to have our school play canceled. I think the petition is virtually bogus based on what Priscilla and Sandra have found so far when looking at the names on it."

"Oh wow," I said, feeling relieved his news wasn't about us personally…this time. "You're not that worried about it?"

"I was meeting with the entire board this morning which was why I wasn't in my office when you stopped by. Thank you again for my flowers and breakfast, by the way. Your thoughtfulness made my day. Anyway, the board is committed to seeing the play through, but they feel like they at least need to hold a special public meeting on Friday. Cait said they'll allow this Roy Halifax an opportunity to speak, and I suspect she'll ask for a rebuttal from someone who supports the play. The board will then have a public vote that same night."

"You don't think anyone on the board will waver under pressure? How many people signed the petition?"

"Seven hundred and fifty," Rome said. "Priscilla and Sandra have been matching the names up to the high school roster, and so far, more than seventy percent of the names they've checked aren't valid. Some are even dead. Priscilla is having a field day with this one."

"You sound pretty confident," I said, smiling at him.

"I have to be because telling those kids we can't produce their play isn't a conversation I want to have with them."

"Nor do I." I decided to adopt Rome's positive approach because focusing on negative energy never had a good outcome. I tucked into my lunch because my break wasn't that long, and I'd only have time for a quick snack after school before we climbed on the bus to head to our next tennis match. "Thank you for lunch," I finally remembered to say.

"My pleasure," Rome said, but I could tell by his voice he was distracted. I looked up and saw that a furrowed brow marred his handsome face.

"What's wrong?"

"What?" he asked, looking up to meet my gaze. "Nothing really. I was just thinking."

"About?" I prompted.

"The conclusions you jumped to when I told you I had news to share. You assumed the bad news was about us. I never thought to ask if you wanted to keep our relationship a secret. I mean, I would understand if you did, but wondered what that would entail. Would you want to go out of town for all our dates, and would it mean that we never slept over at each other's places? I would try if it made you happy, but…"

I reached across the desk and cover his hands. "I would never ask that of you, Rome. What we do off school grounds is our business. I wouldn't have started this with you if I wasn't brave enough to see it through. Leave town for dates," I grumbled. I released his hand and picked up my fork again. "I have every intention of learning what color sheets you keep on your bed," I whispered.

"I could just tell you that," he suggested with a wry smile.

"I want to feel them against my bare skin," I countered.

He swallowed hard, and his light blue eyes practically glowed with hunger. "Change of subject. Quick." I loved that I could affect him so much.

A knock sounded on the doorframe and I glanced up to see Clara, Ellie, and Curtis peeking in the room. I could tell by the dejected look on their faces they too had heard the news.

"We're sorry to disturb your lunch," Ellie said, looking between Rome and me.

"We can come back another time," Curtis suggested, wrapping his hands around Clara's and Ellie's biceps.

"It's okay," I said, waving them in. "I've done enough damage to my mac and cheese."

The trio entered the room and approached my desk.

"We've heard our play is going to get canceled. Is that true?" Clara asked. I was surprised her mother hadn't told her, but maybe she wanted to wait until she had more facts.

"That's not true," Rome said. "A petition was presented to the board requesting they cancel the play."

"But they're not going to, right?" Ellie asked. "We already got the play approved by them. They all read the play before they took a vote."

"They're going to have a public meeting to discuss it and then vote to honor their original decision or reverse it."

"Reverse it?" Curtis asked. "Do you think they will change their minds? Buckle under peer pressure?"

"I don't," Rome said. "I met with the board this morning, and a group of us are working on getting our facts straight so we can have an accurate picture of the challenge we're facing."

"Damn bigots and homophobes," Clara said under her breath.

"Let's not get upset about something that hasn't happened yet," I said calmly. "Let us look into it and have faith that things will work out the way we want them to."

"I'm not so good at placing my faith in other people, Mr. S.," Clara said.

"You can write your next play about that," I teased.

"The music will consist of a bunch of whiny violins," Curtis baited, earning a playful elbow jab from both girls. "Sorry. Bad joke."

"I want you to do your best and not worry about this. Try being kids for once. I hear it's a lot of fun," Rome told them.

"Might I suggest worrying about your tennis matches instead?" I asked Ellie.

"Yes, sir," she said sheepishly.

"We know how much this play means to you, and I assure you it means a lot to us too," Rome told them. "I'm going into that special meeting with the belief we'll be hosting auditions next week as planned."

"Okay," Clara said, sounding perkier. "Moping never fixes anything anyway."

"No, it doesn't," I agreed. "I hate to be rude, but I only have five minutes left with my fella, so do you mind if we talk about this later?"

"Your fella, eh?" Clara asked brightly.

"Awww," Ellie added.

Curtis snorted, but his smile said he approved of the development. "That was the worst thing to tell them if you expect them to clear out. Come on, ladies."

"Okay," Clara and Ellie said, unable to wipe the happy smirks off their faces as they left my classroom.

Rome chuckled. "Well, I guess that punctuates your previous remarks with a resounding exclamation mark. There's no way everyone in this school building won't know about our relationship status by the time school is out."

"And you're sure it's not a problem for you?" I asked.

"I'm more than fine with people knowing you're unavailable." The bell rang, and Rome slowly stood up. "I wish I could give you a good luck kiss before you get on the bus."

"Maybe I can stop by your place later after you have your walk with Howie. We should be back by six."

"You could join us for our walk. I know Howie wouldn't mind."

"I'll call you when I get back in town."

"Please do," Rome said. The room would fill with students any second and there I sat staring at his lips, wishing we were alone. "I… um…need to get going. See you tonight."

"Yo, Mr. S.," Justin said, walking through the door. "What's this I hear about a big science contest?"

Rome stood there with the trays in his hand, quirking a brow at me. "I'll tell you all about it tonight." He nodded and reluctantly headed for the door.

"Yo?" I asked Justin. "The nineties are calling, and they want their stupid vocabulary back."

"Is it true about the contest?" he asked.

"I'm going to discuss it in class. Have a seat and be ready to turn in last night's assignment."

Justin gave me a mock salute, and I glanced up in time to get a wink from Rome before he walked through the door. I was already counting the minutes before I saw him again.

Chapter Thirteen

"For I never saw true beauty till this night."
~William Shakespeare

"Ditto."
~Romeo Bradley

"WHAT DOES IT MEAN WHEN A LADY KEEPS BRINGING OVER casserole dishes?" Howie asked as we strolled down the sidewalk. He led the way with Bess while Jules, Dolly, and I followed behind him. I held Dolly's leash in my left hand and Jules's hand with my right.

"She's romancing you, big guy," Julius told him. I loved how quickly they had bonded when Jules made it back in time to join us for our nightly walk.

Howie even gave me a thumbs-up when Jules wasn't looking. "You think so, Jules?"

"She knows the way to a man's heart is through his stomach. She's wooing you hard."

"Is she a good cook?" I asked.

"Mighty fine cook," Howie said. "Should I invite her to join me one evening?"

"Do you want her company?" I asked.

Howie was silent for a few steps then said, "I guess it would be okay. I'm not really ready to date anyone right now, so I don't want to give her the wrong impression."

"You can always try being honest and up front. That way she can't read more into it than what you're offering," Jules suggested.

"Have you ever known that strategy to work with a woman?"

"I wouldn't know," Jules and I said at the same time, making Howie laugh.

"I guess that's right," he conceded. "I mean, I would like to date someone with a sweet disposition and great sense of humor like hers. If I were ready, that is."

"Does this lady have a name?" Jules asked.

"I've known her for a long time. She goes to my church. She can be a real firecracker if the situation calls for it. Should've retired a long time ago but thinks the school can't get along without her."

I knew then exactly who Howie was talking about. "That's the first time I've heard anyone refer to Priscilla as having a sweet disposition, but I recognized the firecracker comment right off."

"I forgot she was your secretary," Howie said. "She doesn't discuss school business much. She's the kind of person who does more listening than talking." *Since when?* I could hardly get a word in around her. "She values that school and her job."

"She is irreplaceable," I admitted. "People like to tease her because she isn't up to date with modern technology, but she knows things the computer can't tell us."

"I know people call her 'The Dragon' but she uses her ferocity to do good."

"I agree with you, Howie." It sounded to me that maybe my friend was a little more interested in Priscilla than he let on. Maybe he just hadn't figured it out yet, but he would when he was ready.

Jules squeezed my hand to get my attention. I looked at him, and he waggled his brows like he was thinking the same thing. God, I was so excited to have this man in my life.

"Anyway, I'd like to invite her to share the casserole dishes she brings me, but I'm not sure."

"You'll know when the time is right," I assured him.

"How's things going with the play? Ready for auditions next week?" Howie asked, changing the subject. I told him about the latest developments. "Preserving Our Society? POS? Who trusts anyone who sets themselves up for those kinds of jokes?"

"That's what I said," I told him. The three of us erupted into laughter.

"That's like an environmental protection group coming up with a name that has an acronym of COAL or PLASTIC."

"True," Julius agreed. "It doesn't make these POS zealots any less threatening though."

Howie stopped at the intersection and turned to face us. "Also true," he agreed. "What can I do to help you fight these nutters? I need something to do with my days that doesn't include moping and feeling sorry for myself."

"Maybe you could organize a group of people to come and support the kids at the board meeting," Julius suggested.

"Write an op-ed piece for the Blissville Daily News," I offered. "Turn your ire away from potholes and onto hateful people who want us all to go back to living in the fifties."

"Hey, we all know those potholes on Main Street are getting ridiculous. They're only neglecting them to force us in to voting in favor of creating a payroll tax for anyone working in this town and assessing taxes on anyone working outside of Blissville who isn't currently paying city taxes. They think if they wait long enough, we'll get fed up and cave in. The hell we will. Not when revenue continues to grow with every new store that opens up."

"I didn't mean to get you all riled up," I said, patting his shoulder. "Your op-eds are always well-researched and thought out."

"Thank you," Howie said, settling down. "And the fifties were a great era."

"Not if you were gay," I said.

"Or black," Jules countered.

"Or a woman who was nothing more than her husband's property," I added.

"Okay, maybe it wasn't so great when you're not looking through rose-colored glasses," Howie replied. "Can we at least agree there was excellent music in the fifties?"

"Absolutely," Jules and I both said.

"You two are something else together. Even a crotchety, half-blind geezer like me can see it."

"You're not crotchety," I countered.

"You're not a geezer either," Jules said.

"And clearly you're not blind if you can see that we make a handsome couple," I added.

"Enough already," Howie said, waving to cut us off before crossing the street. "You'll make me blush. You two fellas go on back to your place, Rome. I can take it from here."

"We only have to circle back a few blocks once we reach your house," I pointed out.

Howie turned around and grinned when he reached the other sidewalk. "Your yearning is emitting a frequency that's disturbing my hearing aid. Go spend time with your fella."

"What hearing aid?" I asked, knowing damn well he didn't have one.

"What? I can't hear you," Howie shouted back before he turned around and whistled for Bess to follow him.

"I'll have to work on turning the volume down on my want whenever we're in public," I said, smiling at Jules. "Do you want to head back to my place?"

"Oh yeah." We turned around and headed back the way we came.

"Are you hungry?"

"Mmm-hmmm," Julius responded.

"Great. I tried this delicious roasted pork recipe I found on Pinterest for the crockpot. I raised my brow over a few of the ingredients but I'm glad I made it anyway. Who knew adding a bit of lemon juice and soy sauce to chicken broth would combine with the juices from the pork tenderloin to make a delicious gravy?"

"I'm sure it's wonderful, but that isn't what I'm hungry for right now."

I sucked in a sharp breath, and my heart threatened to pound its way out of my chest. Julius must've mistaken my reaction for uncertainty.

"Rome, we don't have to do anything you're not ready for yet."

"I'm ready," I said quickly. "That isn't my issue."

"What's the problem then? Your underwear doesn't match your T-shirt today?" he teased, squeezing my hand.

I couldn't keep the leer from my face when I looked at him and said, "I'm not wearing any underwear."

Jules raked his hazel eyes over my body, lingering on the crotch of my gym shorts before he cleared his throat. "How the hell hadn't I noticed? God, we need to pick up the pace." He wasn't teasing about the last part. We quickened our stride which seemed to make Dolly happy. She was a Labrador trapped in a Dachshund's body.

Once we were back inside my house, Dolly danced in circles while I hung up her leash at the back door and opened the treat jar. "Have you really been good enough to earn this?" I asked, holding the prized goodie in my hand for her to see. *Woof!* That little bark could've said "I'm Daddy's best girl ever" or it could've meant "drop the fucking treat right now or I'll piss in your shoe while you sleep." I gave her the treat because she was definitely the first option and I wanted to avoid the second.

"So, I'm not the only one you like to dangle a treat in front of, huh?"

Rather than reply with words, I slid my fingers between Jules's and led him upstairs to my bedroom. I flipped on the light and tried to see the space through his eyes. A big bed with luxurious linens, a cherry armoire and two matching dressers, and a club chair, ottoman, and end table tucked away in the corner. The colors were a mix of grays and blues, a combination I felt was relaxing and serene.

"That's some bed," Julius said. "I've never seen anything like it."

I looked at him, but his eyes were locked on the four-poster bed made of cherry wood and wrought iron. I didn't think he saw any other part of my room besides the bed. Why did he sound nervous suddenly? It was just a bed. Yes, the headboard and footboard were made of intricate metal work that formed lotus flowers, but it shouldn't have been cause for concern. Then it occurred to me.

"Peter didn't make the bed," I said. "I bought it when I moved to Blissville. You've never seen anything like it because I had it custom made."

"It's a work of art, Rome."

I tugged on Jules's hand so he would turn to face me. "I probably said the same thing when I saw the bed for the first time but seeing you in my room makes me realize I was wrong. That," I said, pointing at the bed, "is a piece of furniture. You are the work of art, and together, we're going to make something devastatingly beautiful."

"English lit majors are such smooth talkers," he said, but I saw how much my words moved him.

"Would you expect anything different from a guy named Romeo?" I teased. "I meant every word." I leaned in for a long, tender kiss then pulled back because there was something important I needed him to hear. "There's been no one else in that bed other than me." I released his hand to remove my shirt. "And I want you there with me. Only you. Over me, under me, or beside me. I just want you there." I placed Jules's palm over my heart, letting him feel the way it raced for him. Only him.

"You completely unravel me, Rome. You seduce me with your body, heart, and your brain. The perfect trifecta, and I want to make you mine."

"I want to be yours." God, I hadn't wanted anything so bad for a very long time. I reached for the hem of his shirt and pulled it over his head, revealing his smooth chest and flawless skin. My hands immediately went to his pecs while he pulled me to him for a hot, needy kiss. I moaned into his mouth as I slid my hands up to wrap around his shoulders and pull him flush against me, needing that skin-on-skin contact. Jules's skin blazed like he had a fever and was burning up from the inside out.

Jules pulled back from the kiss, breathing hard. "Bed."

I missed his heat the second I stepped out of our embrace, but the sooner we undressed, the sooner I could have all of him against me. The fooling around on his sofa the previous evening was amazing, but I wanted—needed—to feel all of him pressed against me, moving inside me.

"Baby, are you sure?" Jules asked once we were completely naked. "I know *this*"—he wrapped his left hand around my aching dick—"is ready, but are you ready here?" He pressed his right hand over my heart then raised his hand to gently caress my temple. "Or here?"

"So ready, Jules."

The walk to my bed felt more like floating on air. Jules pulled back the duvet then slid between my sheets and I followed until every part of me was touching every part of him. First-time sex between a couple tended to be awkward, at least until passion overrode insecurities and bodies took over and did what they were made to do. In my eagerness to taste Jules's lips again, I leaned forward to recapture his mouth at the same time he started to lower his head to lick my nipple. My lips smacked hard against his forehead.

"God, I'm sorry," Jules said. He ran his finger gently over my lips to make sure they hadn't split. In response, I sucked his finger in my mouth and pretended it was his cock. I loved the way his pupils expanded until there was only a thin rim of color showing around the obsidian circles. Alice had her rabbit hole, and I was teetering on the edge of falling into Julius's eyes.

I suddenly rolled him to his back and my knee caught the inside of his thigh when I tried to position myself between them. Julius groaned, and my only recourse was to slide lower in the bed so I could kiss it better. The scent of his arousal drove me insane, and my body took over, driving away my inept clumsiness. I gripped his cock and laved it with my tongue, savoring his taste and the way Julius fisted my hair. I wanted to make him writhe, pant, and moan, so I took him to the back of my throat.

"Unh," Jules grunted. "Maybe we do that when I'm not so worked up, yeah?"

I released his cock from my mouth and circled the flared head with my tongue. "Feels good?"

"Too good. C'mere." I was torn. I wanted to stay right where I was and work his cock with my mouth until his entire body shook with his pending release. Even then, I was tempted to suck and lick until he came, hoping he would shout my name as he spilled down my throat. His pleading eyes were the deciding factor. "I need you now."

Jules's lips met mine when I crawled back up his body then he rolled and pinned me beneath him. Unfortunately, he misjudged the distance to the edge of the bed and cracked his elbow on the nightstand.

"Fuck!" he yelled. I cringed because I knew how bad that had to hurt. We both burst into laughter when he looked down into my eyes. I'd always heard that laughter in bed was a bad thing, but I loved the way Jules's body shook with mirth when I pulled him into my arms. "Have you seen anything more ridiculous in your life?" Jules asked when he could speak again.

"I've never seen anything more beautiful in my life." I sounded like a besotted, sappy fool, but so what. I was too old to be coy with the man I was falling so hard for. "And the night has just begun."

I lifted my head, needing to taste Julius's smile on his lips. We fell into sync then. Our hands sliding over smooth flesh, learning the dips and planes of one another's bodies while needy moans echoed off the walls of my room. I clung to Jules, unable to get enough of him and wishing I could absorb him into my body. Having his dick inside me would be as close as I could get, so I retrieved the lube and condom from the drawer and handed them to him.

He didn't double check to see if I was sure; he saw the certainty in my eyes and the steadiness of my hands. Jules took his time stretching me open while kissing me until I was vibrating with need. His fingers grazed over my prostate but never lingered long enough to put me out of my misery. Once he was certain I was ready, he slid the condom down his erect length and slicked it with more lube.

"Go slow," I urged when the broad head of his cock pressed against my pucker, reminding him it had been a long time for me.

Jules responded by lowering his head and kissing me as he slowly worked his cock inside my body one glorious inch at a time. It was painful at first but then I just felt stretched and full by the time he was buried to the hilt. Jules raised his head and looked down at me. "Still with me?"

"Make me yours," I whispered breathlessly.

Jules began to move then, slow and languid at first, allowing my body time to adjust, then sped up at my urging. "God, yes. More." In case my words weren't enough, I raked my nails down his back until I gripped his ass with both hands and raised my hips up to meet his thrusts. Our sweat-slicked bodies slapped together as we chased our climax, panting and groaning. It was too much and not enough at the same time. I was desperate to come but frantic to make it last at the same time.

I came first with Jules's name on my lips then held him tight in my arms as my spasming clench pulled him over the edge with me. Jules's body stiffened and stilled in my arms for a heartbeat before he started rutting inside me again. I felt the scalding heat from his release through the thin latex barrier as he cried out my name. He didn't stop until I'd milked the last drop from him.

We lay there together touching and kissing for several minutes before he carefully eased out of me.

"Now can I feed you?"

"Shower first?" he countered.

"Sure. I'll go heat up a plate while you—"

"Join me?"

I wasn't passing that up. It turned out the only thing more beautiful than Julius Shepherd naked in my bed was him naked and wet in my shower. My greedy hands touched his strong, muscled body everywhere while I washed him with my body wash. Man, did I like that he smelled like me.

"How do you feel about delaying dinner a little longer?" I asked, looking down at his erect penis in my hand.

Jules lowered himself to the shower floor in front of me, gripped my cock, and looked up at me. "Feed me."

So I did.

Chapter Fourteen

"The only source of knowledge is experience."
~Albert Einstein

"Don't stop until you get it right."
~Julius Shepherd

"IN CLASS TODAY, WE'RE GOING TO BE MAKING OUR OWN BOUNCY polymer," I announced to my seventh period science class. "Which is basically Silly Putty."

"Silly Putty?" Anastasia Collins asked. "We're making kids' toys in chemistry class? I thought this was supposed to be a hardcore science class. I didn't play with Silly Putty as a kid, Mr. Shepherd. I certainly don't want to start now."

"That's great news," I replied. "I didn't say anything about playing with our creation. Anastasia. I said we were going to make it."

"Why?" she asked.

"Because chemistry is the study of matter, and how matter behaves and interacts with other kinds of matter. This experiment is a study of both chemical properties and chemical reactions."

"Surely, there are other things we could make as an experiment. I heard that first period made bubbles."

"Bubbles?" Billy Hill asked from the corner. "You think making bubbles is more mature than Silly Putty? That's just…silly."

"No one asked you, Hillbilly," she fired back.

"Hey, now," I said, holding up my hands. "We're not about to start criticizing each other or revert to name-calling. Anastasia," I said calmly. "Did you know that some of our most common household items are results of failed NASA experiments? Most of the items were deemed unsuitable for our rockets but are extremely useful in our everyday lives."

She rolled her eyes in response and snidely said, "Whatever." That kind of attitude would never fly in my classroom.

"And now you get to write a detailed report about what those household items are and why the experiments failed. It will be due on Monday."

"What?" she asked. "It's Thursday already."

"Keep it up, and it will be due tomorrow."

She pursed her lips together in a firm line indicating just how displeased she was with me, but at least she was pouting silently.

"I know that this is a small school, and you've likely heard what the other classes made today. I introduced a series of experiments today to all my chemistry classes with various levels of difficulty. I will rotate each of the experiments around so that all of you will get a chance to make these projects. Your first experiment will be making Silly Putty. If anyone here doesn't agree with my lesson plan, they can take a zero on the assignment and hang out in the office." I sounded more and more like my mother every day. The woman took no prisoners, and neither would I.

I passed the project worksheet out that included the objective, materials, and procedure. "You'll see under the procedure section there are columns for observations and physical properties beside each ration combination of glue and borax solution. A critical part of being a scientist is recording the data. I will knock a ton of points off your grade if you present me with a perfect specimen of bouncy polymer but don't include your observations. Am I clear?"

"Yes, sir," most everyone said.

"You will fail this assignment if you aren't wearing the appropriate safety gear. Lab coats, safety goggles, and disposable gloves are required as stated in the instructions. Am I clear on that too?"

"Yes, sir."

One person from each team retrieved the safety gear while their lab partner collected the materials they'd need. Once the kids had their backs turned to me, I permitted my gaze to land on the sexy, silver fox observing my class. Looking at him then, no one would guess that we had spent the past three nights together. He was cool, calm, and the ultimate professional who judged my performance in the classroom. He had cheerfully greeted the kids and asked that they pretend he wasn't there. Some of the kids had joked that they'd seen him in several of their classes over the week. Only I knew the magnetism his fancy suit, flesh, and bones hid from the rest of the world.

I had known Rome would be stopping by and had braced myself for the impact of seeing him in my space while surrounded by my students. I didn't speak to him directly when he entered the room, nor did I allow myself to meet his crystalline eyes even though I felt his regard on me. Rome's presence wasn't an official evaluation, we had decided it wouldn't be appropriate, but the board had implemented a new plan for the school district. They wanted him to be familiar with the teachers, their styles, and the classes our school district offered. I knew from dinner conversations how impressed he was by the teachers, students, and curriculum. He was looking forward to doing the same with the elementary and middle schools too.

"I feel like I've waited my whole life to work in a school district where I can have a real impact on the students' lives," he'd said while brushing his teeth last night. Rome's joy and enthusiasm, both in and out of bed, were invigorating and inspiring to me.

I returned my attention to the class once they started to file back to their tables. "My good pal Einstein said, 'The only source of knowledge is experience.' That means we don't stop until we get it right."

"Isn't that a Michael Jackson song?" Aaron Harbinger asked.

"No, Aaron. That's 'Don't Stop 'Til You Get Enough.' Close though," I said. "I simply mean you have to start over if you don't get it right the first time. Work together as a team."

By the time the bell rang, each of the teams had successfully made bouncy polymer in various colors since food coloring was permitted. I could tell Anastasia was more impressed with her "toy" than she anticipated, but I didn't comment on it. Most importantly, they each documented their observations.

"Nice job, everyone! See you tomorrow."

Rome slowly rose to his feet but didn't make his move toward me until the last student crossed the threshold. His strides were predatory, and his pale blue eyes burned with intensity. When Rome reached me, I noticed the skin on his face looked like it was stretched tighter. His body was rock hard and rigid with tension, and he practically shook with how badly he wanted to touch me. I reached for my bottle of water to moisten my mouth which had gone dry.

"Last class," he said tersely.

I smiled then because I knew he wasn't mad. "Was that the final bell?"

"Yes."

"I'm not sure what I'm going to do after school since tennis practice was canceled due to the bad weather. Do you have any ideas about what I could do with my free time?"

"Dinner at my house. Five thirty." That had already been the plan, so I was disappointed I wouldn't be seeing him sooner. "I have to meet with the board to go over our agenda for tomorrow's meeting." I filed away my disappointment because he had something very important to do.

"Duh. It's the 'gay agenda.' Haven't you read the petition?"

Rome snorted. "You know I read every word on the petition at least twice the last time I was naked in bed with you living our 'gay agenda,' or have you forgotten?"

"Not in a million years could I forget that. I'll go home and do some laundry while you're busy so it won't cut into our time together later."

"I'm sorry," Rome said, looking and sounding conflicted.

"Don't be. You're doing something amazing, and I'm going to be so proud of you tomorrow night when you get in front of everyone and stick up for our kids and every marginalized person who's needed a champion."

"Our kids?" Rome quirked a brow.

"An educator doesn't look at their students as just another face or just another number. The students become our kids and their success becomes our motivation. We take every slight against them personally, and we do something about it. You, sexy man, are taking on that fight with the full support of the board and the high school faculty. That POS leader has picked the wrong man, the wrong school, and the wrong town to mess with."

"I really like this side of you, Julius." He leaned closer and lowered his voice another notch. "If I can find a yardstick, can we play bad teacher later tonight? That scolding you delivered was so fucking hot."

"Rome, I need to ask you to leave my classroom now," I said in a stern voice. His response was a needy little whimper in the back of his throat. "Five thirty."

He nodded. "Five thirty," he managed to rasp out.

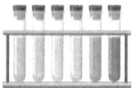

When I pulled into the driveway, Dare was dumping a plastic tub of recyclables into the bigger bin we hauled out with the trash each week. "Well, hello there, Mr. Shepherd. Did you have a good day at school?"

"I certainly did," I said, smiling from ear to ear. "Did you have a good day?"

"There's never a dull day at Curl Up and Dye."

"Really?" I asked. "And just because your day wasn't dull doesn't mean it was good."

"True, but I got enough material from today to laugh about it for weeks. If I wasn't heading over to see my grandpa, I'd tell you all about it. As it is, I'm running behind. Grandpa signed us up for another euchre tournament. He and another resident at his nursing home are locked in a vicious battle until one of them dies. It used to be an annual tournament but the two guys had nagged and griped until it's now a quarterly tournament. We have signals and all kinds of ridiculousness."

"Rome's aunt Astrid would fit right in there."

Dare started walking backward to his house. "You'd just have to bring up his name when I don't have time to grill you. Don't think I haven't noticed your car missing in the driveway a few mornings this week."

I shrugged my shoulders. "I'm not trying to hide anything."

"Good for both of you. I'll see you around." Dare waved then turned around so he could hustle to his car.

After I went up to my apartment, I started my laundry and grabbed a snack. I felt restless and unsettled, and I couldn't put a finger on what was wrong with me. I found myself staring off into space and wondering how Rome's meeting was going which was silly because he'd tell me all about it over dinner. By four, I was making myself crazy and dialed the one person who could verbally slap the stupid out of me. I knew she'd be home watching *Ellen*.

"Hello, baby boy," Mom said warmly. "I was starting to think you lost your phone or forgot my number. I can't recall the last time we went this long without talking on the phone. I hope this means you're up to something five-ten, silver-haired, and sexy."

I couldn't keep the chuckle out of my voice. "I'm neither your baby or a boy, Mama."

"You are if I say so. Did you finally stop fighting the inevitable? Is that why I haven't heard from you?"

"I have started seeing Rome."

"All of him or just parts of him?"

"Mom!"

"Okay, that was a bit of an overstep. I apologize." She knew I'd had dinner at his house Saturday night, but she had no idea we'd been together every night since then. That was more information than I wanted to share with her right then.

"Just know that I'm really happy."

"I know you are, baby. I can hear it in your voice. You have no idea how happy it makes me." It sounded like she was about to start crying which would make me cry too, and that was the last thing I wanted for either one of us. "I can't wait to meet him."

"What makes you think we've reached that level yet?"

"Julius, are you really going to play me like I'm dumb? Hasn't that failed every time you ever tried to attempt it? You're a horrible sneak and liar. You know I'm right."

"True."

"About which part?"

"You're right about everything, Mom."

"Mmm-hmm. I know I am. Marcus FaceTimed me last night, and I got to meet Camilla and Manny. Aren't they beautiful, Julius?"

"They are," I agreed. "I've never seen Marcus this happy."

"I thought I had, but I realize now he was only content before he met Camilla. I know I should be worried that he's too young, but your father and I weren't much older when we started a family, and we turned out okay. If I'm real honest, things have come easily to Marcus up to this point in his life. His athleticism opened doors that made it easy for him to walk through. I'm not saying he hasn't worked his ass off on the football field and in the classroom, but it won't be anything like juggling family, work, and law school."

"We might be putting the cart before the horse." Mom snorted. "Yeah, probably not."

"I cannot wait to see my boys and meet the people who've stolen their hearts." I wanted to argue that my heart was still firmly in my chest, but the words wouldn't come.

"Will you be able to make a trip before Thanksgiving?"

"I hope so, but we're short-staffed at the hospital right now. I'll let you know if I can get away sooner."

"I'll cross my fingers, but I won't hold my breath." My mom had taken an administrative nursing job which came with a sizable raise. I wasn't sure the extra money was worth the additional headaches. My mom was a nurturer and caregiver not a pencil pusher and number cruncher.

We got caught up on all the other things going on in each other's lives, and I lost track of time. I was shocked when I saw the credits on the show start scrolling signaling the hour-long show was over.

"Mom, I have to go. I need to be at Rome's house for dinner in half an hour."

"Call me tomorrow night and let me know how the board meeting goes."

"I will. Love you, Mom."

"Love you too, Julius."

After we hung up, I switched my clothes from the washer to the dryer, took a shower, then carefully chose my outfit for the evening. Rome would expect me to wear a T-shirt and sweats or a pair of shorts, but that isn't the kind of attire a strict teacher would wear. If Rome wanted bad teacher, that is what he'd get.

Chapter Fifteen

"By the pricking of my thumbs, something wicked this way comes."
~William Shakespeare

"We're all born with a superpower that tells us when evil is near."
~Romeo Bradley

I'VE ALWAYS CONSIDERED MYSELF TO BE A MAN WHO RELIES ON SOUND reason and logic, but I've never ignored my gut instincts when it came time to make decisions or analyze a situation. Reason and logic told me everything with the play would go on as planned and the POS group would become a distant memory. Why wouldn't I think that when I looked into the eyes of each board member as they vowed not to let bully tactics from an extremist group pressure them into letting our kids down? They looked at the data Priscilla and Sandra had comprised and said they were convinced this was nothing more than attention-seeking from a group trying to make a name for themselves.

"Bad press is better than no press," Cait said to the group.

"Press?" Earl asked. "You think there will be press?"

That's when I realized that no matter what they said to me privately, things could turn on a dime if a mob of zealots showed up or even a news crew from one of the local news stations. Blissville's proximity to Cincinnati, Dayton, and Columbus made it a distinct possibility that one, or all, of the media outlets had heard about the board meeting.

Cait's reply was swift and succinct. "You better dress up just in case. We want to look good on camera when we fight the good fight for our kids." Earl didn't look too sure, and a few others lowered their eyes instead of meeting mine. I knew when I left the meeting nothing was guaranteed, but I forced the worry away so I could have a good night with Julius.

Julius.

During my drive home, I realized I could face whatever decision the board handed down the next night as long as I had Julius to celebrate or commiserate with afterward. Julius pulled up in front of my house just as I exited my car. I was running behind, and he was a few minutes early. The first thing I noticed was the battered, brown leather bag slung over his shoulder, and then I noticed what he was wearing. I stood and gaped at him as he headed toward me with a confident—make that arrogant—stride. He wore a navy blue suit, pressed white shirt, and a bow tie that matched his pants and jacket. His pants hugged his legs like they were tailored to fit only him. I couldn't wait for him to lose the jacket because I knew his ass would look amazing. Jules had put on a pair of black glasses with rectangular frames that made his hazel eyes look brighter.

"Hello," I said when he stood in front of me. Damn. He made my mouth water.

"Good evening." His voice sounded formal with clipped words and stiff tones. My dick was getting stiff too. "I have prepared a lesson for you."

"School me, baby," I said eagerly, making it nearly impossible for Jules to keep a straight face. His lips quivered for a mere second, but he managed to get it under control. "What's in the bag?"

"You don't get to ask the questions here. *I'm* in charge." *Fuck.* He was so hot.

"We better go inside before I embarrass myself in front of my neighbors." I started to head toward the house, but Jules stepped in front of me, barring my path. He wrapped my tie around his fist then pulled me closer.

"Aren't you forgetting something."

"I will kiss you hello once we get inside."

"She has four legs, dances around in circles, and burrows herself under her blanket instead of sleeping on it. Does that help?"

"I haven't forgotten Dolly. I just thought we could—"

Jules silenced me with a firm shake of his head. "You need to show discipline, and only then will you be rewarded. Hand me the key so I can let myself inside your house while you retrieve your girl."

I silently handed him the keys and walked across Lily's lawn toward her front door. She didn't answer my knock nor was my presence greeted with excited doggy barks. I trotted down the steps and looked around the side of her house. Like many properties in Blissville, Lily and her husband had a detached garage behind the house. I noticed her car wasn't in the driveway, and I'd never seen her park inside the garage. I figured she must've run a quick errand and had taken the dogs with her, so I jogged back to my house and found Jules sitting stiffly in the club chair facing the door. He had his leg raised and folded so his right ankle was propped up on his left knee. I noticed the outline of his hard-on through his pants and knew he was as turned on as I was. Then I saw the ruler lying across his lap.

"Oh fuck." I'd never experimented with power play and spankings before, but the hot look in Jules's eyes told me I wanted to give it a try.

"Where's Dolly?" God, his voice was rich and dominant. "I gave you an assignment, and it looks like you've failed to complete it."

"But…"

"I don't want to hear any excuses out of you. You need to learn a lesson." Jules lowered his right leg and patted his muscled thigh with the ruler. "Get over here and lie across my lap."

"Yes, sir," I said. In my haste to cross the room, I hooked my leg on the coffee table and tripped. Instead of sexily presenting my ass to him for a good whacking, I fell into his lap and nearly tagged his nuts with my knee. Julius released all the air in his lungs with an *oof*. "Fuck me," I growled, feeling my face turn from a warm, sexy flush to a burning-with-embarrassment red. "I'm so sorry."

Julius blinked his eyes, and the stern countenance was gone. He held me tight against his chest as his head fell back against the chair, and he laughed harder than I had ever heard him laugh before. I joined in because I knew he wasn't laughing *at* me. Julius didn't have a mean bone in his body. It was the ridiculousness of the situation that had both of our eyes filling with tears.

"I've ruined the mood," I said.

Julius took my hand and pressed it against his bulge. "Not a chance." *Whack*. Julius slapped the ruler against the palm of his hand. "Across my lap, Dr. Bradley."

I scrambled to do as he commanded and was rewarded when his big hand massaged one ass cheek then the other. "Fuck, I love this ass."

"I love that you love my ass."

"Silent, Dr. Bradley. I didn't give you permission to speak." *Whack*.

The sting of the ruler through my pants startled me. I jerked and cried, "Oh!" Warmth began to spread out across my ass cheek from the spot of impact. "Oh my."

"Was that too hard?" Jules asked, sounding alarmed. He massaged my ass until the smarting lessened.

"No it just caught me off guard. It stung at first then my flesh started to heat up." I involuntarily rubbed my dick against his thigh, seeking friction.

"I've never done this before, and I don't want to go too far."

"I'm a kink rookie too. You'd think an old guy like me would've at least tried a little spanking before now."

Jules removed his hand and the ruler came back down on my other cheek with a resounding *crack*. "You're not old. Knock it off."

"Yes, sir." God, I never knew a show of dominance could be such a turn on. I trusted Julius and knew he'd stop if it got to be too much for me.

I heard the clatter of the ruler hitting the hardwood floor then Jules said, "I think we need to get a few things straight."

"I don't want to be straight."

"To your feet, Dr. Bradley."

I got to my feet and stood in front of him. Jules looked at me with so much need and longing that I almost wanted to say we forget the chit chat and get to fucking.

"We're going to try a different type of teaching method today," Jules said. "Positive reinforcement."

"Sounds promising."

"Take off your jacket," Jules instructed.

I removed my jacket and tossed it aside not caring where it landed.

Jules patted his thighs. "Straddle me. I want you looking in my eyes so you can see the truth." I straddled his lap and watched as he loosened his tie and unbuttoned his shirt. He lifted my palm and placed it over his heart. "I want you to feel the truth too."

It was hard to keep my hand from roaming all over his body, but I could see how important this was to him. Jules's heart pounded beneath my palm. "I feel it," I whispered.

"Good. My racing heart doesn't care that you're seventeen years older than me." Jules lifted his hands and deftly loosened my tie and opened my shirt. Leaning forward, he placed his lips over my speeding heart. "Your heart doesn't seem to mind that I'm younger."

"No," I agreed.

"So, it's all up here then," Jules said, gently tapping my temple. "Remember when I said I would trust you to know what you wanted?" I nodded. "You need to trust me too. You're the man I want. You're the guy I couldn't get out of my head since the day we met nearly six months ago when the school board hired us. Did you think that jolt of awareness was one-sided?"

"Yes," I confessed.

Jules leaned forward and licked a path from my collarbone to my ear before he sucked the lobe into his mouth. "You were so wrong. Lust hit me like a donkey kick to the nuts."

"Ouch," I said, easing my free hand between his legs to massage his balls through his dress pants.

"I almost convinced myself that I had imagined the electricity arcing between us once I returned to Philly to finish out the school year." Jules chortled then reached for my belt. "It was merely simmering quietly beneath the surface until I saw you again." Metal clanked as Jules released my belt. "Then I saw you out jogging early one morning. Hot. Sweaty. Shirtless." He leaned forward and licked a nipple while unbuttoning and unzipping my trousers. "Christ, you're the hottest man I know. Do you feel how much I want you?"

"Yes, but the part of my brain that's still functioning says it's only lust and this will pass when someone closer to your age comes along."

Jules removed his hands from my body long enough to retrieve a bottle of lube he'd hidden in the cushions when he set up his scene. My ass puckered when he poured a generous amount on his middle finger.

Jules captured my mouth in a searing kiss while he slid his hand beneath my underwear. He pressed his slicked finger against my pucker and ripped his mouth from mine. Jules circled the rim of my ass but didn't push inside. "Do I have your attention now?"

"Yes."

Jules slid just the tip of his finger inside my ass, making me whimper for more. "It isn't just your body that stimulates me, Rome." He eased the digit inside me a little further, breaching the first ring of muscles. "Your intelligence drives me wild." Jules pushed in to his first knuckle then rotated his wrist.

"Christ," I said, fighting the urge to sink down and fuck myself on his finger.

"Are you listening?"

"Uh huh."

"Your kind heart makes me want to be a better man." Jules inched inside a little deeper then crooked his finger to press against my gland. I made no attempt to stifle my moans of need and pleasure. "There is nothing I want to change about you, Rome. Nothing. Do you believe I'm a man who knows what he wants?"

"Yes." I did trust that.

Jules circled my gland with the tip of his finger then nudged harder against it as he kissed a path up my neck. "Good. Have faith in me." Jules bit my neck. "Trust me." He tagged my prostate again then massaged it. "Believe me." Circle. Tag. Circle. Tag. God, he sent me reeling.

Could it really be that simple?

"I want you to remember this moment every time doubt creeps in. Will you try to do that for me?"

"Yes," I whimpered.

Jules rewarded my answer with a passionate kiss. One slick finger became two and he continued to work me open while I let my hands roam freely over his beautiful body. When he thought I was ready, he stood up holding me against him like I weighed nothing. Instead of carrying me to my bedroom, Jules laid me across the coffee table, propped my calves over his shoulder, and continued my lesson on positive reinforcement until my toes curled and he wiped out every negative thought in my head.

Lesson learned.

The forecast for Friday said there would be clear skies and sunshine, but I awoke to a deluge of rain hitting my roof and windows thirty minutes before my alarm went off. Julius appeared to be sleeping soundly, so I brushed my teeth then headed downstairs to start the coffee. Since I was already up, I decided the day called for a nice breakfast.

I had just finished frying the sausage links when Julius and Dolly joined me in the kitchen. I welcomed his minty-fresh kiss and loved the way he looked wearing nothing but a pair of boxers and T-shirt.

"Will Dolly go out in this kind of weather?" Julius asked, peering out the window.

"Yeah," I replied. "She takes two steps off the patio and does her business as fast as she can."

"Come on, Miss Dolly. Let's get our business done."

"I keep a towel in the laundry room around the corner for days like these."

I cracked eggs in a bowl, added milk, vanilla, and cinnamon and whisked it all together to make French toast batter. I had the first two pieces sizzling in the skillet when Jules and Dolly returned to the kitchen. I watched over my shoulder as Dolly did her dance while Jules got her treat.

"Who's a good girl?" Jules asked. Dolly answered with a soft *woof* and immediately received her treat.

Jules walked up behind me, slid his arms around my waist, and rested his chin on my shoulder. "Smells delicious."

"I felt like I needed to kick this day off on the right foot."

"I was thinking morning sex, but this works too," Jules said. He turned his head and kissed the sensitive spot behind my ear.

"Who said we can't do both?"

"Even better."

Breakfast was tasty, the sex was delicious, but my mood started diminishing once we parted ways to drive to school separately. I tried to shake off the gloom, but it hung over me like my own personal rain cloud. For my first act of the day, I burned myself when I sloshed hot coffee on my hand. It kicked off a series of misfortunate events that made me want to go back home and hide under the covers. The highlight had to be when I jammed up the Xerox machine when I tried to put together copies of my speech for the board members. The copier was the size of a VW Beetle, had two dozen places where paper could go in or come out, and featured more buttons and options than the Starship Enterprise. This bastard could print on both sides, correlate those pages into a binder for a presentation, or staple the documents together. I had no clue where to start first, so I just fed my presentation into it. Instead of sucking one page in, it took all of them and made a horrible grinding sound before it stopped working altogether. I was just grateful smoke wasn't billowing from the damn thing. I wasn't prone to tantrums, but I was ready to kick that—

"What are you doing?" Priscilla asked angrily. "Since when do you make your own copies?"

"You were at lunch," I said, aiming my most charming smile at her.

"Save that for your boyfriend and get out of my way." She elbowed her way past me and pushed a button to open the belly of the beast. As much as she hated technology, she sure knew all the ins and outs of the copier. "Here's the problem," she said, tugging on the papers I'd fed the beast until they were free. "You forgot to take the staple out before you fed the document."

"Oh," I said sheepishly. "Sorry."

Priscilla's annoyance faded when she turned to me holding my speech in her tiny hands. "You're a mess today. Normally you only trip all over yourself when Julius is around, but today…" Her words trailed away. "Get ahold of yourself, Rome. The kids are counting on you."

I nodded. "That's why I was trying to make copies of my speech. I just needed to do something to keep busy and be prepared."

"You *are* prepared." I watched in horror as she ripped my prepared speech in half then in fourths.

"Why'd you do that?"

"You don't need fancy words on a piece of paper, Rome. You need to speak from your heart." She dumped the pieces of paper in the trash bin beside the copier.

"But—"

"No buts about it. Speak with conviction and share your story. Talk about how much this play would've meant to you as a kid."

She was right. There wasn't a single hateful thing Roy Halifax could say I hadn't heard before, nor a situation he could present I hadn't already overcome.

"Be yourself because no one can represent those kids and our district better than you can tonight." She crooked her finger for me to lean down, and she kissed my cheek.

"Should I be jealous?"

I turned and found Jules standing behind us holding a cafeteria tray laden with food. His warm smile said he wasn't the least bit concerned about the peck on the cheek Priscilla gave me. "Pizza day," I said, sniffing the air appreciatively.

"I know you're probably busy, but I had an extended break since the kids are going to a pep rally in the gym. I thought I'd treat you to lunch for once."

"Your timing is perfect, Julius," Priscilla said. "I think I'll go over and watch the pep rally. Sandra is already over there, and none of the board members are in the office right now. You guys can close the door and have some quiet time."

I felt my cheeks turn pink. "We're not—"

"I didn't say you were," Priscilla said. "I used the words quiet and time. You're the only one whose mind went straight to the gutter." She closed the copier then walked to her desk where she pulled her purse out of the bottom drawer. "All you men love to jump to conclusions and make assumptions. Don't know why I even bother," she muttered as she left.

"That can't all be about you," Julius said. "Howie must've tried to let her down easy or something."

"That's my guess," I agreed, watching her through the door as she walked toward the high school. At least the rain had finally let up. I faced Julius once more and said, "I'm so glad to see you."

"Rough morning?" he asked, following me into the office.

Regardless of what Priscilla said, I left my door open and took a seat at the table in the corner of my office. "I really would love to close us in here together and maybe steal a kiss, but it's not worth the risk. I don't care who knows we're dating, but I will not touch you intimately on school grounds."

"We could always pretend later. You can call me down to your office." Jules waggled his brows suggestively.

"Yeah, that roleplaying thing didn't work out so well last night."

"Last night was perfect," Julius said in a low, husky voice. "As was the night before that and the night before that... You see where I'm going with this."

"I do."

"You're going to be amazing at the meeting tonight. I heard what Miss Priscilla said and she's right. I didn't interrupt the cute little pep talk until she went to make moves on my guy."

"I'm all yours, Jules."

He smiled because he liked hearing it.

Chapter Sixteen

"Play is the highest form of research."
~Albert Einstein

"Delayed gratification is the highest form of foreplay."
~Julius Shepherd

ROME EXPECTED ME TO RETURN HIS SENTIMENT RIGHT AWAY BUT IN-stead, I said, "Good. Now eat your pizza." His light blue eyes held mine, searching. I saw a flicker of uncertainty, but then he blinked, and it was gone. Rome took a bite of his pizza while I chewed over the brief reaction I saw on his face. Did he worry he spoke too soon? Did he think I wasn't as invested in our relationship or my feelings weren't as strong as his? If so, he was very wrong. I would give him as many positive reinforcement lessons as it took for him to realize I was exactly where I wanted to be.

"I'm all yours too, Rome."

He stopped eating and narrowed his eyes at me before he slowly resumed chewing. When he finished, he took a sip of the apple juice I'd brought him. "You're trying to kill me, aren't you?"

I chuckled. "No. Why would you say that?"

"You know how clumsy I get when I'm around you. For Christ's sake, I can barely walk and talk at the same time when you look at me. I forget to breathe sometimes when we're in the same room." His voice was deep and gravelly, his face was flushed with want, and joy radiated from his crystalline eyes. "Yet, you make a declaration like that while I'm chewing? It's a miracle you're not having to perform the Heimlich right now."

"It would give me an excuse for some mouth-to-mouth action," I quipped.

"Yeah, I'd suggest we give it a try when we're alone, but so far we're batting zero."

"I think we have the kissing thing down to an art," I countered. I'd never heard my voice sound so rough and raw. Who knew banter could be considered foreplay?

Rome leaned forward and lowered his voice to a whisper. "I meant the other stuff. You know, me tripping over the table and falling on you."

I leaned forward and lowered my tone to match his. The last thing we needed was someone overhearing us. "You landed right where I wanted you. And besides, you're not clumsy."

"What am I then?"

"Eager, and it's a huge turn-on."

"Really?" Rome sounded completely dumfounded by the notion. "How can you find that remotely sexy?"

"You might not know this, but I've had plenty of time to observe you without you knowing it. You move gracefully, speak eloquently and with sharp intelligence, and conduct your business with a level of professionalism I find incredibly sexy."

"You do?" he asked.

"Oh yeah. So sexy."

"Then how in the world can you find my stumbling and stuttering sexy too?"

I reached across the desk and covered his hand with mine. "Because only *I* affect you that way. With everyone else, there's a cool aloofness about you even when your smile and tone of voice is warm.

You're friendly but unattainable because they don't reach you on an elemental level. *I* break through those barriers and rattle your cage. And I like it. What you find ridiculous and awkward, I find alluring and real. I don't want a smooth operator. I don't want to be handled. Well, I do, but you know what I mean." Rome's wry smile said he wished he could *handle* me right then. My dick was hardening and lengthening in my pants, and I needed to pull myself together. His office wasn't the right place for this conversation, but I couldn't let him spend another second doubting that I wanted him. I started to pull my hand from his, but he rotated his wrist and recaptured it.

Rome lifted my hand and placed a kiss on my wrist, letting his lips linger there so he could feel the way my pulse raced for him. I couldn't look away from the hungriness I saw in his eyes. If anyone popped their head in the office, they might think he looked like a vampire about to pierce my veins with his fangs. I saw only a wolfish man who wanted to devour and ravish me. My ass pucker tensed, wanting to be filled.

Priscilla's ringing phone snapped us out of our lusty fog. Rome placed one last quick kiss on my wrist and released my hand.

"So, anyway, what are you doing for Thanksgiving?" I asked, needing to talk about anything that wasn't sexy or could be twisted into something sexy.

"We usually go to Ashley and Ben's for dinner, but they're going skiing in Vale that weekend. Mom and Dad decided they would go to the nursing home and spend the day with Aunt Astrid and her friends. They invited me to join them, of course."

"Would you like to spend the day with my family?"

Rome looked surprised by my invitation at first, but then he blessed me with the prettiest smile I had ever seen on another person. "Really? You don't think they would mind?"

"My mom has been 'silver fox' this and 'silver fox' that since I first mentioned you. Marcus is dying to meet the guy who's turned me 'sappy.' Camilla and Manny may not realize it yet, but they can't wait to meet you too."

"You talked about me to your mom?"

"More than I realized. It didn't take her long to recognize my attraction to you. She looked up your photo on the internet and began hounding me about taking chances."

"When?" Rome asked.

"When what?" I wasn't following his question.

"I want to know when you first mentioned my name to your mom," he explained.

"The first day we met." I smiled at his stunned reaction.

"I know you said you felt the attraction that day, but I'm surprised you mentioned me to your mom." Rome chuckled. "You were sure good at hiding your reaction. You looked like you couldn't get away from me fast enough."

"I was in a hurry to get away from the way you made me feel. I was already overwhelmed by the sudden changes occurring in my life, and there you were, making me feel breathless and stuff."

"And stuff? What kind of stuff?" I quirked a brow in response. "Okay, this isn't the place to have this conversation. Maybe these little lunches aren't such a good idea."

"We'll learn to behave. I heard that delayed gratification is an excellent form of foreplay." There I was causing trouble after I had lightly scolded him for doing the same thing.

"Eat!" Rome said, pointing to my plate. "You haven't taken the first bite."

I wanted to close the door and nibble on him, but instead, I picked up my rectangle of pizza and took a bite. It was surprisingly good. I forked a few bites of my salad in my mouth then recalled the first night I went to Rome's house for dinner. I chortled as I remembered the way his face flushed from embarrassment.

"I know damn well what you're thinking right now," he said, pointing at my salad with his fork. He was trying to look and sound stern, but his quivering lips and the humor glinting in his eyes gave him away. "I swear these kids only create their secret language to make the rest of us look stupid. You'll have to ask my sister about the time I learned what 'Netflix and chill' really meant."

"Oh no," I said. "I'm not waiting until I meet your sister to hear all about it." I pointed my plastic fork at him. "Let's hear it."

Rome groaned. "You're going to think I'm an old fool."

"Rome, you're not old and you're definitely not foolish. I want to hear the story."

"We have a family dinner at least once a month, and we rotate houses so one person isn't doing all the work. One particular visit to Ashley and Ben's, I announced I was going home to Netflix and chill. My oldest niece, Lauren, said 'good for you, Uncle Rome.' I didn't understand why rushing home to binge-watch *Miss Fisher's Murder Mysteries* earned such high praise from her, but I liked that she thought I was cool."

"Uh oh," I said, sensing trouble.

"Yeah," he agreed huskily. "So, I said as much as I liked to Netflix and chill, I would prefer to find a nice guy to join me. The look on her face. She was horrified and said, 'TMI, Uncle Rome.' I was thwarted by a language that might as well be foreign to me."

I couldn't contain my laughter if someone offered me a million dollars. Luckily, Rome laughed right along with me instead of getting pissed. How could he not? It was fucking hilarious.

"But wait! There's more," he said, sounding like an infomercial. "At my old high school, one of the boys bragged to his buddies in the hallway that he received a hummer the night before, and I heartily congratulated the kid and gave him a fist bump. It was much later that I realized he was talking about getting a blow job and not a new SUV."

"I...can't..." I laughed until I gasped for air and tears ran down my face.

"Do you realize we spend as much time laughing together as we do anything else?" Rome asked when the laughter started to fade.

"It's so wonderful I'm not even mad that it's at my expense most of the time."

No one affected me the way he did. I laughed harder, my heart beat faster, and my senses were heightened until he was all I could taste, feel, see, and hear. Just him. I cupped his handsome face and stroked my thumb over his square jawline. "There's nothing I would change about us, Rome. Nothing."

He leaned into my touch, closed his eyes, and sighed. It felt like he truly believed we could have something real and sustaining for the first time. When he opened his eyes, I knew I was right. No doubt. No hesitation. Only soul-deep gratification. "Me either."

My watch buzzed when my timer went off. I'd set it before I came over with lunch because getting lost in his eyes was a big possibility.

"That's my cue to head back." I started to put my plate back on the tray, but Rome stopped me.

"Either finish eating your pizza here or eat it on the way back to class. I'll take the tray back to the cafeteria because I have more time than you do."

"Are you sure?"

"Positive," he replied with a firm nod. "Wise people told me I'm as prepared for this meeting as I'm going to be because all I have to do is speak from the heart."

"That's what I want to hear," I told him.

I finished off my pizza then battled the urge to kiss Rome good-bye. In the end, I leaned my forehead against his, sharing air with him for a few seconds before I pulled away. "I'll see you in a few hours."

"Yes, you will."

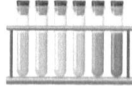

The board had debated whether having the meeting in the school gym on a Friday night before a home football game was wise. They worried the Blissville residents' main focus would be on the game, and only the POS group would show up for the public meeting. They were wrong. The gym bleachers were already packed with students and parents by the time I arrived. They held up signs supporting the play, the kids who wrote it, and the school board for putting it on. Looking around the gym, it was easy to tell who the POS members were by the scowls they wore on their face. So many people kept filing in that we had to set up rows of folding chairs on the basketball court to accommodate them. They wore shirts or sweatshirts showing off their school spirit. I knew most of them were dressed to attend the game, but it warmed my heart to see so many of them stop by the board meeting first.

Priscilla gave me a friendly wave and an encouraging smile from the front row of the bleachers. I winked at her and gave a thumbs up to Howie who sat beside her. The older man's face turned pink, but he smiled shyly. I was glad to see the big guy was no longer in the doghouse.

I joined the faculty standing along the wall opposite from where Roy Halifax and his POS posse waited for the meeting to start. They'd huddled together with lowered heads and joined hands, praying for God's intervention on their behalf. In my head, I imagined the men would all look like Joe Dirt or Dog the Bounty Hunter, and the women would resemble the infamous county clerk from Kentucky who refused to issue marriage licenses to same-sex applicants. That was my ignorance and own prejudices talking, and I should've known better. Hatred didn't discriminate. It resided in the hearts of people regardless of their race, education, religion, or orientation. Knowing that, I was still surprised to see them look so…ordinary. They didn't dress or style their hair differently. They hadn't showed up with an angry mob with protest signs, but I wasn't fooled. This was a group of deceitful people who threw together a phony petition thinking the board would back down under pressure.

They broke apart when the board members and Rome entered the gym and filled the empty chairs on either side of the podium. Across from the board, a lone table was set up with two chairs and a microphone. One of the men broke away from the group after hugs and handshakes from his supporters and approached the table. He nodded to the board and sat down.

Caitlyn Simpson rose from her chair and approached the podium. She smiled at the crowd and acknowledged Roy Halifax with a nod then turned on the microphone. "Good evening. I want to thank everyone for coming tonight. I would ask that the crowd remain quiet throughout the meeting and that we all show respect to those speaking. Anyone who disrupts the meeting will be escorted out of the building." She gestured toward the door to my right and we all turned to see a mountain of a man standing just inside the gym. Marcus had football players on his team that would envy the expanse of shoulders on the cop. Of course, maybe the impression of his size had more to do with the fact his perfectly pressed uniform was at least two sizes too small. His eyes locked on mine, and he smiled before swaggering his way toward me. He was sexy for sure with his dark hair, obsidian eyes, and perfectly trimmed mustache and goatee, but not sexier than my silver fox who claimed more and more of my heart each day.

I turned my attention back toward the proceedings without acknowledging him. My gaze clashed with Rome's and an amused smile curved the right side of his mouth before he returned his attention to Caitlyn.

"Mr. Halifax, the floor is yours. To keep this meeting running smoothly, I'm going to limit you to fifteen minutes, and then we'll hear a rebuttal from our superintendent, Dr. Romeo Bradley."

"Yes, ma'am," Roy said. "Thank you for hearing me out."

"The floor is yours and the time starts now."

"Madame President, board, Dr. Bradley," he said politely. "I'm here today on behalf of Preserve Our Society to ask that you reverse your decision to permit these high school kids from performing *Inside*

Out as the school play." He started in on all the reasons why a play pushing a "liberal agenda" would tear down the foundation of the American family.

I tuned him out and kept my eyes locked on Rome's face. Roy Halifax wasn't saying anything I hadn't heard before, and I had no interest in hearing it again. I just hoped his poison arrows weren't piercing the hearts of the vulnerable kids in the stands. How many of those kids sitting in the crowd were wrestling with their identities? I didn't just mean their sexuality, either. I meant their whole being. There was so much damn pressure on these kids to know exactly what they wanted for their futures that they didn't have time to just…be.

I tuned back in when Halifax said, "That's all I have to say. Thank you for listening." I noticed the time on the huge clock hanging on the adjacent wall. I'd just lost twelve minutes of my life I could never get back.

"Thank you, Mr. Halifax. The board will now hear from Dr. Romeo Bradley."

I watched as my man rose from his seat and strode to the podium with confidence and poise. He stole my breath away. I was beyond proud that he was mine, and I was his. Rome greeted the crowd and the board with fondness and Mr. Halifax with civility before he began his speech.

"I cannot begin to tell you how much I would've loved seeing a play like *Inside Out* when I was a teenager. Maybe I wouldn't have felt so alone and isolated thinking that I was the only kid in the school who felt different from everyone else. For me, I felt like the odd man out because I wasn't attracted to girls like the other guys were. Other kids in my school probably felt odd because their skin color was different, or they had less money than some of the others, or maybe they practiced a different religion than the majority of the student body. Then there are the physical things we hate about our bodies. We weren't tall enough, skinny enough, and we weren't athletic enough. Maybe a student wanted to be a dancer, but her parents said a law degree was the only acceptable path. Haven't we all felt like we didn't fit in at some time in our lives?

"*Inside Out* isn't about pushing any kind of agenda, Mr. Halifax. The play isn't about religion or politics; it's about humanity, sir. I've read this play in its entirety twice because I've been asked to direct it. There is not one scene in the play that doesn't depict the kind of humanity we should all strive for. We aren't telling kids they should be gay, we're telling them we love them if they are. We're telling a kid the sum of their value isn't based on their appearance, socioeconomic status, religion, or orientation, but the kind of human being they are and how they treat others, Mr. Halifax. There are no sexual, political, or violent situations in this play. These are kids navigating the challenges they face while pulling strength from those around them. In my opinion, this play should be performed by every high school in the country. That's all I have to say, Madame President. Thank you for the opportunity to share my feelings."

Rome's eyes sought mine once he returned to his chair, and I let the huge smile on my face speak for me.

Caitlyn rose to her feet and faced the rest of the board members. I couldn't hear what she said but they all shook their heads in response to whatever she asked. "Once again, I want to thank everyone for coming. I've just asked the board if we need to have a discussion before we vote, and they've each declined. All of those in favor of upholding the board's approval of *Inside Out* as our school play say aye."

Every member of the board raised their hand and said, "Aye."

"There you have it. The show must go on," Cynthia said. Cheers erupted in the gymnasium as the student body celebrated their victory. I saw Clara, Ellie, and Curtis clinging to each other in a group hug.

"Hi," a deep voice said from beside me. I turned and looked at the cop who'd moved even closer at some point during the meeting. "I'm Joey." He extended his hand which I accepted with a friendly smile.

"Hi. I'm taken."

"Figures," he said with a snort. "It's good to meet you anyway."

"Likewise."

Joey ambled a few feet away and returned his attention to the POS members who huddled together across the gym talking animatedly. Many of the students greeted me or gave me high fives as they left the gymnasium and headed to the football game that was set to kick off in ninety minutes. Rome spoke with the board members for a few more minutes before he sought me out.

"Congratulations, Dr. Fancy Pants."

"You've just been biding your time to use that phrase."

"Yep," I admitted.

"I'm so relieved this is over," Rome said with a sigh. "I'm looking forward to auditions next week."

I just happened to glance across the gym and caught the POS group staring at us. I figured we hadn't heard the last of them, but I wasn't about to let them ruin our night. "Want a date for the football game tonight?"

"That would be a first for me," Rome said. "There was no way I could've gone with a boyfriend when I was in high school."

"It wasn't acceptable when I was in high school either, and that was only ten years ago," I pointed out. "I didn't officially come out until I was in college."

"It's a date then."

Beneath the full moon and the Friday night lights, Rome and I cheered with the crowd as the Blissville Bulldogs beat the East Carter Cardinals twenty-eight to zero. Somewhere in the fourth quarter, I had an epiphany that was bigger than the victory over hate and our cross-county rivals. I, Julius Aaron Shepherd, was in love with Rome Fancy Pants Bradley.

The following night was the homecoming dance. I had signed up to chaperone before we started dating and regretted the loss of a quiet Saturday night at home together. I couldn't recall when I started to think of his house as home, but more and more of my stuff ended up there, and I rarely stayed in the garage apartment anymore. I'd only gone home long enough to dress in my snazzy suit and grab some more clean clothes.

"We better get a move on or else we're going to be late," Rome said, jogging down the steps. "Oh." He skittered to a halt. He wasn't used to seeing me in formal clothes since I normally wore khakis and a BHS polo shirt when I taught. The only other time I dressed formally was during our positive reinforcement lesson. "Jules, you look breathtaking." I knew I looked fine in my navy blue suit and red bow tie, but I only had eyes for him. He'd chosen a dove gray suit I'd never seen before and paired it with a lavender shirt a few shades lighter than the tie he wore.

"You look beautiful," I said.

"I wanted to look nice since this is the first homecoming I'm attending with a date." He crooked his finger at me to follow him into the kitchen. "I have a surprise for you." Rome shifted several things around in his refrigerator and pulled out a clear plastic box he'd hidden inside. "I wasn't sure what color suit you were going to wear, so I went with ivory roses and baby's breath." I could tell Rome was nervous because he spoke fast and struggled to open the box with the boutonnieres inside.

I placed my hand on the back of his neck, and he jerked his gaze up to meet mine. I moved in with my preferred method of calming him. The kiss was short, but it did the trick. "They're beautiful, and I will wear this proudly tonight." I adored the dazed look on his face and the way his hands shook. Taking the box from him, I said, "Let me." I chose a boutonniere from the box then set it on the counter. "You're my first homecoming date too," I confessed as I pinned the rose to his lapel. "I'm glad I waited and can share this first with you."

"Jules," Rome whispered my name like it was a prayer. "I wish I could hold you in my arms and dance tonight."

"We will when we get home. We'll turn the lights down low, open a bottle of wine, and dance as long as we want." Rome's eyes lit up when I referred to his house as home.

"I'm going to be thinking about holding you in my arms every time our eyes meet across the gym floor."

"I'll be thinking about what happens afterward," I confessed. "You've heard of the term dancing your socks off, right?" Rome nodded. "I won't stop there. We'll keep dancing until all our clothes hit the floor and I'm holding you skin-to-skin in my arms."

"Wow. You scientists sure know how to heat a man's blood."

"Pin your flower on me," I said huskily. I wanted everyone to see I belonged to him.

Rome picked the flower up from the box and pinned it to my jacket. "There. I didn't even stab you."

The energy in the gymnasium was high and contagious, preventing me from pouting too hard. The glaring overhead fluorescents were turned off and temporary lights were set up to illuminate the makeshift dance floor. Some of the lights were shining through prisms and projecting rainbows onto the walls and floor like you'd see from a disco ball. The DJ played the perfect mix of fast and slow dances, and I enjoyed watching the kids dance and celebrate. I especially loved the times my eyes caught Rome's across the dark room. I knew he was remembering the promise I made to him before we left.

I smiled especially wickedly when "Lights Down Low" by Max started to play. The kids took to the floor to slow dance while I stared into Rome's eyes. So much longing and need passed between us.

When we got back home, I replayed the song so we could have our own dance. Rome's lips were on my neck and my hands were in his hair as we turned slow circles in the living room. As I promised, I didn't stop dancing with him until we were both stripped bare.

"I need you," I whispered against Rome's neck once I removed his shirt.

Rome shoved my pants to the floor and gripped my ass. "I want inside you."

"Touch me." I wrapped Rome's hand around my cock. He stroked me until I pulled away and dropped to my knees in front of him.

Rome fisted his dick and painted my lips with his precum. "Taste me."

"Make love to me," I pleaded when I could no longer handle the emptiness. When Rome sank inside my heat, there wasn't a part of us that wasn't connected in some way. I loved being tangled up in his arms and legs. We clung to each other like we couldn't stand the thought of letting go. Both of us came to Blissville for fresh starts but what we found was more than either of us had bargained for.

"Inside out," I whispered against Rome's neck once I lay replete against his dewy body. It was both the name of the play that brought us together and the way he made me feel. Everything inside me was laid bare for Rome to see. Instead of feeling vulnerable, I felt strong, desired, and adored.

"I feel it too."

Chapter Seventeen

"I would not wish any companion in the world but you."
~William Shakespeare

"Hashtag keeper! What? I'm not that old."
~Romeo Bradley

I T WASN'T LIKE ME TO BURY MY HEAD IN THE SAND AND NOT TACKLE touchy subjects head-on. I guess some would say my head was engaged elsewhere, and they weren't wrong. Who the hell could blame me? There wasn't one thing about Julius I didn't adore. I lived for his smiles and found ways to earn one every chance I got. His laughter was a gift that sent ripples of joy throughout my body. And his brain? There was nothing sexier on this planet than an intelligent man, and he was one of the smartest I'd had the privilege to know. Speaking of sexy, I discovered pleasure in ways I never knew existed. Julius made me feel twenty-eight again too.

It was no wonder a week had passed without me realizing it, and auditions for the school play were upon us without me having a conversation with three precocious and wickedly talented teens.

"Are you nervous?" Julius had asked me at lunch.

"Yeah," I admitted. "This play is their baby. How could I even think about asking them not to audition for the roles?"

"'Cause you're Dr. Mean Ass," Julius quipped then chuckled when I groaned. "I'm just teasing you. You haven't decided to exclude them from performing in the play. You've decided to have a discussion with them about what is fair to everyone who wants to participate. You're doing the right thing." I knew he was right, but doing the right thing was seldom easy.

Imagine my surprise when Clara, Ellie, and Curtis showed up before auditions and asked to have a chat with Julius and me.

"Are you three ready for tonight?" I asked.

"It doesn't seem real to me," Clara asked.

"Me either," Curtis admitted.

"I keep thinking my alarm is going to wake me up any second now," Ellie added. "This play means more to us than we can possibly express."

"We know," Julius told Ellie. "We could feel it when we read the words you wrote."

"Because this means the world to us," Clara said, "we want the best possible cast to perform the roles we created."

Here we go, I thought.

"We decided that we're too close to the characters we created to perform them," Curtis said. "I know that sounds weird to you, doesn't it?"

Relief washed over me. "Not at all. Many writers don't act out their own roles. Many directors have never acted."

"I'm a musician who can't carry a tune in a bucket," Julius told them. "I can write melodies all day long, but I can't write lyrics."

"It takes all types of talent to put on any kind of production," I told the kids. "I'm impressed that you're willing to step aside and put the play first. That couldn't have been an easy decision."

"We're not exactly stepping away entirely, or at least, we hope not," Ellie said. "We'd like to assist you with the production."

"Oh?" I asked, raising a brow. "What did you have in mind?"

"I would really like to assist Mr. Shepherd and Mrs. Hoffenburger with the music," Curtis replied, looking at Julius with hopeful eyes.

"I'd love that, Curtis," Julius said.

"I'd be way too bossy as a director's assistant," Clara said, "so I'd really like to help with costumes, props, and setting scenes."

"I think you'd do a great job at that," I told Clara then looked at Ellie. "Does that mean you're stuck with me?"

She giggled. "It's probably the other way around, Dr. B. I'm not looking to tell you how to direct the play. I just want to help however I can."

"I'm grateful to have your assistance," I assured her. "I think I'm going to require more from the three of you though." They exchanged looks between them but silently waited for me to continue. "I would like your input during auditions." Clara's eyes widened excitedly, Ellie did a little dance in place, and Curtis beamed his approval through his smile. I held up my hand to regain their attention. "I'm still going to have the final say, but I want to hear your opinions."

"Dr. Bradley, that's just…" Clara's words trailed off as emotion swelled inside her.

Ellie looped her arm around Clara's shoulders. "I think she was going to say amazing."

"Or thoughtful," Curtis added.

"Julius and Curtis will provide feedback on musicality. Ellie and Clara, you'll give me your thoughts on stage presence. Sound good?" The three teens nodded while Jules smiled his approval. I wished for the hundredth time that day we were at his home or mine so I could lean forward and kiss him without repercussions.

I kept expecting some sort of retaliation from the POS group, but so far, they'd remained quiet. I wasn't foolish enough to think I'd heard the last of them, but I would take advantage of the peace for as long as I had it. That meant I'd keep my lips to myself and not go borrowing trouble.

We had posted audition signups once we'd worked out a production schedule. I don't think any of us were expecting a fourth of the student body to sign up. Even then, I figured several would change their minds by the time auditions rolled around. Kids lived in the moment and a month to them was like eighteen months to everyone else. Still, I had to plan auditions based on the number of kids who had signed up, so I allowed for four nights. I sorted the signups by the role they were trying out for and made a firm schedule so Jules and I could see sixty kids a night. I allowed for fifteen auditions per hour and scheduled a dinner break at the midway point. Having three extra sets of eyes and ears was really going to help.

I wasn't surprised most of the kids wanted to audition for the three lead roles of Alexandra, Diego, and Tiffany. There were also more than a dozen supporting roles for their parents, classmates, and teachers, so I decided to alternate audition slots between the various roles to keep things fresh. I didn't want three Alexandra auditions in a row followed by four Diegos then five Tiffanys. They would all start to sound and look alike if I did that.

Armed with audition sheets, the five of us kicked off the first night of tryouts. In addition to acting and singing abilities, I was looking for stage presence and passion for the role. Which meant, I had one very important question to ask each person about the role they were auditioning for. The first person to take center stage was Mark Vaughn, a freshman.

"Hello, Mark. First, we'd all like to thank you for auditioning tonight. I see you've chosen to audition for the role of Diego Sandoval. In a few words, can you tell me why you think you're a good fit to play him?"

"The name assigned to me at birth was Marissa. I know what it feels like to look in the mirror and not recognize the person I see. It never matched who I was on the inside. I understand Diego's struggles even if they weren't the same as my own. I think that's the point of this play."

Mark's words were like a fist to my gut, knocking the breath from me. It took a few seconds before I could acknowledge his answer.

"Very true. Thank you for sharing. You can begin reading the script when you're ready."

Mark closed his eyes, took a deep breath, and slowly exhaled the air from his lungs. When he reopened his eyes, I could see he was completely in character. Mark looked distraught and somehow disheveled without doing anything to his clothes or hair. It was the power of presence I was looking for, a command of expression that conveyed everything he felt without uttering a single word. Then he opened his mouth and blew me away.

"Who is this face in the mirror that the world truly doesn't know?" His voice quavered with emotion. *"They say they love me, but how can this be true when they don't know who I am? Will they still want me if they know the truth? Will I still be the son they adore? Will they continue to brag about the things I do that make them proud, or will Diego Sandoval cease to exist? If Diego is no more, then who will I be? The queer kid? The outcast? The one without a family? Without a home? I want to have faith, but I'm afraid. I would pray for God's help, but he supposedly hates me. I'm not ready to show the real me, so I'll keep on being the one everyone loves until I find the courage to be the one they might all hate."*

I was ready to applaud, but that would've been unprofessional. I didn't want the kid leaving here thinking he would get the part. Hell, we had two hundred and thirty-nine kids left to audition. "Thank you, Mark. Are you ready to sing a portion of Diego's solo?"

"Yes, sir."

Julius hit play on the remote that turned on the sound system hidden backstage. It was very high tech which was why no one entrusted it to my care after word spread like wildfire about my incident with the copier. Once Julius's music began to play, I forgot the world existed until Mark began to sing with so much emotion. I felt tears welling in my eyes and glanced over to catch Curtis's reaction. This role was so personal to him, and I wanted to see how he felt about someone else singing his song. Curtis didn't bother to hide the tears sliding down his face. Clara wrapped her arms around his shoulders and leaned into him as she cried too. Ellie just looked like she was completely gobsmacked. Julius reached beneath the table and squeezed my knee, pulling my attention to him. He was enchanted, and it was okay that I wasn't the one who put the look of unbridled joy on his face. That moment right there with the four of them was the reason I loved theater so damn much.

"Thank you for such an inspiring performance, Mark," I said after he finished.

"Thank you for the opportunity."

We sat at a table below the stage in the cafetorium as more students made their way to the center of the stage and performed for us. I could tell when one of the kids was especially moved by something they saw on stage because they would gasp, sit eerily still, or feverishly write notes on the sheets in front of them. As for the adults on the panel, I reached for Jules's hand beneath the table a few times, and he bumped his knee into mine while we calmly made notes.

I'd placed an order to have pizza delivered during our break before I knew dinner for two needed to be dinner for five. Luckily, I'd ordered an extra-large, and there were plenty of slices to go around. The delivery guy had brought enough paper plates and napkins, so we were all set.

"We couldn't," Clara said when I offered her a slice.

"We shouldn't," Ellie said.

"I'll eat their share," Curtis said, diving in for a slice.

"What's everyone drinking?" Jules asked on his way to the vending machine.

"We couldn't," Clara said again, sounding like a broken record.

Curtis snorted and said, "Ellie wants a Mountain Dew, Clara wants a Dr. Pepper, and I'll take a Sierra Mist. Thanks, Mr. S." He turned to his friends. "It's rude to reject a kind offer."

"It is," I agreed. "Eat up. We don't have a lot of time before the next round of auditions start."

"Yes, sir," Clara said.

"I think Mark Vaughn is the perfect guy to play the role of Diego," Curtis said after he consumed two slices and looked longingly at the remaining pizza. Julius nudged the box in his direction and Curtis helped himself.

I agreed with him but said, "We still have three days and dozens of potential Diegos left to audition. We need to give the other kids a fair shot."

Curtis nodded. "I agree with you, Dr. B. I'm going to keep an open mind and give the other kids a fair shot, but my gut tells me Mark is the one."

"Me too," Clara and Ellie said.

"I know it was just the first night of auditions, but he blew me away," Ellie told me.

"Ditto," Clara added. "His stage presence, delivery, and the passion he put into his performance gave me chills."

"The dude can sing like it's no one's business too," Julius said. I gave him a look that conveyed he wasn't helping. He just shrugged.

"He's definitely at the top of my list for Diego right now too," I admitted. "Open minds though, right?" Everyone nodded in agreement.

Thirty more students graced the stage over the next two hours. Afterward, Clara, Ellie, and Curtis handed over their audition sheets to me before they left. Once we arrived home, Julius poured wine while I ran over to Lily's to pick up Dolly. I found Julius waiting for me on the sofa in my favorite room of the house. He'd chosen an Ella Fitzgerald album to play in the background while we looked through the audition notes the five of us had made.

I sat beside him and accepted the glass of wine he offered. I took my first sip and sighed. "You're getting really good at picking out wines."

"Now that I know what you like, I find it fun experimenting with the different brands." Jules swirled the glass around then inhaled deeply, mimicking a scene from a movie we'd watched over the weekend. "I'm getting floral and citrus undertones."

"I'm not that pretentious," I said, nudging my shoulder into his. "Don't you dare swish it around in your mouth and spit it out either."

"Spitters are quitters," Jules replied with a leering smile on his face.

Of course, I'd just taken my first sip of wine when he said that. "You're so mean," I said once I safely swallowed my wine. "You're lucky I didn't spray your face with…" My words trailed off when he smiled wickedly.

"We have work to do," I said, pointing to the stack. "Normally, I'd let tonight's performances settle before I start culling the herd, but there are just too many. I figured we would sort them into three categories: no, yes, and maybe for a different role. There were a few kids who acted wonderfully but they lacked the musicality needed for the lead roles. I could see a couple of them playing different parts if they were interested."

"I made that notation on several sheets too," Julius said.

"I'm curious to see how our remarks compare. But first, I need to do something I've been thinking about since we left the house this morning." I set both our wine glasses on the table then straddled his lap and took his face in both my hands. "I missed you today." I saw him at lunch and during auditions, but he knew what I meant. It was so hard to be in the same room with Jules and not be able to touch or kiss him. I had to be careful of what I said or how I acted around him. Our homes were our sanctuary where we could be ourselves to kiss, strip each other down, and make love while Ella sang to us.

We eventually got around to reviewing notes and drinking the wine he'd poured for us. I wasn't surprised to see Jules and I had made similar notes on the audition sheets, but I was amazed to see the three teens were in sync with us nearly every step of the way. I thought it bode well for the remaining three nights of auditions.

At the end of the week, the five of us met in my office to go over our next step. No one had come close to matching Mark's performance for Diego, so he was our unanimous choice for that role. As for Alexandra and Tiffany, I had whittled it down to three possibilities for each character. Some of the kids we passed over for the main roles, were our first choices for the supporting cast. We didn't know if they would be interested in those roles. Some kids would be too upset and others would be excited for the opportunity.

"Callbacks?" Clara asked.

"It's the only fair way," I said. "This time, I want to see the performances back-to-back."

"Then that's what we'll do," Ellie said.

We held the callbacks on Monday and finalized the cast on Wednesday evening.

"The real work begins now," I told them. "Are you ready?"

The teens nodded eagerly while Julius smiled at me.

"Out you go," I told the kids, shooing them out of my office. I knew what Julius was ready for, and it was rude to keep my man waiting. Maybe it should've scared me how hard and fast I fell for Julius, but I was too busy being enamored to allow doubt to take root and grow.

The following week at school was insanely busy with Julius and me running in every direction except toward each other. Jules had his final three tennis matches of the season, I observed classes in the elementary school every day which prevented us from having lunch together, and the first rehearsals for *Inside Out* began in the evenings. We made as much time for one another as we could. I went to his tennis matches because I knew how proud he was of the team; Julius came to the play rehearsals even though he didn't know anything about acting. I passionately loved theater and working with the kids, and I was ecstatic he wanted to share this with me. We kicked rehearsals off by sitting in a circle so they could begin memorizing lines. It was rough going at first, but with patient coaching, they went from saying the lines with little to no inflection and expression to projecting passion and emotion. By Thursday, the cast still relied on their scripts, but they were up and moving through the scenes. The kids soaked up my instructions like little sponges, and I knew they'd blow the audience away with their performances.

I made arrangements to use the Getty Theatre for a few rehearsals so the kids could experience the environment and get a feel for the difference in the stage size. Our first opportunity came the first week of rehearsals, and the kids were excited to stand on the historic stage. Even so, the long week had taken its toll on everyone, and the kids started to get a little sloppy and slap-happy.

"I don't want your symphony, Mom," Mark said to Carrie Ambrose, who played Diego's mom. *"I want compassion and love."*

Carrie's eyes got big when she heard Mark's blooper, but I had instructed them to ignore mistakes and continue with their lines. I thought Carrie was going to pull it off, but when she opened her mouth to say her lines, a loud squeak came out instead. She covered her mouth in shock then dissolved into uncontrollable laughter.

Mark started laughing too and looked at me for guidance. "What's so funny?"

I was trying hard to keep my composure, but Julius didn't bother with pretense. It was all I could do to keep from pulling him in my arms and kissing his neck. Feeling his joy vibrating beneath my lips was one of my favorite things, and because we laughed a lot, I got to experience it often. He smiled at me, his heart in his eyes, and I knew he was reading my mind.

"You told her you didn't want her symphony instead of sympathy," I told Mark.

"I did?" he asked. "How embarrassing."

"Not at all," I assured him. "This has been a very long week, and you've all worked so hard. I don't think one tiny mistake is embarrassing at all. You want to know a secret about me that might help you feel better?" Mark nodded eagerly. "I couldn't say cinnamon properly until I was seventeen. To this day, if I try to say it too fast, it comes out as cimmanon instead."

Mark laughed but looked skeptical like maybe I was just saying that to make him feel better.

"I used to say chimaney instead of chimney," Julius said. "I still catch myself saying it sometimes."

"Really?"

"We all do it, Mark," I said. "Try not to let it ruin a stellar week. You are doing awesome. All of you are." I didn't think we would get much more productivity out of the kids after the long week. Many of the students also had competed in sporting events, and I wanted to do something fun. I just needed feedback from the director of music first. I leaned closer to him. "Do you mind if we knock off a little early and have a little fun?"

"What did you have in mind?" Jules asked, his voice low and husky. I pinned Jules with a look that promised retribution once we were alone. Flirting in front of the kids was off-limits, and he knew it. "You're the one who brought it up."

"I meant something we could do fun for the kids. I thought they might like to hear the music for the play." Only the play creators had heard the full score up to that point. The kids with singing parts heard snippets of the music during auditions.

"Rome, that's an amazing idea. The equipment backstage is much more advanced than what we have at the school."

"Leave that to me," I assured him. "I've had plenty of experience in that department."

"Can I get everyone on the stage?" I asked loud enough for the kids offstage to hear.

"Hey, do you think we should be having some adult supervision backstage to make sure no shenanigans are going on? There are some dark corners back there."

"What dark corners?" I asked. "Maybe you should show me." It was Jules's turn to give me *the* look. "Yeah, we'll need to get some volunteers when we come back in a few weeks." I faced the eager kids waiting for me to say something. "Is anyone interested in hearing the score that Jul...um...Mr. Shepherd wrote for the play?"

"Yeah!" our thespians yelled excitedly.

"Even you, Mark? You were so convincing about your distaste for symphonies."

"Dr. Bradley." Mark groaned and covered his face, but we could still hear his laughter.

I borrowed Jules's phone and took it backstage. There was a slot for a USB port in the sound system and several different connector cords to choose from. I found the right cord, plugged the phone in, and found the score on it. I started the music then rushed back to the stage because I wanted to see their expressions when they heard it for the first time.

Their eyes widened when the first few notes began to play. Some of the kids closed their eyes and swayed with the music while others looked as if they were in a trance. I saw the kids with the singing parts refer to their scripts. Their mouths moved as they timed the lyrics with the music. Then I looked at Julius, the man who captured my heart so completely. He was observing the kids too with a huge smile on his face and joy in his eyes. Then he turned his gaze to me, and the joy morphed into something greater. I sucked in a sharp breath because I recognized and returned the emotion shining back at me.

Toward the end of the score, parents had begun filing in to watch the last minutes of rehearsal. When the last song ended, I released the kids to the parents inside the theater. Some of the older kids drove themselves, and I walked the rest out to the parking lot where their folks were waiting in their cars. Once I was sure everyone had left, I walked back inside the theater to retrieve my guy. I couldn't wait to get Julius home and tell him something very important. I jerked to a stop when I saw him standing in the middle of the stage. The score had started over again, and Julius must've played around with some of the lighting equipment because the stage was bathed in darkness except for hundreds of tiny pinprick lights that looked like stars. I realized I couldn't wait another second to tell Julius how I felt about him.

I took a step toward Julius followed by another and another until I stood in front of him. It was a miracle I hadn't tripped over my own two feet, but I was too caught up in the moment to be nervous. Julius's face lit up with love for me. I didn't need to hear the words to know how he felt, but I needed to say them to Julius. I placed my hand over my heart and spoke from my soul.

"How do I love thee? Let me count the ways.
I love thee to the depth and breadth and height
My soul can reach, when feeling out of sight
For the ends of being and ideal grace.
I love thee to the level of every day's
Most quiet need, by sun and candle-light.
I love thee freely, as men strive for right.
I love thee purely, as they turn from praise.
I love thee with passion put to use
In my old griefs, and with my childhood's faith.
I love thee with a love I seemed to lose
With my lost saints. I love thee with the breath,
Smiles, tears, of all my life; and, if God choose,
I shall but love thee better after death."

The Elizabeth Barrett Browning sonnet became my favorite the first time I read it, but I never expected to recite it to another person as a declaration of my affection. "From the depth of my soul, I love thee, Julius."

Julius closed his eyes briefly, and the tears that had pooled in them slid down his beautiful face. I reached up and wiped the wet trails away, and he did the same for me. I hadn't even realized I was crying until then.

"I love you too, Rome. God, do I love you."

The few inches separating us were suddenly too much. We stepped into each other at the same time. My arms circled his neck while his wrapped around my waist. We weren't at school, the kids had already gone home, and there was no reason I couldn't kiss the man I loved. Julius must've drawn the same conclusion because our mouths moved together at the same time as if on cue.

"You English lit guys," Jules said shakily. "Say it again."

"I love you."

Later at home, I whispered the words as I ghosted kisses all over his body. Julius repeated them to me as his actions mirrored mine. When we joined our bodies together, we said, "I love you," at the same time. Two hearts, two souls, and one accord.

Chapter Eighteen

"Silence. Speak not but what may benefit others or yourself;
avoid trifling conversation."
~Benjamin Franklin

"Pick your battles; know when to speak and when to ignore."
~Julius Shepherd

"WHO ARE YOU SUPPOSED TO BE AGAIN?" I ASKED ROME AS he tied a cape around his neck and reached for a wig. We'd rented a hotel room in Columbus so we could attend his friend's Halloween party and be in town the next morning to have brunch with his family. I was really looking forward to meeting them.

"Isn't it obvious?" he asked with a quirked brow. The wig was dark brown, wavy, and nearly touched Rome's shoulders when he had it positioned correctly.

I stood back and gave him another once-over. Rome wore black, shiny shoes with large gold buckles, and ivory stockings beneath blue velvet pants that ended at his knees. He paired it with a dou-ble-breasted, velvet jacket in the same color of blue and an ivory silk shirt that tied at his throat. He capped off his outfit with a black satin cape.

"I have no idea. I can tell by the outfit it's the late nineteenth century though."

Rome slipped his arm around my waist and nuzzled his lips against my neck. "'I can resist everything except temptation.'"

"I've heard that one, but I'm not sure which of the lecherous poets said it."

"Lecherous poets?" Rome scoffed. "Is that what you think of me when I write you such beautiful words?"

"It loses the wow factor when you send your poems in a text message."

Rome covered his heart like he was in pain then cleared his throat. "'Roses are red, violets are blue. I'm naked in your bed, and I'm waiting for you.' Tell me that didn't motivate you to wrap up your parent conferences and get home quicker."

"Lecherous poets," I pointed out. "You didn't woo me with words about my eyes or my lips or the way I made you feel. You wanted me to come home and fuck you."

"That's romantic," Rome countered. "And it worked."

"Hell yes, it did. I still don't know who you dressed up as."

"Oscar Wilde," he said on a disappointed huff. "You're going to freeze in your costume."

"We're not walking a great distance, right?"

"We're taking a Lyft there and back. That way neither of us need to worry about drinking and driving. We can just relax and have a good time." Rome raked his hot eyes over the expanse of legs showing between the hem of my too-short shorts and my crew socks with the red stripes around the top. "I'm not sure I'll like other guys ogling your legs in those shorts."

"I'm not sure I'll like them looking at those velvet pants clinging to your ass either."

"You're going to be the only man I want in that house," Rome said, leaning forward to kiss me.

"I only want you too."

Rome's smile said he loved hearing the words, but I started

wondering lately if he believed them. He still made occasional comments about our age difference in the guise of a joke, usually referencing that a movie, song, or a show was way before my time. He always chuckled, but I couldn't help but think perhaps he was more bothered by our age difference than I realized. Maybe it was time to bring out the bad teacher again to give another positive reinforcement lesson.

I wanted to address his comments and clear the air, but not before we were due at his friend's house. I didn't want to risk creating tension and ruin our night. Instead, I leaned forward and kissed him long and hard, hoping he could feel how much I wanted to be with him. I'd told Rome that I was in love with him, but I needed him to feel it deep down in his marrow.

Rome's eyes stayed closed a few heartbeats after I pulled back from the kiss. I saw desire and adoration in his gaze when he looked at me once more. "We could just stay here and order room service."

"And hurt your friend's feelings? We at least need to make an appearance."

"Fine," Rome conceded. "We're not staying long though."

Sometimes five minutes is too long in certain circumstances. I knew I was far out of my league when the hired car drove down a long driveway that ran alongside a rectangular reflection pool. I was stunned when the driveway curved, and the Greek revival house came into view.

"Holy crap," I whispered to myself as I slid from the car.

Rome thanked the Lyft driver then placed his palm at the small of my back and led me up the huge steps toward the front door. The porch had wide marble columns extending up to the roofline of the house. There was a second-story balcony that overlooked the front of the property and would offer spectacular views of the city.

"I forgot how pretentious this house was," Rome said in reply. It wasn't a remark I expected him to make considering the people inside were supposed to be his friends. It made me uneasy for the first time that night, and I suspected it wouldn't be the last. "We won't be bobbing for apples at this Halloween party."

I snorted. "I should hope not."

"Is that another one of those sayings?" Rome asked me, sounding alarmed. "What did I imply?"

"It's a blow job this time," I said, "but it's while one of us sits in a hot tub or pool."

"Underwater then?" Rome asked inquisitively. "I can see where that one at least makes sense."

Before I could suggest we try it in private, the door opened wide, and a lady dressed as Marie Antoinette greeted us.

"Rome, darling," she said, but it sounded like dahling. The woman greeted him with an air kiss then stood back to rake her eyes over him. "You look different."

He chuckled and said, "I should hope so, Cybil. This is a costume party after all."

"Don't be cute," she said, patting his chest almost possessively. "Then again, you can't help being cute."

Rome's fingers tensed against my lower back then he slid his hand over to hook my waist and pull me into him. "Cybil, this man is the reason I 'look different.' Say hello to Julius and please stand aside so we can come in. It's freezing out here."

Cybil's eyes widened as if she hadn't noticed me standing there while she pawed my guy. Her pale, shrewd eyes raked over me from head to toe. The smile she gave me was cold and calculating. "Charmed to meet you, Julien." She sounded anything but, and I was certain she deliberately said my name wrong to let me know I was of no importance to her. That's okay. Rome knew my name very well and cried it out every time I made him come. This little harpy's opinion meant nothing to me.

"Are you going to let us in or do I need to call the driver back?" Rome asked.

"Don't be silly, Romeo," she breathlessly said before stepping aside.

"Who put you in front of the door?" he asked once we stepped inside the expansive, marble and gold foyer. Pretentious was an understatement.

"I was watching for you, of course," she purred. I just bet she was. She glanced at me once more before an evil smile spread across her face. "You didn't tell Frank or Heather that you were bringing a date."

"I didn't tell them I was bringing my *boyfriend* because they didn't ask me to RSVP. They've always told me any friend of mine is a friend of theirs."

"Sure, but they didn't mean it." She was the snidest, most hateful person I'd run across in a very long time.

"We're leaving," Rome said, firmly gripping my bicep. "I'll call Frank in the morning and explain to him that his sister insulted my boyfriend before we were two steps inside his home."

"I'm not insulting your *boyfriend*," Cybil said backpedaling. "I'm insulting my brother and his wife's attempts at matchmaking." Her eyes roamed over my body again. "No wonder none of their choices did anything for you."

"What the hell do you mean by that?" Rome demanded.

"Come now, Rome. I've seen the guys they've tried to fix you up with after Peter died. The one they lured here tonight isn't any better than the others. Your boyfriend is much younger, more vibrant, and I bet a lot better in—"

"There you are," said a husky voice from behind Cybil. I couldn't see what the man looked like with Cybil's tall wig blocking my line of sight. "Cyb, let my guy in. Rome, I have someone I want you to… Oh," the bear of a man said when he walked around Cybil and saw me standing in the doorway. "I didn't know you were bringing a guest."

"I brought my boyfriend, Julius," Rome explained.

The man's friendly smile when he looked at me contrasted with his roguish pirate costume. "Well, I feel really silly for not knowing. I might've made an ass out of myself."

"No more than Cybil already has," Rome assured him. "Your heart, however, is always in the right place. Your days of worrying about me are over. Frank, I'd like to introduce you to Julius Shepherd."

"It's good to meet you, Julius." Frank's hand was the size of a baseball mitt and could really hurt a person if he was inclined. His handshake was firm but friendly, and he slapped my shoulder after he dropped my hand. "Welcome to my home. Any friend of Rome's is a friend of mine."

Cybil snorted before gracefully walking away. I hoped she was going to seek out the poor schmuck invited to the party as Rome's potential Mr. Right to tell him the deal was off.

"Please don't take anything she says to heart. She's um…she's a difficult person."

I turned my gaze away from the cold woman to meet her brother's warm, brown eyes. "Thank you."

"I recognize that you came as Arthur Ashe, Julius, but who the hell are you supposed to be, Rome?"

My boyfriend started spouting quotes that were obviously not ringing any bells for Frank. "All of my friends are Neanderthals."

"Who is here, dear?"

The mountain of a man moved to the side and allowed us to see the newcomer. She was tall, svelte, and dressed like a flapper girl from the roaring twenties. "Oh, it's Rome. How are you, darling? I'm so glad you made it. I wasn't sure you'd pick up on the subtle words I used."

"What's she going on about?" Frank asked, turning his attention to his wife. "Did you coerce Rome to attend the party?"

"I did no such thing," she said, frowning at her husband.

"It was the adult version of 'be there or be square.' There was something about not taking no for an answer also," Rome told Frank.

"Hello, I'm Heather," the stunning woman said, pulling my attention away from their friendly banter. She extended a gloved hand to me and I accepted it.

"I'm Julius," I said. "It's lovely to meet you. You have a beautiful home." It wasn't my style, but I could still appreciate fine craftsmanship.

"It'll do," Heather said casually. "Of course, it's really hard for you to form an opinion when you've only seen the foyer."

"Well, it's pretty impressive," I said, gesturing to the curving, ornate double staircase that led to the second story.

Gripping my elbow with her dainty hand, she tipped her head toward the bustling belly of the house. "Would you like a tour? Your boyfriend has obviously forgotten his manners and was prepared to linger in the foyer the entire night."

"I'd love a tour," I replied politely.

She started forward, and I went with her since we were joined at the elbow. "Nice costume, by the way. Frank's parents met Arthur Ashe a few times. They were big fans of his during his tennis career and later became large donors to his foundations. They host a gala every year to support them. Maybe you'd like to attend?"

"That's very thoughtful," I said, noncommittally. Fancy galas and fundraisers weren't my thing unless I was playing in the orchestra at one. I sucked at inane chatter and small talk. I preferred meaningful conversations and even good-natured debates over discussing the weather or struggling to find the right things to ask strangers. No, galas and fundraisers weren't my kind of thing, but I'd do it for Rome if he missed this part of the life he left behind. *Did he miss it?* He rarely talked about his past, and I assumed it was because he wanted to focus on his future with me. Maybe the answer wasn't as simplistic as I'd thought.

"Do you mind if I take you around and introduce you while I give you a tour of the house?" Heather asked. Her expression was warm and sincere, so I nodded. She glanced over her shoulder and snickered. "I see some things haven't changed. Rome hasn't magically become comfortable in this environment." Her remark quieted some of my unease.

"I don't mind introductions," I replied, even though I would've preferred to stay in the foyer with Rome. I wanted to watch him interact with his friend more. Frank and Heather were obviously important to him, and I wanted to get to know them. Not only that, I wasn't eager to run into Cybil again, or anyone like her.

"Don't worry, they're not all like Cybil," she whispered then laughed when she saw my reaction. "You didn't speak your thoughts out loud. I just know how my sister-in-law is." Heather released a long-suffering sigh. "I can't believe she and my Frank share DNA and were raised in the same home. They're nothing alike. My husband is warm, kind, and generous to a fault. Cybil is, well… You've met her."

"What's her problem with me?" I asked, feeling like I could trust Heather.

"It's not really about you, love," Heather said, patting my forearm with her free hand. "She can't fathom that anyone she wants, man or woman, won't return her desire and affection."

"Really?" I asked.

"She's quite narcissistic."

"You don't say?"

"Yep. The first stop in the grand tour is my kitchen. I will have you know that I can barely boil water, but when I do, I need a state-of-the-art setup."

"Wow," I said looking around the immense room. It looked like something I'd seen on HGTV. Chefs and servers moved all over the kitchen like busy bees prepping appetizers for the guests.

"Pretentious as fuck," Heather said, shocking a snort out of me. "What? It's true. I'm from a blue-collar family, and even twenty-five years later, Frank's kind of wealth still makes me queasy."

"Isn't it your wealth too?"

"So the law says, but in here"—she patted her chest then tapped her temple—"I'm still the girl living from paycheck to paycheck. It's created a lot of trouble for us over the years."

"From outside influences?" I asked.

"And strife between Frank and me. He wanted me to just forget everything I knew and be the wife he needed. I tried, and I still do, but on some days, I just want to put on a pair of leggings, a ratty old sweatshirt from my college days, and curl up in a chair to read. I have board meetings or committee obligations almost every day of the week."

"I have an idea," I told her. "One weekend, you should come to Blissville and stay with us. I know the perfect spot for you to curl up and read."

"Can I wear my leggings and ratty sweatshirt?"

"I wouldn't have it any other way."

"What's the catch?" Heather asked, narrowing her eyes.

"No catch. You can say I need your help coming up with a school fundraiser to raise money for my Ohio Science Olympiad team."

"That's a great idea," she said excitedly. "I really could help out during my visit so I wouldn't be lying to my husband."

"I already have my fundraiser set up for the spring, but we can talk about it to ease any guilt you might feel about sitting and reading undisturbed for hours at a time."

"You're a genius, Julius."

"My mother says so," I said, bumping my shoulder against hers.

"You're a man of science then?"

"Among other things," I replied vaguely. I reserved talking about my music with my inner circle. "I'm definitely passionate about teaching advanced sciences at Blissville High School."

"You know a thing or two about chemistry then," she teased.

"Are you referring to my relationship with Rome?" I asked uneasily. Was she indicating that chemistry was lacking between us?

"Honey, it doesn't take a scientist or require special goggles to see the chemistry arcing between you and Rome. You can't possibly know how much it means to see him looking so happy." Heather stopped walking and faced me. "I just want to be certain it's not the kind of chemistry that burns white hot at first then fizzles out because sustaining that level of heat and intensity for long periods of time is impossible. I want it to be a slow burn that builds up over time, binding you closer every passing year."

I had the urge to pull back from her and go find Rome. Was it because I was insulted or because Heather had spoken my biggest fear out loud? Most of the time, I ignored the tiny nagging voice that cautioned me that Rome and I had moved too fast. When love was new and the passion was explosive, it was easy to convince yourself the differences between you were no big deal. Love will conquer everything and all that jazz. The truth was, love wasn't always enough. If differences couldn't be bridged and compromises found, no amount of passion could sustain a relationship for the long haul. My scientific brain knew compatibility needed to be an equal component to love and chemistry in the relationship equation, while my musician's soul only knew Rome made my heart sing. Did Rome and I have the perfect trifecta working for us? Prior to seeing this part of his life, I would've said yes. After meeting his friends, I had some doubts I couldn't ignore.

Heather shook her head and snorted derisively. "Look at me getting all emotional." I returned my gaze to hers and saw tears swimming in her eyes. "You really love him. It's written all over your face right now."

"I—"

"Don't say another word. I had no right to say that to you. I'm acting as supercilious as some of the pompous windbags you're about to meet."

"Oh joy," I said dryly.

"Stick by me, kid. I've got your back."

"Kid?" I arched a brow dramatically so she wouldn't know her arrow had pierced through my armor.

"I meant that as a term of endearment and not a crack at the age gap between you and Rome." Heather's hand slid down my arm until she laced her fingers with mine. "You'll need thicker skin if you're going to come out of this party alive."

I figured she was being dramatic, but she wasn't. While some of the people she introduced me to were nice or polite, some were downright snide. They didn't bother to hide their surprise that I was Rome's boyfriend. Of course, they weren't bold enough to say what it was about me that stunned them, but it didn't matter. Their message was clear: I didn't belong in their world; therefore, I couldn't possibly belong in Rome's.

Speaking of my guy, where the hell was he? I'd tried to discreetly search the room while trying to appear engaged in the conversations going on around me but didn't spot Rome anywhere. Everything was fine with Heather by my side, but the claws came out the moment she was called away for an emergency in the kitchen. Questions changed from polite but indifferent to rude and probing.

"Who are your people?"

"My people?" It took me a second to realize they weren't referring to my ethnicity. They wanted to know if I came from an affluent family. Then again, had I been as white as Rome, they would've naturally assumed my attendance meant I had good social standing in their community. "My mother is a nurse and my father drove a taxi cab." They didn't gasp in horror, but it was close. I looked around the room once more, hoping to find Rome but didn't see him with any of the assholes. I decided I'd had enough separation and politely excused myself from the group to go find him. I was tempted to rescind Heather's invitation to our—Rome's—house after she abandoned me to the wolves.

Heather had told me the general direction of Frank's study during our tour, and I wondered if that was where my man had gotten off to. If not, she'd said there was a bathroom close by, and I could just pop in there to catch my breath and center myself.

As I walked down the corridor, a familiar voice coming through a partially open door stopped me in my tracks. "Ted, you don't have anything to worry about. I could tell you made a good impression on

Rome. He probably went to order a car to send the whelp back to the litter."

"Don't be crude, Cybil," a man said. I didn't recognize his voice, so I hadn't met him yet. "Now I guess we know why he's never shown any interest in the rest of us. He wants younger guys."

Cybil snorted. "It's a midlife crisis, my pet. Nothing more. You'll be in Rome's bed by Thanksgiving, if not sooner. When you are, I want *all* the juicy details."

"Not a chance," Ted told her.

My stomach pitched and rolled. I continued down the hallway, hoping they didn't see me walk by. I found the bathroom door further down the hall but was upset to find it was already occupied. I didn't want to walk toward the study again and risk running into Cybil or overhear more of her poison. I had decided to peek inside the rest of the rooms down the hall to see if any of them had a door that led outside, but the bathroom door suddenly opened.

Rome's pale blue eyes widened in surprise and his lips curved into a joyous smile. He didn't look like a man who wanted to get rid of me. "There's my guy," he said. "I've been—"

I cut him off by pressing my lips to his while walking him back inside the bathroom and shutting us inside.

Chapter Nineteen

"Hell is empty and the devils are here."
~William Shakespeare

"Bill said it best."
~Romeo Bradley

ONE HAND WENT TO CUP JULIUS'S HEAD WHILE THE OTHER WENT to his waist. Energy pulsed through Julius's body making him tremble. I wanted to think it was lust, but the desperation I tasted on his lips was mixed with something else. Fear?

I broke our kiss after several minutes and leaned my forehead against his while I sucked air into my lungs. "Maybe you should run off at parties more often if you're going to kiss me like that when we reunite."

"Run off?" Julius asked, pulling away from me. His hazel eyes turned a darker shade of brown as his temper rose. "I'm not the one who hid away with my buddy while leaving me with *those* people."

"I'm sorry, love. Were they terrible?"

I shrugged. "Not when Heather was with me."

"She's good people," I said softly.

"Except when she's trying to fix you up with other men," Julius said. I loved the flash of possessiveness I saw in his eyes and his fingers flexing against the small of my back.

"That was all Frank. Heather gave up on trying to find someone for me to love a long time ago." Jules took a shaky breath, and I hated being the reason he was so unhappy. "I'll fix this," I said, pulling out my phone from my jacket pocket.

"Who are you calling? The Party Etiquette Police? The Douchebag Collector? If so, they're going to need a bus to haul all of them away."

"I'm hiring a Lyft to pick us up. These people have clearly made you uncomfortable, and I—"

Jules took the phone out of my hand and slid it back inside my pocket. "Huh-uh. They're not running me off. You've chosen me. I'm the one you love, and they'll need to get used to it. Especially, Ted. He's not going to find himself between your sheets by Thanksgiving or sooner."

"Jules, what the hell are you talking about?"

"Just a little conversation I overheard between Cybil and Ted while I was looking for the bathroom," he said. "I've caught many snippets of conversation tonight, and the consensus between them is that you're going through a midlife crisis." Jules had kept his voice light, but the humor didn't reach his eyes and his gorgeous smile didn't greet me.

"Fuck them and the horse they rode here on."

"Horse?" Jules asked. This time his hazel brown eyes sparkled with mirth.

"Fine. They would've arrived in luxury sedans to flaunt their wealth and make up for other things that aren't as impressive. You've heard of little dick syndrome."

"I've heard of short man syndrome," Jules countered.

"Same logic applies. Overcompensating." We shared a quick chuckle, but I knew the situation called for more than laughter, and we weren't leaving the bathroom until I set the record straight. "The only two people here I consider my friends are Frank and Heather. At times, Frank is a little disconnected from reality because of his wealth, but he's a good man. You don't find a more warm-hearted woman than Heather. I was excited for them to meet the man I love, but I realize now this isn't the right setting. The demands of hosting a party aren't allowing them to really get to know you. I don't give a damn about what the rest of those people think. This isn't my scene. You know the real me, Jules. I'm the guy who likes to listen to scratchy records and read literature written more than a hundred years ago. I'm the man who is crazy about you. Let's just say our goodbyes to Frank and Heather and head back to our hotel. Did you see the size of that bathtub? It's big enough for two."

"Backing down from a challenge isn't my thing, Rome. I'm not saying I want to go out there and pick a fight or flaunt that I'm the man sharing your bed in front of Ted, but... Okay, I might want to rub our love in Cybil's and Ted's faces a little bit, but I'm better than that. I'm better than them."

"You are," I agreed wholeheartedly. "What is the point of staying when neither of us want to be here? It's not like our livelihoods depend on our attendance. We both know how precious time truly is, and we won't get these hours back, baby. I could be drinking wine with you in a tub, touching you, loving you. This isn't retreating or backing down from a challenge. This is us thumbing our noses at their pompous bullshit to do what we really want. That's the ultimate freedom."

I saw the moment when my words sank in because the tension melted from his body, and his eyes softened. "I want to hear more about your life before we met. I want to hear about your life with Peter."

"I'll tell you anything you want to know. I just thought talking about Peter might be uncomfortable for you."

"Not talking about him makes me feel like you're not as ready to move on as you say. Like maybe it hurts too much. That's how it was with my dad for a long time. I couldn't look at his picture or talk about the memories without feeling like someone fed me through a paper shredder. Now, I find comfort in reliving those memories with my mom and Marc."

I nodded because he was right. I'd gone through those same phases of grief after losing Peter. "Frank took me to his study to show me a new piece of artwork. I thought that was code for wanting to grill me about the new man in my life, but he really did have a new piece of artwork. He's going on and on about the painter's genius technique and the raw power in every stroke. I saw an ordinary sail-boat riding the waves, so I tuned him out. That's when I noticed the crude metal sculpture Peter had made for him in shop class during their senior year of high school. I was drawn to it like a magnet and forgot I was in the same room with Frank. I left him yammering about his painting and hoisted the heavy piece off the shelf. None of us come from wealthy backgrounds, but Frank had lofty dreams. Peter bent and shaped a piece of metal to look like a horseshoe and welded it to a base. It's crude as hell, but it's Frank's prized possession. Peter told him horseshoes were a symbol of wealth and prosperity. Frank wanted those things, and Peter wanted him to have them.

"A few years ago, I wouldn't have been able to look at that statue let alone pick it up. Tonight, I held it in my hands and smiled as memories of conversations about the statue replayed in my mind. Peter wanted him to get rid of it or at least let him make a nicer piece, but Frank only wanted the original one. It was his lucky charm. Anyway, Frank left the room at some point during my trip down memory lane. I don't know how long I was alone before Cybil and Ted found me."

"Cybil thinks she saw a spark between you and Ted."

"Not a chance," I said firmly. "The huge smile I had on my face was all for you, love."

"I thought you were reminiscing about your life with Peter."

"I was at first, and then like always, my thoughts turned to you. Peter was my past, and you are my future, Julius. I'm always going to choose you."

Tears swam in Julius's eyes and his voice sounded husky when he said, "Damn, you English lit guys have serious game."

Someone knocked loudly on the bathroom door. "Rome, are you in there?" Heather asked.

"Maybe," I replied. "Who is looking for me?"

"No one," she said sassily. "I'm looking for my new best friend. You get to see Julius all the time, and I've only just met him. Either send him out or let me hide in there with you."

Julius tipped his head back and laughed before he pulled from my embrace to open the door. Heather slipped inside the bathroom, and Julius tucked her beneath his arm. "Miss me?"

"For Christ's sake," Heather groused. "I get called into the kitchen to put out the stupidest fire and—"

"Literal or figurative?" I asked.

"Really, Rome?" Heather didn't bother hiding her annoyance with me as she cuddled closer to Julius. "There was a mix-up with the menu that apparently had a huge impact on the world. We have starving kids in this country, but these caterers only care about appetizers I can't even pronounce. Anyway, I returned to the party and my Julius is gone."

"*My* Julius," I reminded her. "How do you know the caterers aren't as concerned as you are about the plight of starving children just because they're wanting to please you? People can be upset about more than one thing."

Heather tipped her head back and looked at Julius. "Why do you put up with him?"

Julius looked away from Heather and locked his gaze on mine. "I love him."

"Awww," Heather said. "He's easy to love, even if it's annoying that he's always right."

"I'm not *always* right."

"You're planning your escape, aren't you?" Heather asked, changing the subject. "I know how much you loathe these parties, but can't you stay a little longer?"

"How about we make a deal?" I offered. "Julius and I leave now before I say things to these people that I've repressed for twenty years, and we'll come back when it can just be the four of us. I know you've missed me, and I've missed you too. This party isn't how I'd choose to spend time with you and Frank."

"Are you telling me the truth, Romeo Bradley, or are you saying anything to escape?"

"While it's true I'd chew my own leg off to free myself from the shackles of this party, I'd never lie to you. I'm sorry I've pulled away from you guys since moving to Blissville, and I—"

"It started before then," Heather stated.

"Okay, yes," I admitted, "but it doesn't have to be that way. I can have my new life and still keep the best parts of my old one too."

Heather dropped her arm from around Julius's waist and launched herself into my arms. "I'm holding you to your promise."

"I love you, Heather. I'm sorry if I ever gave you reason to doubt it."

She sniffled against my chest. "You can make it up to me when I come stay at your house."

"What's that?" I asked, looking to Julius for answers. He grinned sheepishly.

"Julius invited me for a weekend visit. I get to wear leggings, my ratty sweatshirt, and curl up in a chair and read. Doesn't that sound like heaven?"

"It does," I agreed. "You're welcome anytime."

Another knock sounded on the door. "Heather, are you in there?" Frank asked. Julius snorted then opened the door for Frank. Instead of coming in, my big bear of a friend assessed the situation from the doorway. "Who made you cry?" he asked his wife. "I'll throw them out on their ass."

Heather released me and walked into her husband's strong arms. They reminded me of Kong and Ann Darrow. "These are happy tears," she said to her husband. "Rome and Julius have another party to get to, but they assured me that the four of us will get together soon so we can get to know the man who stole Rome's heart."

Frank quirked a brow. He knew damn well I didn't have someplace else to be unless it was a private party for two. "That sounds perfect," he said to me then turned his attention to his wife. "Sweetheart, the caterer is looking for you."

"Not again," she grumbled. "I'm ordering pizza and wings for our next party." She rose up on her toes and gave Frank a quick kiss. "You promised, Rome," she tossed over her shoulder as she exited the room.

"Everything okay?" Frank asked, looking first at Jules and then me.

"Everything is perfect. Don't let us keep you from your party. I'm going to order a ride through my handy app."

"You'll do no such thing," Frank said firmly. "Stevens will take you anywhere you want to go."

"It's very thoughtful of you to offer your driver, but Stevens might be enjoying a night off."

"Nonsense," Frank said, fishing his phone out of his pirate's coat. I recognized that tone of voice. It was no use arguing with him. "Stevens, I need you to give Rome and his boyfriend a ride back to their hotel." Frank listened to his driver's response then thanked him before hanging up. "He'll pull the car around in ten minutes."

"How do you know we're going back to our hotel and not another party?" I asked.

Frank's answer was an eye roll and a snort. "It was really nice to meet you, Julius. I'm looking forward to getting to know you better."

"I'm looking forward to it too, Frank," Jules said, shaking the man's hand.

"I guess I better head back to the party where I'll either receive unsolicited investment advice or ignore attempts to solicit my backing for the next big thing. You guys have a good night."

Frank wrapped me up in a bear hug before he left Julius and me alone.

"What exactly does Frank do for a living?" Julius asked me once we were waiting on the front porch for Stevens to pick us up.

I pulled Julius into my arms to offer him my warmth. "Software and cybersecurity development. He could be every bit as rich as the big guys if he moved to Silicon Valley, but he didn't want to uproot the life he built here."

"Neither of them sounds very happy," Julius said. "Maybe a change of pace and scenery is what they need." Jules's insightfulness amazed me. He'd pointed out something to me that I should've seen a long time ago. "It sure worked out for us."

"Who's the charmer now?" I asked as Stevens pulled up in front of the house in a black, Mercedes SUV.

"I'll show you charm."

Chapter Twenty

"Life need not be easy, provided only that it's not empty."
~Lise Meitner

"Nothing worth having is easy. Surround yourself with love, not stuff."
~Julius Shepherd

NEITHER OF US SAID MUCH ON THE RIDE BACK TO THE HOTEL BE-yond Rome telling Stevens where we were staying. I'd learned early on that Rome and I communicated in many ways that didn't involve words. We could have an entire conversation with just our eyes, but my favorite form of nonverbal communication was touch. The firm way he held my hand in the back seat of the Mercedes said he didn't want to be apart from me, the press of his hand to the small of my back when we walked through the hotel lobby said he claimed me as his own, and the tender press of his lips against mine in the elevator said he cherished me.

"I haven't taken a bubble bath since I was a kid," I confessed once the tub began to fill with fragrant bubbles. "I'm not sure I'll like it."

"It's not a deal breaker if you don't," Rome said, letting his cape fall to the bathroom floor. He pulled his jacket off next and dropped it down too before going to work on his frilly, silk shirt.

"You're a bit messy," I said, pulling my polo shirt over my head.

I folded the shirt and set it on top of the counter. "But I won't hold it against you."

"You're a bit of a neat freak," Rome countered. "But I can live with it."

I crossed the brief space and replaced his hands on the fastenings of his velvet pants with my own. "I've been wanting to strip these off since the moment I saw you in them."

"Yeah? Well, I've been wanting to do this all night long." Rome slipped his hand beneath the hem of my shorty shorts, ran his warm palm up my inner thigh, and cupped my package. I started hardening and lengthening once he began massaging me with firm, confident strokes. "God, I love how you respond to me."

I pushed his pants down to his thighs then cupped his luscious ass, loving how he moaned. "I love how needy you sound right now."

Rome's response came in the form of a long, wet kiss that, combined with his fondling, made it nearly impossible for me to think of anything else except how good he'd feel wrapped around my cock. I could tell things between us were quickly heating up, and the conversation I wanted to have would soon be forgotten if I didn't put the brakes on. Rome had said all the right things in the bathroom in Frank and Heather's house, but I needed more. Walking into the lavish party was the first time I'd felt insecure about our young relationship.

I reluctantly broke our kiss but didn't go very far. "I thought we were going to talk?" I whispered against his lips.

"So, let's talk. We can do it naked in the bathtub so we both get what we want. Compromise, yeah? I will bare my soul, but I'd prefer to do it while wrapped around you. We can get everything out in the open and wash it away." Suddenly, the idea of taking a bubble bath didn't sound so ridiculous.

We stripped the rest of our clothes off and sank down in the bubbles. Rome, true to his word, straddled my hips and got as close to me as he could without burrowing inside me. His hands roamed over my body as he talked about a life and love that didn't include me.

It should've hurt me on some level, but his adoring expression and soothing caresses on my face, chest, shoulders, and back showed he was with *me*, not living in the past. *I* was his future. Instead of being jealous, I was grateful Rome had been loved so thoroughly.

"Our relationship wasn't perfect, and we had our share of problems," he confided. "We fought hard when we disagreed. Nothing physical," he corrected when he saw and felt me tense. "Raised voices, a few slammed doors, and I spent many nights on the couch in our tiny apartment or in the spare bedroom once we purchased our house."

"What kinds of things did you argue about?"

"The same stuff as everyone else. I know the heterosexual world would expect us to have a bitch-slapping throwdown over who was better between Bette and Cher, but it was always about finances, jobs, not having enough time together, and the biggest battle was over family."

"He didn't like your family?" The idea was a little bothersome since I was meeting them in the morning.

"No, he loved my family, and I adored his," Rome replied.

"I'm confused," I admitted. "Did you fight over where you would go for the holidays then? I'm sure it's hard to blend families and traditions in a way that doesn't leave a family feeling excluded or second best."

Rome chuckled. "That wasn't it either." I could tell he wasn't comfortable answering the question but there was no way I was letting him off the hook. I decided to wait patiently while he chose his words. "We fought about having children. That is the one area that I don't think couples can compromise on without someone becoming bitter."

Ah. Things clicked into place. I knew Rome wanted to be a father even if he hadn't told me. I saw the dozens of pictures of his nieces all over his house, and he fussed over babies every time we came across one in public. He was dad material, and the idea of him never fulfilling that dream made my heart ache. "You wanted children, but Peter didn't."

"Yes," Rome admitted. "I didn't realize it at first. The idea of us adopting kids was so far out of reach for the longest time. Suddenly our gay friends are adopting kids or hiring surrogates, and I began to hope we would do the same someday." Rome shook his head. "I was so caught up in my fantasies I didn't notice Peter's lack of enthusiasm each time one of our friends expanded their family until one night he exploded in our bedroom. We'd just come home from another baby shower I had dragged him to, and he was sick to death of baby talk. 'I thought the whole point of being gay men was not being held to heteronormative bullshit standards. Marriage and babies weren't in the cards for us. I was fine with that. Fuck! I even liked that I wasn't constrained like my straight friends.' I remember so clearly how angry he was. I was stunned because he didn't seem upset about the commitment ceremony we'd had two years prior. Constrained? He sounded like our relationship was a prison. God, I was crushed."

"I'm so sorry," I whispered, running my nose along his.

"He left on a long business trip the following morning. It was the first time he ever left the house without kissing me goodbye or telling me he loved me. I thought it was the end for us, but Peter called me once he reached his hotel room that night. He cried and apologized for hurting me and promised we would talk about it more once we got home. He said he was just afraid we would lose *us*, and I had to admit I'd already seen signs of it with our friends. We never had a conversation that didn't revolve around their kids. I loved it, but Peter didn't.

"When he got home, we didn't talk about the big divide. Instead, both of us went on a mission to prove our point to the other. I tried to show Peter we didn't have to lose *us*, and he tried to demonstrate that we were perfect just the way we were, and he should've been more than enough for me."

"Exactly how did you two try to accomplish this? It sounds like a really bad rom com."

"I started offering to babysit kids for our friends so Peter could see how much fun our life could be. Who didn't like playing with Play-Doh and Barbies? Turns out Peter didn't. I thought baking cookies with kids was fun, but all he saw was the mess left behind. As for Peter, he started taking me on lavish vacations. Every time one of our friends shared a picture of a kid on their phone, Peter showed a photo from our latest adventure. A few of our friends would remark on how jealous they were that we could just pick up and go when we wanted, or that we could have sex whenever we wanted. Peter would get this smug smile on his face and look at me like 'See! They regret it.' But every single time, our friends would smile and say they still wouldn't trade places with us."

"Uh oh. I bet you returned his smug smile."

"Baby, I showed more teeth than the Grinch."

"Had you come to a compromise before Peter died?"

"No," Rome said, shaking his head sadly. "We would let the conversation drop for months at a time to avoid arguing, but it still hung over our heads like an ominous cloud."

"What do you think would've happened if Peter hadn't died?"

"We would've drifted apart and found people who wanted the same things we did, or we would've become grumpy, bitter old men. I would've chosen to walk away and be grateful for all the memories we'd made together, but Peter would've rather hung on to what he knew, even if it wasn't what was best for him."

"How long did it take you to realize that truth after he died?" I asked softly.

"Five years, give or take a few months. You know what happens when you lose someone you love. All you can remember was how great they were. The things that annoyed you no longer seemed valid. It took a long time for me to realize as much as Peter and I loved each other, we weren't *in love* with each other anymore. We were bound together by history and friendship, and it's terribly hard to let go sometimes. Jules, being with you has driven that home harder than any epiphany I had before we met. The way you make me feel... It's like nothing I've ever known, and I will never accept anything less ever again. Not if I live for one more year or live to be one hundred. You are everything I want, need, and cherish. You."

Tears stung the back of my eyes. "I've never been in love until I met you. I knew lust and desire, but not this." We leaned toward each other at the same time and knocked heads.

"Damn," Rome swore angrily. "Will I ever stop ruining our moments with my clumsiness?"

"I think we share the blame." I cupped the back of his head and held him in place for the kiss we'd both sought. By the time our lips parted, I was done talking about the love and hurt from Rome's past; I only wanted to think about pleasing him in the present. "We need to get out of this bathtub."

"You didn't enjoy it?"

"No. I think you're sexy as fuck all wet and sudsy, but this space is too limited for what I want to do."

Rome pulled the stopper to let out the water then we got out of the tub and toweled off. Rather than risk Rome tripping over something on the way to the sprawling bed, I hoisted him over my shoulder and carried him fireman style. He gasped in surprise and playfully slapped my ass.

I wasn't gentle when I laid him on the bed. I settled over Rome, aligning our hard dicks together, but he had a different kind of foreplay in mind. I didn't put up a fight when he rolled me to my back and kissed a path down my body before taking my dick inside his talented mouth. I never knew how sexy eye contact during sex was until I met Rome, and I loved the way his gaze held me spellbound as his lips and tongue cherished me.

"C'mere," I said when I reached my breaking point. "I want you inside me now."

Rome reluctantly released my dick and crawled up my body.

After carefully stretching me open with slick fingers, he sheathed his cock and pressed inside me. Like always, the world faded away and he was the only thing I could see, feel, or hear. He was the maestro, my body was his instrument, and the score we created together was the most beautiful I'd ever heard. The tempo of our lovemaking reminded me of a symphony. A graceful minuet gave way to an explosive sonata as we chased our climax. Afterward, our song faded into a lilting melody as we lay together in a heap of tangled, sweaty limbs. It was so beautiful I wanted to recreate it for Rome so he could carry our music with him everywhere.

The next morning, we headed to Ashley and Ben's house for the all-important first meet and greet. Rome told me not to worry and assured me his family was already in love with me because he was. I decided to take him at his word instead of worrying.

Ashley and Ben's house wasn't as grand as Frank and Heather's, but it wasn't too far off.

"Don't worry," Rome said, squeezing my hand as we approached the front door. "The inside is as warm and inviting as the welcome you're going to receive from my family."

The door jerked open before we reached it to reveal two angry teenagers. I recognized them as Michele and Laurel from the numerous photos Rome displayed around his home.

"This is all your fault, Uncle Rome," Michele practically spat out. "I hope you're happy now."

"What's my fault, lamb?"

"Ugh! I thought you stopped calling me by that name," she replied, sounding even angrier.

"We haven't slept in two days," Laurel whined.

"Michele and Laurel," Ashley said in a warning tone as she walked up behind them. She had a baby swaddled against her chest in a sling and managed to look both exhausted and beautiful at the same time. "Let Rome and Julius in right this minute."

"What's going on?" Rome asked. A huge smile spread across his face. "You didn't."

"Not yet" the girls both said.

"We're just babysitting this weekend, but Dad calls it a trial run for when we adopt a baby," Laurel said.

The baby let out a soft, pitiful cry and Ashley cooed to him. The girls looked at each other and winced.

"We're horrible people," Michele told her sister.

"The worst," Laurel agreed. "We make babies cry."

"Um, hello," Rome said. "Who's the handsome fella?"

"His name is Jacob, and he belongs to friends of ours," Ashley explained. "They had to go out of town for a funeral, and I volunteered to watch the little guy. And now I want a baby."

"Can we at least come in? Maybe Jacob wants to meet Julius even if you don't," Rome said.

"Don't be silly," Ashley said. "I've been waiting for this moment forever. Girls, get out of the doorway and let them inside. I raised you to have better manners than this. Julius, welcome to our home. I apologize for the chaos and ridiculous way you were greeted by my uncouth daughters. Rome, you can feed this little guy so I can help Ben in the kitchen."

We followed Ashley to the back of the house where Rome's parents, Astrid and Ben, waited for us. Rome made quick introductions before he practically elbowed his mother out of the way to get to Jacob.

"Ashley wants me to feed the baby so she can help Ben in the kitchen," Rome said smugly.

Michele handed Rome a bottle and hovered close by like she was afraid Rome might drop him. I think she liked the idea of a little brother more than she let on. Laurel kept her distance still, but she kept glancing over at him.

"Four brothers," Rome softly teased to antagonize his nieces without disturbing the baby.

Rome was right about his family. They were warm and made me feel very welcome. They didn't care about the differences in our ages or backgrounds; they only cared that I made him happy. There was never an awkward silence between conversations, and their questions about my background came from a place of getting to know me. Astrid loved hearing about my days of playing in the orchestra and was excited that I'd written the score for the play.

"I cannot wait to see the production," she said, squeezing both my hands in her frail ones.

Rome's dad and I talked about our favorite shows on the Science channel. "Do you think there's alien life on other planets?" he asked me.

"I think it would be arrogant to believe otherwise," I replied.

I learned his mother also loved trying out new IPAs. "The next time you come to Columbus, I'll take you to Carmichaels. It's my favorite pub, and they only serve IPAs there."

"I'm looking forward to it," I told her. She was pleased to know Rome always kept my favorite IPA on hand. "You raised a wonderful man, Amelia." She kissed my cheek and squeezed me extra tight.

"Oh, how I've prayed for you," she whispered before releasing me.

I chatted with the girls about school and their hobbies. Michele was a tennis player like me, and I was happy to hear that Laurel liked to play chess. We agreed future matches were a must. Conversation continued over brunch, and Ben and Ashley shared more about what they did.

Rome and I cleared the table and cleaned the kitchen after brunch so Ashley and Ben could kick up their feet and rest. After we finished, Rome announced we were heading back to Blissville to get ready for the next work week. I was embraced and hugged like they'd known me longer than a few hours, and returning their affection felt natural and right.

The day was as perfect as could be until Rome received a phone call from Caitlyn Simpson informing us the POS group had struck again.

Chapter Twenty-One

"Never argue with stupid people, they will drag you down to their level and then beat you with experience."
~Mark Twain

"Rolling around in the gutter with stupid people only leaves you stinking like them. Rise above it; be smarter."
~Romeo Bradley

"WHICH TIE WOULD LOOK BEST IN A TELEVISION INTERVIEW with the investigative reporter from Channel Eleven news?" I asked Julius Monday morning, holding my top two picks up in front of me. "Dark red or navy blue?"

Julius rose from the bed and shook his head. "Neither." He walked into my closet and returned with a pale lavender tie. "This one is my favorite. Wear it and know that I'm there with you."

I exchanged the red and blue ties for the lavender one. "I wore this tie on the day the board hired me."

"I know," he said. "We were hired the same day, remember?"

"Of course, I remember. My first official act as the superintendent was to greet the new science teacher. I'm surprised you remember my tie."

"I remember everything about you." Julius took the tie from my fingers and looped it around my neck. He used it to tug me closer to him for a kiss. "I'm so damn proud of you, Rome. You could've let

Cait's phone call ruin your day, but you didn't."

I wouldn't let the latest development with POS destroy what had started out as a perfect day. We'd slept in late, made love, then spent a wonderful couple of hours with my family. I hadn't lied to Julius when I said my family would love him, but it still made my heart all warm and fuzzy to see how quickly he was absorbed by them. My nieces had loved making boasts that they could beat him at tennis and chess, he geeked out with my dad over science talk and aliens, talked theater with Astrid, and bonded over beer with my mom. If I hadn't been holding the baby, I would've jumped to my feet and did some ridiculous double fist pump while whooping about how right I was.

I was high on life when Cait called to let me know she'd received an interview request from Channel Eleven news. The POS group had flooded them with complaints and false stories about the play, the board's handling of their complaint, and alleged that I was engaging in inappropriate behavior in front of impressionable students. Me? What had I done? My mind replayed all the times I longed to acknowledge Julius as mine in some way but refrained because it wouldn't be professional. Not just because we were two gay men, but because of our positions in the school. Other married teachers in the district kept their personal lives just as private as we did which was next to impossible in such a small town. Julius and I weren't breaking any rules, and we didn't so much as hold hands during the school day. The allegations were false, but they could still negatively impact my career.

"I wasn't sacrificing valuable time with you to fret over those hateful bastards."

"That's the spirit. This will work in our favor, babe. I just know it."

Julius and I worked as a team in the kitchen. I cooked the sausage and browned the toast while he made the egg white omelets with spinach, tomatoes, and feta cheese. I would've left the dishes for later, but it would bug Julius all day long, so we tidied up, topped off our coffee mugs, and headed to work. Julius rode with me since tennis season was over, neither of us had meetings planned after school, and play rehearsal didn't start until six o'clock. Well, if the board didn't change their mind after the latest stunt. Damn, I hoped they stayed strong and didn't back down from the bullies. The kids would be so crushed. Julius must have sensed the tension rising in me because he laid his hand on my knee. I loved how he intuitively knew when I needed his touch.

I placed my hand on top of his and squeezed. "You know what would really make me feel better?"

Julius chuckled. "I could guess."

"That too, but I was thinking about heading into Goodville to get some Christmas decorations. I decided to get all new stuff for my new house."

"*Christmas decorations?* It's not even November yet. Can't we celebrate Thanksgiving first? I have much to be grateful for this year."

"I do too, love, but I didn't plan to decorate until after Thanksgiving."

"Why today then?" Julius asked.

"All the good stuff will be gone if we don't grab it now. I want to buy the decorations and store them until it's time to decorate."

"Which is?"

"After Thanksgiving," I said.

"I can live with that. I'm in."

"I should warn you that 'after thanksgiving' sometimes means once the feast is cleared away and the kitchen is cleaned." I gave him my best innocent smile.

Julius just shook his head. "Warn a dude. How crazy do you get with your Christmas decorations?"

"On a scale from one to ten, with one being Scrooge and ten being Griswold, I'd say I'm about a seven. I'm a firm believer in making things merry and gay." Jules groaned. "I promise that my decorating will be the epitome of tasteful and timeless. There won't be a single gaudy decoration anywhere."

Julius scrutinized me intently. "I don't believe you for a minute."

I loved how easily he distracted me from negative thoughts during the short drive to the school. I turned to face him once I'd parked in front of the school board building. "Regardless of what happens today, I get to go home with you. That's all that matters to me, Jules." I reached over and caressed his face, letting my thumb linger over his lips.

"I'll see you at lunch," Jules said, looking as hesitant as I was to part ways. "Walking tacos today. I'll grab extra napkins for you to tuck into your collar so you don't ruin your lucky tie. I know how enthusiastic you get on taco day."

"Good call, love."

Once inside the building, I found Priscilla at her desk in front of my office. She was looking extra dragon-ish while pulling guard duty which meant she'd already heard the news. "You're looking pretty damn chipper for a man who's about to be interviewed by Charles Zimmerman. That guy is a real ballbuster."

"I'm wearing my lucky tie, Pris," I said cheerfully. "What's not to be chipper about?"

"The Hammer is coming. That's why." I got a kick out of the nickname the news station had given their investigative reporter.

"What have I done to earn his anger?" I asked. "I haven't cheated senior citizens out of their money, and I'm not a corrupt contractor. The man doesn't scare me."

"That's true, but still. He's—"

"Don't you worry about me, Pris. I need to focus all my energy on the looming budget meeting later this week. Will you hold my calls until after I meet with The Hammer?"

"You got it. No one gets to you without going through me. They don't call me The Dragon for nothing."

I winked at her before heading into my office. Once alone, I inhaled deeply and exhaled slowly. Everything would be all right, and I refused to entertain any other thoughts. Cait called my cell phone as soon as I sat down.

"Good morning, Cait. I'm surprised it took you this long to call me," I teased.

"Anything earlier would've been indecent. I'm sorry to call your personal phone. I knew better than to try to reach you on your office phone since all your calls are routed through Priscilla and not the voicemail system the rest of the district uses. I just want to wish you good luck."

"You won't be here?" I asked.

"No. I have a court hearing in fifteen minutes. It shouldn't take long, but I won't make it back to Blissville in time. You don't need me there anyway. You've got this, Rome. I know you'll handle that bruiser just fine and make our district proud. You were the right man for this job in the spring, and you're the right man now. Nothing has changed. I just needed you to know it."

"Your support means a lot to me, Cait. Thank you."

"I gotta run. I'll see you later this morning."

"Good luck!"

The Hammer arrived with his cameraman at seven fifty. His voice was as big as he was, and I heard him greet Priscilla politely and ask to speak with me. I rose from my chair and crossed the room to open my door. Priscilla scowled at the man and looked like she was about to give him a piece of her mind.

"Gentlemen," I said cheerfully. "Come in." I stepped aside to let them pass before I poked my head out the doorway and mouthed "behave" to Priscilla. "I would say it's an honor to meet you, but I'm afraid I'd be lying under these circumstances."

Charles Zimmerman guffawed and shook my hand before dropping down in the chair in front of my desk. It squeaked in protest under his bulk. The investigative reporter wasn't overweight, but he was carrying a lot of muscle on his broad frame. "I'm not here for the reason you think, Mr. Bradley."

"Dr. Bradley," I said, but softened my correction with a

good-natured smile. "You're not here to investigate my conduct as superintendent or talk about the play our school *will* perform in January?"

"No." He chuckled at my raised brow. "I want to hear about your encounters with a hate group that's operating illegally as a 501c3 non-profit organization."

"They were granted nonprofit organization status?" I asked.

Charles nodded. "Religious groups can apply for a 501c3, but they have to follow the same rules as all other nonprofits."

"Can I ask which rules you suspect they've broken?"

"I don't suspect, Dr. Bradley. I have hard evidence to back up my claim. Normally, I would tell you to watch the show because of ratings and such, but I'll make an exception since you were clearly targeted by this POS"—a wry grin spread across his face—"organization. And, I would hate for the supportive crowd outside to turn into an angry mob."

"Crowd?"

"You didn't know there are at least fifty people gathered in front of the school with signs showing their support for you and the play?"

"No," I said. "I hadn't been informed." I had to swallow hard to dislodge the lump of emotion in my throat. "How long ago did POS start flooding your email asking for help?"

"The week after they were shut down by the school board. I had other investigations going on and didn't have the time to dedicate to digging into their background. I reached out to your school board president first and she sent me a copy of the play for me to read. I'm sure she thought that would be the end of it. That's what I thought too when I sent an email to Mr. Halifax telling him I wouldn't be investigating his allegations after reading the school play. There was no agenda being pushed on the kids except encouragement to be decent human beings. He didn't like my answer and turned his ire on you instead."

"Me? I haven't done anything wrong."

"He seems to think differently. I received a lengthy email that reeked of homophobia and it included a photo of you kissing a man I presume is your boyfriend or husband."

"Photo? What photo? I haven't so much as held my boyfriend's hand on school grounds."

"The two of you were kissing on what appeared to be a stage."

The Getty. It was the night I told Julius I was in love with him after blurting out my favorite sonnet. I was outraged and sickened that Roy Halifax witnessed one of the most beautiful moments in my life. How had I not sensed his evil lurking? "There were no kids in the theater at the time. I had personally supervised the younger kids getting picked up by their parents and watched the older kids drive away in their cars. That means that asshole was stalking me."

"He was outraged that the parents weren't concerned about leaving their kids in your care, so he was going to look out for them."

"By hiding in the shadows and snapping photos of private moments. How dare he?"

"That's what I thought too, so I decided to investigate this case after all, but not in the way he expected. I decided to dig into his background and the nonprofit organization he runs."

"And you've discovered that they're not legally operating under the 501c3 rules?"

"Correct. It would be easier to tell you the tax codes they didn't break than it would be to list the ones they trampled all over without bothering to cover their tracks. They're either as stupid as their acronym implies or completely careless. Either way, I'm going to do my best to destroy their credibility."

"How do I come in?" I sounded as confused as I felt.

"I just want you to tell us about your interactions with him."

"I've only had one interaction with him at the school board meeting. I never spoke with him before or after. I had no idea he was following me around."

"I obtained a copy of the board meeting transcript, but I'd just like a few sound bites to go with it. The focus will be on exposing POS and Roy Halifax."

"Okay. Let's do this."

The Hammer only asked me two brief questions then allowed me to talk about the incident with POS. I talked mostly about the support we received from the school board and the community of Blissville.

After he left, Priscilla came into my office to give me a high five. "Love always wins," she said.

Between the phone calls and unexpected visits, my morning was completely unproductive, but it was hard to be upset when everyone was so excited. I was feeling especially festive when Julius and I went shopping for Christmas decorations after school.

"Merry and gay," I reminded him as the cashier began ringing up our purchases.

"Totally Griswold," he countered.

"Hush, or I'm coming back for the inflatables this weekend."

"If you want them, you better grab them now," the cashier said.

"See," I said. "Don't act like you weren't putting things in the cart left and right either."

"I guess your 'merry and gay' is contagious."

I snorted. "I think I saw that same accusation in the POS complaint against me."

Julius stored the Christmas loot away then made dinner so we wouldn't be corralling teenagers on an empty stomach. Rehearsal went off without a hitch, and we were home by nine which gave us enough time to shower, grab a snack, and settle in for the news at ten. I cringed a little when I saw myself on the news but was pleased I sounded calm and spoke eloquently. There was no keeping the grin off my face when Charles Zimmerman dropped the hammer on Roy Halifax and his POS group. The hatemonger sputtered and stuttered when he found out that The Hammer had already sent a copy of his findings to the Carter County Sheriff's office and the Ohio attorney general.

"Justice," Jules and I both said at once.

I was glad that Roy Halifax was getting what he deserved, but I was still sickened by the thought of him trailing after Jules and me.

"Put it out of your head," Jules said, knowing where my mind had gone.

"I can't."

"Let me help you drive out the ugly so you can focus on the beautiful."

And he did.

Chapter Twenty-Two

"For who would live if life held no allurements?"
~Lewis Howard Latimer

"A life that doesn't arouse you from slumber and tempt you with challenges might be cleaner and easier, but it's also boring. Thrill me; let's get messy."
~Julius Shepherd

THE POS SITUATION KEPT US ON EDGE FOR THE FIRST FEW WEEKS after the story aired on Channel Eleven news. Who could blame us? The hate group had worked quietly to disrupt the play without us knowing, so common sense made you wonder what else the group planned. Would they boldly retaliate this time? Were they a danger to us or the kids? Roy Halifax had already stalked Rome and me without us knowing it. Wasn't that an indication the man could be unhinged?

God, I was so pissed when Rome told me about the photo, and even more concerned what Roy would do with it going forward. We couldn't possibly hope it would always land in a fair-minded person's inbox. Rome had asked Cait if she wanted him to step down, but she assured him a letter of resignation would be immediately put through the shredder. She reiterated what we knew in our hearts; we hadn't done anything wrong. Rome had even asked Ashley if she thought we should obtain a restraining order, but the man had never physically threatened any of us. She encouraged us to file an official complaint with the local law enforcement, both for documentation and to see if they'd patrol by our house more frequently. *Our house.* I loved hearing people say that.

"Do you want me to go to the police station to file the report?" Rome had a series of meetings coming up after school, and I had more free time than he did since tennis was over.

"Why? So that muscled hunk in the too-tight uniform can try and take you away from me? I bet he'd offer to keep a really close eye on you. Probably stand over your bed and watch you sleep." The last part creeped me out and made me shiver. Rome laughed, and I knew he wasn't seriously worried about the cop's interest.

Just in case though, I said, "Knock it off. No one is going to take me away from you, and you're the only one I don't mind watching me sleep."

We went to the police station together, and I tried not to laugh when Rome placed his hand possessively on the small of my back when Officer Simanski was the one who took our complaint. The cop's flirty side from the night of the board meeting disappeared when he heard our concerns.

"This is the part I really hate," Officer Simanski said. "I will file your complaint to get it on the record, but right now, there's not much we can do. I can ask the captain if patrol can swing by your house a few times during their shifts, but without a direct threat…" His expression contorted and looked like he'd sucked on a lemon, but maybe it was because his words tasted nasty in his mouth.

"My sister is an attorney, so we knew there wasn't anything you could do besides document the claim, Officer," Rome assured him.

"I'm serious about asking for extra patrolling," he said. "Dr. Bradley, I have your address on the complaint. Can I have your address too, Mr. Shepherd?"

"We live together," I replied without thinking. "I do have my own residence, but I'm never there."

"Okay, so I'll just ask if we can patrol this one address then."

"Thank you for your time," Rome said, shaking the officer's hand.

"I just wish I could do more."

"You're doing what the law allows. We wouldn't ask you to go beyond that," I said, offering my hand to him. The big guy's hand dwarfed mine but there wasn't a single tingle or buzz when our skin touched. Only Rome made my skin come alive.

On the way out of the police station, Rome leaned close and said, "Make sure we're pulling the bedroom curtains extra tight." I just rolled my eyes and looped my arm around his waist. Rome stopped suddenly in the middle of the parking lot and turned to me. "I like what you said inside the station."

"Which part?" I asked, even though I knew.

"The part about us living together. I know we've unofficially lived together for some time, but I want to make it official. I know you're locked into a lease, and I'm not asking you to break it, but I want to move your things out of *your* place and into *our* place."

The smile on my face grew until it hurt. "Dare already told me he'd rip up the lease if I wanted to officially move out."

"When?" Rome asked.

"A few weeks after we started dating. I'd only stopped by long enough to take my trash to the curb for pickup. He told me he'd never stand in the way of love. I kind of laughed him off, but I knew even then how much you meant to me."

"So let's make it official. Move in with me."

I looked at our surroundings and chuckled. "You English lit guys aren't always so suave. Asking me to move in with you while standing in the middle of the parking lot at the police station? How will I ever top this moment?"

"Spontaneity is supposed to be sexy. I can ask again with a bottle of wine and a crackling fire in the background if you prefer."

"I prefer honest and sincere which is exactly what I got."

"Is that a yes then?"

"It's a hell yes." I didn't just see his joyous smile, I tasted it when I pressed my lips to his. "Let's go home."

"Where you can try and top me…um… I mean my proposal… um—" I pressed my lips to his for a second time to stop the nervous rambling. There was no doubt in my mind there would be some topping going on in my future, and I was also just as certain there would be a proposal for a deeper commitment between us down the road.

"Let's go home."

"Permutations and combinations. Who can tell me the difference?" I asked my seventh period class the Wednesday before the Thanksgiving break. They looked at me with annoyance in their eyes because they expected to goof off the last class of the day. It was a good thing Anastasia's family got an early start to their vacation travel plans or else she'd really let me have it.

"Are you seriously giving us homework?" Ben asked.

"Did I list homework in your syllabus, Mr. Devers?"

"No, sir."

"Then I hadn't planned on giving you homework. I can change my mind if you like."

"No, sir."

"Permutations and combinations," I repeated. "Anyone? This is the lesson we're tackling on Monday, so I thought I would plant the seed and give it time to root."

"Permutations and combinations are the same thing," Jill said. "They're groups of things that you put together to make something else."

"You're partially right, Ms. Skellson. The difference between permutations and combinations is the order. Permutations require a specific order where combinations do not. This theory doesn't just apply to science. There are many recipes you can jack up if you don't combine the ingredients in a specific order. Think about your locker *combination*. You all have three numbers to unlock it, correct?" They all nodded. "Can you use those same three numbers randomly or must they be in order?"

"In order," Randy said.

"That's an example of a permutation. Our experiments next week are going to be fun," I said waggling my brows. "We'll see who is paying attention and who isn't."

"Are we finally going to utilize the face shields?" Travis asked excitedly.

"I worry about you sometimes, Travis," I teased. The kid was way too excited about the possibility of needing a face shield for experiments. He just laughed and shook his head. "If this were a philosophy class, we'd talk about permutations and combinations in relation to fate. Are our lives guided by preordained permutations or do we just throw in a bunch of stuff to see how it turns out? Do we have destinies or opportunities?"

"Preordained permutations," Derrick said confidently.

"I think we just close our eyes and toss in the ingredients," Molly Sue countered.

I hadn't expected the kids to start debating fate vs chance in my classroom, but I wasn't mad about it. A teacher could learn a lot about their students by listening. Before any of us realized it, the forty-five minutes had passed, and they were free for a long weekend. My heart swelled with happiness when every single kid in my class wished me a Happy Thanksgiving. Some of them even included Rome in their well-wishes.

I was excited to kick off our first holiday season together, but sad my mom had to cancel her travel plans due to some crisis at the hospital. She was devastated she didn't get to see her boys and meet Rome,

Camilla, and Manny, but promised she would be there the first weekend in December even if it meant quitting her job.

"I don't think that's a bad idea," I'd told her on the phone when she called me on Monday evening. She'd sounded so upset, and it made my heart ache. "You're miserable in your new position. I think it's time for a big change."

"How big?" she asked suspiciously.

"You should quit your job and move here."

"To Whoville?" she asked.

"Mom, you're starting to sound like Marcus," I teased. "Yes, you should move to Blissville or Cincinnati if you prefer to stay in a bigger city. My garage apartment is paid up until February, so you could always stay there. You and Dare would go together like peas and carrots."

"I'm not sure I want to make such a big change, J."

"Mom, how many weeks of vacation do you have left?" I asked.

"Three," she admitted.

"And you lose that time if you don't take it, right?"

"Yes, but—"

"Take them, Mom. Stay in the apartment for three weeks. Get to know the people Marc and I love. Take time to breathe and bake and celebrate the holiday with us. Please."

"That does sound heavenly."

"While you're here, you can update your resume and look at employment opportunities. There are tons of hospitals around here."

"One thing at a time. I'll inform HR that I'm taking my vacation. They can just deal with it like they expect me to every damn day."

"That's my mama," I'd said proudly.

Rome had taken the entire week off to prep for the feast he planned for our guests which included Camilla's parents. Rather than making Marc and Camilla split time between the families, Rome thought it would be a nice gesture to invite everyone. I watched in shock as my normally messy man turned into a super-neat freak when we started cleaning for company. Apparently, that meant cleaning the closets because it's where I found him when I got home from school, not in the kitchen like I expected.

"Is there something you want to tell me?" I asked. Dolly got up from her blanket nest by the door and came to welcome me home. "Hi, baby girl. Miss me?" I cradled her against my chest and she licked my chin. "I missed you too, but I'm not licking your chin."

"How about mine?" Rome asked, peeking around the closet door. "Hi, love."

"Hi. What's going on?" I asked, gesturing to the mess he'd made inside the closet.

"I'm getting ready."

"To go back in the closet? Are you making a nest in there?"

"No," Rome replied, rolling his eyes. "It's part of my annual Thanksgiving cleaning ritual."

"I don't think Mr. and Mrs. Álvarez are planning to look in there," I said when he disappeared out of sight. I put Dolly back down then made myself comfortable on our bed. I'd helped clean the house too, of course, but I was drawing the line at cleaning the closets when we could be making love. This was a side to him I hadn't seen, and I found it completely adorable. "So, are you making room for new stuff?"

"No," he said from somewhere inside his walk-in closet. I saw a shirt sail through the air and land in the pile in the center of the closet floor. That was the Rome I knew and loved. I pulled my polo over my head and dropped it beside the bed then reached for my belt. "I want everything to be tidy and organized for the New Year."

"So you can mess it up again in a week?" I asked, shoving my pants and underwear to my thighs.

"You think you know me so well, don't you? I'll have you know—" Rome's words died when he saw me working my dick up and down. He blinked a few times then licked his lips.

"You'll have me know what?" I asked him.

I heard a crash which meant Rome dropped whatever he held

in his hands. Then he practically tripped over his own two feet when he cleared the doorway. "Close your eyes, Dolly. Dad and Daddy are about to kick off this holiday right."

Sometime later, I roused from my post-coital nap. "Do I smell burnt toast or am I having a stroke?" I asked.

Rome snorted from somewhere in the room. I sat up and saw that he was back in the closet again, and the pile of stuff in the center had tripled. He poked his head around the door and grinned. "It's burnt toast. My handsome guy came home and distracted me, so I forgot I was toasting bread for my homemade stuffing. Luckily, I bought extra bread, but that means we'll have to use store-bought croutons instead of my homemade ones."

"Oh, the horror," I gasped then yawned. "Where are you getting your energy?"

"Is that a crack about my age?"

"You know it's not."

"I'm just happy," he said. "I'm going to need your help in the kitchen later. We have plenty of casseroles to prep."

"Where are you going to bake all these casseroles? We only have the one oven, and it will be stuffed with that forty-pound turkey you got from the butcher."

"It's only twenty-two pounds," he said, ducking back inside the closet. "Lily and her husband are going to her in-laws, so she said I could borrow her oven tomorrow."

"We're going to need a double oven," I told him. "My mom has one, and it made the holidays so much easier for her. Or," I said after consideration, "you could ask the guests to bring a casserole dish with them. That's what most families do."

"Next year," he said, but I knew he was dismissing the idea. My grandmother was the same way. She never let anyone bring any food or clean up afterward. I'd have to work on Rome because that was just insane, especially as our lives expanded to include more people.

The feast we prepared would impress Scott Conant. I missed

having my mother there so much, but we FaceTimed her so she could meet Camilla's parents and feel like she was there with us.

"I have big news," she said once we all finished the initial greetings.

"I'm coming to Ohio next week and won't be leaving until after the New Year, *if* I leave at all.

"Julius, I'm going to accept your gracious offer and stay at your apartment while I enjoy a much-needed break."

I was too excited to ask how she was able to stay an entire month if she only had three weeks of vacation to use. My mom was a sensible woman, and I had no reason to question her.

"No, you must stay with us," Rome said. "I have a spare bedroom."

"Huh-uh," Mom said, shaking her head. "I won't be an intrusive mother in-law. We'll get to spend plenty of time together, but we'll have our separate spaces too."

"You won't win," I whispered to Rome when it looked like he would argue.

Seeing Rome with kids always made my heart so happy, and I looked forward to us having kids of our own. That thought reminded me of the remark I made in class about permutations and combinations. The components of the formula were the same: two men and a baby. The difference between combination and permutation was in the order. Combination implied we could adopt a baby just as we were: two men who were committed to each other. A permutation implied the components should be applied in a specific order, and for Rome and me, that would include marriage before adoption. Old fashioned, yes, but I knew it was the outcome both of us wanted.

Mama arrived the following week like she promised, and she held tight to Rome when we picked her up from the airport. They'd talked, video chatted, and texted a lot over the last few months, but it couldn't compare to meeting in person. She cried, and Rome got choked up too. I just stood there grinning like an idiot waiting for my turn as people walked by smiling at the spectacle they made.

"I've waited for you for such a long time, Romeo Bradley," my mom said, cupping his cheek.

"Mom, are you trying to steal my guy?" I asked.

"Hush," she said, waving her hand in my general direction. "You're even more beautiful in person."

"I was about to say the same thing about you," Rome said, hugging her again.

"We're due at the Álvarez's house for dinner in an hour. Camilla said her mom makes the best empanadas," I said. They continued to ignore me as Mom gushed about how happy Rome made me, and he in turn told her that I was the best thing to ever happen to him.

"Oh, my heart," Mama said, clutching her chest. Then she turned to face me. "You never stood a chance at resisting him, Son." It was true; I hadn't. Just like I knew she didn't stand a chance of resisting the charm of Blissville and the lure of being close to both her sons while they built lives with the people they loved. It came as no surprise to me when Mama announced she wasn't returning to Philly other than to sell her home. She spent part of her vacation interviewing for jobs at hospitals nearby and looking for a quaint home to buy in Blissville.

The next month flew by in a whirlwind of decorating, eating, play rehearsals, eating, parties, eating, a holiday parade, eating, shopping, and more eating. There were a lot of festivities and even more eating, but through it all there was so much love and happiness. The level of sappiness surpassed the sappiest movie ever to grace the Hallmark Channel. I mean, seriously. Two men move to a new town for fresh starts, fall in love, and live happily ever after.

As exciting as it was to be surrounded by our families, I was grateful that Rome and I carved out quite a bit of time just for us. We had plans to combine both sides of our families for one huge bash at Ashley's on Christmas day, but Christmas Eve belonged to just us. I made an intimate dinner for two, we drank wine, exchanged gifts, and made love by the Christmas tree lights while listening to the song

I recorded for Rome as one of his gifts. I had almost drifted to sleep when I noticed Rome had replaced the picture in the built-in frame on the entertainment center. Instead of Rome and Peter staring into each other's eyes, there was a picture of us kissing on the stage the first night Rome told me he loved me.

"When did you do that?" I asked, pointing to the frame.

Rome didn't lift his head off my chest. "A while ago," he said sleepily. "Turns out that homophobic asshat can take a good picture."

"Where'd you get it?"

"The Hammer," Rome said then yawned. "Out of the blue, he emailed it to me. He said the origin of the picture shouldn't take away from the beauty of the moment."

"The Hammer said that?" I asked suspiciously.

"I might be paraphrasing, but it's still the truth."

"Why didn't you tell me?"

"I didn't want to make a big fuss out of it. I loved Peter, and I'll always be grateful for our memories. You're the one, Jules. You're the love of my life, and I want everyone to see it when they come into our home. Over the years, that picture will change to show our love evolving and our lives expanding."

I imagined a picture of us holding a baby or a toddler between us. We would kiss our child's cheek at the same time while someone snapped a picture of us. Later, there would be us at graduations, and weddings, and every other big moment in our family's life. Our faces and bodies would change over time, wrinkles and age spots would mar our skin, our eyes would cloud over with cataracts, and our hearing would turn to shit, but one thing would remain the same: Romeo and Julius forever.

Epilogue

"My bounty is as boundless as the sea. My love as deep. The more I give to thee, the more I have, for both are infinite."
~William Shakespeare

"Love is the ultimate superpower. The more you love, the more you're loved in return. Love is boundless, depthless, and knows no limits."
~Romeo Bradley

I KNEW I WOULD BE EMOTIONAL WHEN I STOOD OFF TO THE SIDE OF THE stage and watched the kids perform their heart out for our families, friends, and our community. I knew there would also be relief because Roy Halifax and his little band of haters were nowhere to be found when the sheriff went to arrest them. It turned out they were more afraid of the charges the attorney general filed against them than they were of two men in love. I wasn't the least bit surprised, but it allowed me to forget about them and just enjoy the play that brought Julius and me together.

Every line spoken, every song that was sung, and Julius's beautiful music performed by the high school band in the orchestra pit was precious to me and the man gripping my hand. We found ourselves holding our breath, laughing out loud, and silently cheering them on when they got to parts that worried them the most. There were plenty of mistakes made, but that happens with every performance. Lines are flubbed or forgotten, songs are sung off-key, and the band wasn't exactly up to the same standard as Jules, but none of that mattered. It was all about the message. The kids wanted us to really see and hear them. They wanted to turn us inside out, and there wasn't a dry eye in the theater when the last line was delivered.

When the curtains came down, Clara, Ellie, and Curtis bullrushed us, nearly knocking us over.

"Thank you so much," Curtis said through his tears. "This means everything to us."

"We love you, Dr. Bradley and Mr. S., but not in a creepy way," Clara said.

"Yeah, what they said," Ellie added.

The performers gathered behind the red velvet curtains waiting for their curtain call while the crowd continued to cheer wildly.

"Thank you for letting us be part of something special," Julius told them.

"The message in your play is bigger than the three of you, or even the five of us," I told them. "This is something everyone can relate to regardless of how they look, their financial situation, or how they love. We're proud to have played a role in making this play a reality."

Over their heads, I saw the curtain go up and the actors join hands and take their bow. The cheers got even louder so they bowed again. Mark Vaughn stood at the end of the front row, and he turned and waved for the five of us to join them.

"Should we?" Ellie asked, biting her lip.

"The three of you need to go out there and receive the praise for what you created," I said. "Smile big because Channel Eleven is here."

"What?" Clara asked.

"Didn't I tell you that?" They shook their heads. "Huh, I guess we can keep some secrets in this town after all." I had to obtain signed permission from their parents to allow the news channel to record the production and for the interviews with The Hammer that were to follow during the after-party. He wanted to do a special about these kids, their message, and how the small town of Blissville turned out to love and support them. "Go on and take the stage."

Ellie's chin wobbled as she pulled her best friends with her onto the stage. I didn't think the crowd could get any louder, but I was wrong. They waved to the audience, took a bow like the performers, then turned to face us. Clara, Ellie, and Curtis waved their hands for us to join them too.

"I look a mess," I said to Jules.

"You look beautiful," he countered. "We don't want to let the kids down now." Jules held out his hand for me to join him. "Are you coming with me?"

In his eyes, I saw my future. In his smile, I rediscovered joy. In his heart, I made my home. This man turned me inside out, and I would follow him anywhere.

The End!

Want to be the first to know about my book releases and have access to extra content? You can sign up for my newsletter here: eepurl.com/dlhPYj

My favorite place to hang out and chat with my readers is my Facebook group. Would you like to be a member of Aimee's Dye Hards? We'd love to have you! Go here: www.facebook.com/groups/AimeesDyeHards

Acknowledgments

First, I need to thank my husband and children for their constant support and encouragement. It's not easy living with a writer who often disappears into a fictional world for long periods of time. They do so many things to help me out so that I can realize my dream. I love you guys more than words can ever express.

To my creative dream team, thanks seem hardly enough for all that you do. Miranda Vescio of V8 Editing and Proofreading, thank you for your tireless work, feedback, and many laughs while editing. Jay Aheer of Simply Defined art is an incredible artist, and I love how she brings my words to life. Stacey Blake of Champagne Formats is also an amazing artist who does incredible interior formatting, illustrating, and designing for e-books and paperbacks. Let's not forget Judy Zweifel of Judy's' Proofreading. She does an amazing job of finding the tiniest details that make a book shine.

To my lovely PA, Michelle Slagan. I'm not sure how I ever did this without you. I love you to the moon and back!

Lastly, I am so grateful for my beta readers and the honest feedback they provide me. Thank you for all that you do, Racheal, Kim, Dana, Jodie, Michael, Michelle, Brittany, and Laurel.

About

AIMEE NICOLE WALKER

Ever since she was a little girl, Aimee Nicole Walker entertained herself with stories that popped into her head. Now she gets paid to tell those stories to other people. She wears many titles—wife, mom, and animal lover are just a few of them. Her absolute favorite title is champion of the happily ever after. Love inspires everything she does, music keeps her sane, and coffee is the magic elixir that fuels her day.

I'd love to hear from you.

You can reach me at:

Twitter: twitter.com/AimeeNWalker

Facebook: www.facebook.com/aimeenicole.walker

Instagram: instagram.com/aimeenicolewalker

Blog: AimeeNicoleWalker.blogspot.com